*For Tammy,
...and this one,
too!*

The Nothing That Is Not There

This book is forthe Class of 1966
and especially for Chuck Jurvelin

and

in memory of Sharon Coyle

Also by Tim Jollymore

Listener in the Snow (2014)

Observation Hill, a novel of class and murder (2015)

The Advent of Elizabeth (2016)

Lake Stories and Other Tales (2017)

People You've Been Before (2019)

The Final Confession of Saint Augustine (2022)

The Nothing That Is Not There

Tim Jollymore

FINNS WAY
BOOKS

Acknowledgments

I acknowledge my debt to Wallace Stevens whose interest in metaphysical naturalism spawned *The Snow Man,* my epigram, from which I take the story's title and the inspiration for the book itself. Stevens said, "The world about us would be desolate except for the world within us," something that moves much of the action of this story.

I give thanks to the people of Northern Minnesota, to the many Ojibwe people who passed down stories and cultural information to the present day, and to those who foresaw the need to preserve wilderness.

I thank Davis Hammet Proulx who years ago told of a windigo chase, a tale that eventually grew into *Listener in the Snow* and this book as well.

Tim Jollymore

July 2023

The Nothing That Is Not There. Copyright © June 20, 2023 by Tim Jollymore. All rights reserved.

Printed in the United States of America. For information, address Finns Way Books™, 2244 Lakeshore Avenue, Third Floor, Number Four, Oakland, California, 94606; or contact www.finnswaybooks.com

For information on Finns Way Reading Group Guides, please contact Finns Way Books™ by electronic mail at finnswaybooks@gmail.com.

Four lines of Roy Orbison's song *Pretty Woman* appear on page thirty-seven.

ISBN 978-0-9985288-9-2

The Snow Man

One must have a mind of winter
To regard the frost and the boughs
Of the pine-trees crusted with snow;

And have been cold a long time
To behold the junipers shagged with ice,
The spruces rough in the distant glitter

Of the January sun; and not to think
Of any misery in the sound of the wind,
In the sound of a few leaves,

Which is the sound of the land
Full of the same wind
That is blowing in the same bare place

For the listener, who listens in the snow,
And, nothing himself, beholds
Nothing that is not there and the nothing that is.

Wallace Stevens, 1922

The Nothing That Is Not There

RELATIONSHIPS

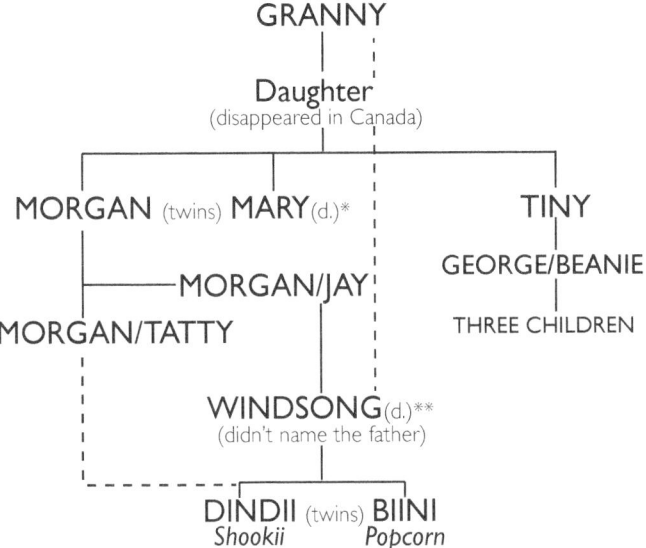

Objective Case

Listener in the Snow

In 1957 Morgan Langille's twin sister Mary freezes to death during a misguided windigo* chase through the winter woods outside of Thief Lake, Minnesota. To avoid prosecution for organizing the deadly escapade, Morgan adopts her sister's name. Months later she gives birth to a daughter, Windsong, and within a year, leaves the infant with Granny, who raises the girl. Morgan, now calling herself Mary, exits Thief Lake to build a new life in Florida. She leaves her lover Jay and the incarcerated other organizer, Roscoe, behind.

By 1963, Morgan meets and marries Tatty Langille, a half-Mi'kmaq, half-Finnish orphaned college student whose father complex steers him to dependence on women. Tatty knows nothing of Morgan's previous life, and they settle into a productive existence in Tallahassee, Florida. Tatty is disturbed by Morgan's occasional, violent melt-downs, but remains loyal and loving.

Back in Minnesota, when Windsong, now grown, is about to deliver twins of her own, Morgan responds to the pull northward and draws Tatty with her to Thief Lake. It is December, 1977, the beginning of *Listener in the Snow*. The story shows Tatty flying to Minneapolis, <u>driving through</u> the snowstorm of the century northward

---

*The Native American flesh-eating windigo is an evil spirit rooted in the forest or lakes. It can appear in any form.

to the Canadian border to Thief Lake. Each hour brings him stranger and stranger experiences.

Along the way, Tatty meets the clownish Danny and Cooley at a roadside doughnut shop. He tails truckers in the throes of the storm, following their red running lights. He is disturbed by windigo stories Morgan had told him, and swerves his car in answer to their howls in the blow of the storm. Close to Thief Lake, he is sent into a ravine by an outsized magical buck, a windigo deer, and is struck unconscious.

Rescued by Jay, a local medical tech, Tatty is brought to Tillie's Tavern, where a handful of denizens of the lake are weathering the storm. This is the place he was warned against visiting, a bar where the bear man of Thief Lake, Roscoe Lucci, holds mad court with the ghost of Mary (Morgan's sister) and recollections of the twenty-years-past windigo chase he led that brought Mary death and his own jailing for it.

In a downward spiral of angst, violence, and anger, Roscoe threatens Tatty, fights his tavern partner, Jay, Tatty's rescuer, and, when she arrives, wrestles with Morgan who he is half convinced is Mary his own former lover. Morgan burst into the tavern, and with a kick breaks Roscoe's collarbone, but fails to disarm the burly bear man who stabs Jay, killing him. Tatty is aghast, confused, and cannot but learn in a few hours all that history of hurt and terror.

Roscoe escapes. A day later, Tatty discovers him hiding in Granny's garage. So deeply involved with the bear man's story now, Tatty avoids betraying the killer to the other members of Granny's household. During the evening, just after a native burial of Windsong, Granny cross examines Tatty, finally claiming he is a seer. "He sees from afar," she tells those assembled.

Next morning, the household is awakened to the roar of the Snowcat Roscoe is commandeering for an escape to Canada. Danny, Cooley, and Tatty follow quickly on snowmobiles, chasing Roscoe into the middle of Thief Lake. When the ice begins to break up on these three, and Roscoe, too, Tatty takes one of the machines to the shoreline and up a hill to escape the disaster. Cooley and Danny pursue, but turn back when the ice floe Roscoe is on breaks free, upends, and tosses the bear man into the icy waters.

Tatty, observing from the hilltop, sees Roscoe go under the ice floe that totally flips upside down. He is distracted, though, by a sound behind him which turns to a vision of his long-dead father. In a mystical action, Tatty passes through that ghost and into a new kind of understanding.

After a week-long illness, Tatty relates the whole of his story, *Listener in the Snow*, to his brother-in-law, Tiny, in a fish house out on the frozen lake. On his way back to shore once again, he mulls over a decision he must make: Will he return to Florida without Morgan, or will he stay at Thief Lake to save his marriage and adopt Windsong's parentless twins?

The Nothing That Is Not There

The twins Dindii and Biini are born, December 1977. Their adoptive father, Tatty, becomes postmaster in Thief Lake. Morgan is their adoptive mother and blood-grandmother who now pursues arts, crafts, and "personal" interests at the lake.

Dindii is cruelly burned in a kitchen fire at age seven.

The twins grow apart.

The following year, Morgan falls in love with an itinerant radio preacher, Teddy Good, who will visit the lake each summer, also running an international summer camp nearby. In Teddy's wooden luxury boat, the Saint Muggsy, he and Morgan cruise the summer nights away, together under the stars. Tatty tolerates the affair as long as he is able to shield the children from its effects.

Their lives proceed estranged but tranquil until in 1987 Roscoe Lucci, in spirit and/or body reappears. Roscoe mystically foretells the reopening of Tillie's and dictates the strengthening of Tatty's fatherhood. From that point on the family is hurled into a streaming vortex of passion, action, and reconstitution that inform the ensuing family story. The story of Morgan, Tatty and the twins plays out against the backdrop of anti-government and anti-Native sentiment at the lake that increases tension inside and out of the family's concerns, leading, finally, to Morgan's demise.

Infancy

 ## Morgan from Beyond   1

Back in what the song calls "the good old world," I was frozen to the spirit of my sister when she stepped inside what Roscoe called "that horrible light." For years afterward, I hid, a fugitive, behind Mary's name. Then back in the north again—it must be two decades now, I cannot tell time anymore (there is no time here)—I burned for the soul of yet another twin sister, like the twin who died for me. That night my last breath blew out across Thief Lake, the place I was born. The place I died.

My remains mixed with the char of the half-destroyed Tillie's Tavern, a place I had, at one time safe in Florida, wished never to set foot in again. I was led there, though, by the bumbling of my wanting-to-do-the-right-thing husband who, by virtue of his Algonquin or his Finnish blood, or both, couldn't say "no" to our twins. It seemed that the more I wanted to avoid that watering hole, the more it drew me back.

At last, I owned the dump, more or less. I kept it shut until I couldn't any more. Then, I died there in a second story fire set by crazed denizens of the lake. Who was it? Who, I ask, had spawned such fools as those over the years? I don't know. Maybe I gave birth to the mayhem or was one of the nut-cases, and like the rest (Scummy and Roscoe, the Olsen's crowd, and Preacher Ted, to name a few) had to pay for my wickedness with my life. Still, my penance, if that is what I suffered, or fate, which is more likely, perfected my vision, which became as clear as the reflected sky over the lake on a still summer day. Some parts of that night are dark, smoky, and unclear. So I don't know who set the fire. Whoever it was saw me, I'm sure, and thought I was Dindii, my daughter. Funny, most every other detail is as crisp as a January morning after a snowfall.

As if I'm in an aerie overlooking the lake and town spanning space and time, I see my twin granddaughters grow together, then, nearly adults, split apart, like my sister Mary and I did years before, all of us four clashing with the fury of faith, freezing, and fire.

And what do I see? The past:

Up among the birches over the lake, fifteen and more years back, I see my husband clapping-away with numbed hands a vision of his howling father to become more of a man than the man who raised him. Note, I say *more of*.

Out on the lake, that same day, I see Roscoe Lucci finally meeting the windigo he'd fled from all his dastardly life, those two slipping down an upraised ice slab into winter waters, to be seen on the earth never again.

In that cursed tavern I couldn't be shut of, I again see Scummy—a man I had loved in youth and for decades after—taking a broken beer bottle in the gut, bleeding out for telling, at long last, his tightly-held secrets about me, our child, Windsong, and the yearslong lies he told to his best friend.

Closer to the present (I think) I hear the snort of resentment. I see it blown, the bomb of insurrection: good men—not ordinary fools—holding knives to each others' throats, guns to each others' temples. I see government men's entrails in the snow. Hatred under bushy eyebrows flashing forth.

I see that goddamned preacher, Teddy, a silver-tongued garter snake, twining one of my girls around his twisted form, taking her far from the lake, from her sister, from me, from her home. Curse the man. He'd had me body and soul, too.

I see ancient ways despoiled; I see even the white's foreign ways deposed.

I ask, "How could my youthful good intentions and love stir up such mayhem?" I finally tried to outwait my bad luck. I settled on the warmth of Florida to shelter me. Try as I might, though, the cold fingers of the Canadian borderlands pulled at me and drew me back. I risked a cozy home, a settled life, and a good-enough marriage for a chance to mend a wrong, to atone for barrelsful of sin—and for what? Death, destruction, damaged lives in another generation? Best I had stayed in Tallahassee.

What of that Florida marriage?

It wasn't much to begin with, and it didn't grow much better. Tatty, my dear windbag of a husband, busied himself fleeing the ghosts of his half-Algonquin half-Finnish heritage. He probably still believes he chose the Finnish side. I wonder. If he didn't want to be Indian, why did he marry one? He was, and very much still is, a man who doesn't know himself. Or maybe, knowing himself very well, is one who doesn't want to admit to his own life. Was his wavering the reason for my knife-throwing and plate-smashing in the midnight kitchens of our early years? I'll admit to my own rage, but Tatty's romantic idea of life with me didn't help matters at all.

Still, the man had a practical side that came in mighty handy for the way things go in this land. He could sure turn a dollar. He sold more storm shutters than six better Floridian men and provided for us well. He was faithful to a fault, and that left him open to being moved in the directions I wished him to go whenever I wanted. It took just a slight push from behind to place him where he had no yen to be. That was how we wound up in what he called "this god-awful refrigerator." How could he desire to freeze up here when he had never even donned a jacket much less a parka and mukluks? Getting him to come was not a problem. I simply up and left him gaping in the sun on the patio. Getting him to stay around, though, took around seven of us: Roscoe and Scummy, me and Granny, the twin babies, and, of course, my well-connected brother, Tiny. Still, Tatty made it easier, deciding on his own in favor of love.

Tatty used money and the security it provided to fill a cavity in his manhood. Sure, I lured him with both, like a good fisherwoman tickling a northern pike with a wiggling minnow. He took the bait and swallowed. I simply tugged the line,

My brother, Tiny, pulled the strings when McKinnon, the postmaster, conveniently kicked the bucket. Maybe he had some help, I don't know. Anyway, Tatty's practical side did the rest. You don't get a Presidential appointment every day. And even though Carter had never even heard of Thief Lake much less Tatty Langille, he knew how to bestow favor and how to pay back, too.

My husband took the moose by the antlers and became the best postmaster in decades—easy since McKinnon had just bungled around for over a half century—and resurrected the failing general store that housed the post office, making it a stout money maker and meeting place for the scattered community at the lake. He did some good. I guess I loved him enough until Teddy Good the preacher arrived.

And what of those twins?

First of all, you already know I was a twin. Mary was identical with me in face and physique but opposite in demeanor. I was out there, wild. She reserved herself for the important times—like the time she stepped between me and Roscoe's windigo-light. Mary quietly threw everything away for little old me. So, as different as I was inside, I paid her back, I suppose, by being as much like her exterior as I could. That brought me to Tatty. It also confused Roscoe, and made Scummy a liar, or at the very least a secret-keeper.

Mary and I were both pregnant at the time she froze to death. I still wonder if she thought Roscoe's baby was worth less than Jay's, the one I carried. That was how Windsong came to be, and she was whom I left at the lake with Granny. The old woman had raised Mary and me, and I thought she could fare as well with Windsong. I guess Mary wouldn't have done that.

Well, I did.

Then twenty years later I returned to help deliver Windsong's twins. Coming back for their birth would solve everything, or so I thought.

 The Thief Lake Post Office 2

"Tatty, you have a story to tell." Having listened for hours in the dark and closeness of his ice house, Tiny summed up my entire future in seven words.

Then—it has been nearly twenty years since—fixing to leave my brother-in-law's fish house set over the best walleye hole on Thief Lake, having for the first time told my story of the listener in the snow, Tiny set me on the path to repeat my tale, not just while I walked over that frozen lake back to shore but for all time in my life.

Not convinced right off, I'd replied, "Sure, if anyone has the patience to hear it." The shimmer of light rising into the interior gloom of the dun little fish cabin shone from the angling holes cut into the ice floor of the cabin. The rays played over Tiny's face.

"It needs more telling." He sat, his squat form bulky, emphatic, and sure.

On the mile-and-a-half trudge back, over two-foot-thick ice to the snow-banked shore, I used the time to consider the weight of Tiny's simple direction.

If my story needed more telling, that could not be done back home in Tallahassee. No one there would have the fortitude or interest to hear me out. Not a soul there would care. Nor would anyone in Florida understand its import. I might, if I returned, live on a bar stool, elbow to mahogany, blathering nonsense to drunks who would only shake their heads without a sense of what was told. So, to find a sympathetic audience who could parse the meaning of my telling, I would have to stay in the frigid north, what my wife, Morgan, once named "that god-awful refrigerator."

If I were to stay in Minnesota, though, it was certain that I must become father to the newborn, orphaned twins whom Morgan—it had become clear to all, even to me who was snowblind and reluctant to understand, that she was grandmother to those girls—was set on rearing, not just parenting anywhere, but nurturing those two on the very lake where she had been born, where she had also abandoned first her sister, and then the twins' mother, Windsong, two decades before.

I did not think too deeply about it on my slog over the snow-covered expanse of ice, but staying on Thief Lake meant I must give up my interest in the profitable Florida storm shutter business that had sustained Morgan and me since we married fifteen years before. While the fish houses at my back slowly grew smaller as my distance from them increased—the white smoke streams from the potbellied stoves weaving together in the still, frigid air—finally resolving to black dots in a sea of white, I ticked off the arguments. My reasoning evolved slowly with each step on hard packed snow.

I feared the freezing weather that had already done its best to kill me. I did not like snow; I had been buried in it twice since arriving. Winter darkness depressed me.

Further, I had never wanted a child, much less two, nor did I want to share the love-of-my-life with infants. The whole idea of parenthood, due to my troubled upbringing at the hands of a drunken father, filled me with dread.

I had no idea how to support myself in this strange and spare white-pine woods bordering Canada. I was no lumberjack nor fisherman. I had never harvested wild rice, *manomin*, either.

My arguments against staying were strong, and at the beginning of my trek to shore, Tiny's words felt more condemnation than admonition or suggestion.

Still, prior to the week I was down with a fever, incoherent in the god-awful Minnesotan refrigerator, I had lived more intensely in three days and nights than before in all the tepid thirty-eight years in my sun-drenched birthplace of Florida. Like it or not, I could see no way out of the emptiness of the north. Leaving Tiny's fish house behind, by the time I reached the shore that day and passed by Tillie's Tavern, the site of wild truth-telling and carnage, I knew I must stay.

I must learn to be a father to the girls. I could reform and preserve my marriage in the process, but I had to find something profitable and useful to do at Thief Lake. Only then could I tell my story and be at peace with myself.

Mine was not much of a plan, but as is often the case, whether we want to admit to it or not, happenstance brings in a unanimous verdict. An accident provided resolution to my dilemma.

The week before my visit to Tiny's fish house, when I was down with fever, Oliver McKinnon, aged eighty-eight, the local postmaster for nearly sixty years, fell off the stepladder while setting his wife's funeral urn high on a garage shelf. Two days later, Ollie followed her example and eventually found his own urn.

Once on my feet, I came on, first as McKinnon's temporary replacement, then, all arranged by my brother-in-law, Tiny, in a permanent appointment by the President and Senate. I took the mantle and title of Postmaster at

Thief Lake, Minnesota, the first Native and the first Finn to hold the position. Of course, Morgan's history—her sister's weird death and Scummy's murder at Tillie's—came up in the official vetting process, but somehow Tiny and Morgan were able to deflect difficult questions. I had not really been involved and, of course, knew nothing. I have yet to discover if Tiny, who had enormous and singular influence well beyond his cozy little fish house and his maple syrup distillery surrounded by acres of leaky trees, already had this favor in mind at the time I first visited him out on the ice and told him all the story, or if my wife conjured him afterward to bestow honor and income on her husband and, thus, require me to remain at the lake. Now, after twenty-two years of sorting mail and telling stories, having nestled into the life of the lake community of which the post office is the daily center, and having raised our girls, the details hardly matter, although I've often thought that Tiny must have held some smut over the 8th district Minnesota Representative. Also, the investigating agent had gone to high school with Tiny.

What *has* counted is the location of the post office, not so much physically but socially in the middle of town, and I use the term *town* loosely since the settlement at Thief Lake was spread widely here and there along the shores and concentrated only at the south side where the pavement ended and a pair of two-track dirt roads fed off east and west, serving one shore and another. The post office marked the edge of the tarmac and the beginning of town. Two hundred yards further on, stood three fishing resorts, Olsen's, Johnson's, and Nelson's, each with a boat landing, beer bar, and two with restaurants serving succulent fried chicken dinners, all three hugging an inlet that fed to the lake proper and served as a fisherman's marina. At the end to the west, standing off by itself, its property fringed by gigantic white and Norway pines, was the only two-story building at the lake: Tillie's Tavern, a place that had played an outsized role in the village going back before the days of the infamous bear man of Thief Lake, Roscoe Lucci, and Jay "Scummy" Martinen, Roscoe's friend, business partner, and last-known victim.

At the time of my first visit with Tiny, out on the frozen lake, Tillie's was closed, shut first by the sheriff during his investigation of Jay's murder, then by the probate court while the mess of violent death of one partner in the bar and the haunting disappearance of the other played out. Tillie's remained closed all during the prolonged search at the bottom of Thief Lake for Roscoe's body after the ice retreated in April that year. Since both Roscoe and Scummy each thought, at one time, they were Windsong's father, they had written business wills naming each other as primary heirs and Windsong as their successor. So, three years later, the possession of the tavern descended on Morgan, in trust favoring the twins.

Morgan made no move to reopen Tillie's, as if boarding-up windows and doors could hold dangerous ghosts at bay and shelter Dindiisi and Biinishii, called Dindii and Biini, our twin girls, from spirits shackled inside the building.

For all those years, I thought that those djin played havoc only in my dreams. In truth, they were waiting to be loosed through the conniving of an itinerant, jet-setter preacher, my born-again daughter, Biini, and Dindii her not-so-identical sister who leaned into native shaman rites. The mayhem, coming immediately on the reopening of Tillie's, flared into a deadly midnight fire and has given me yet another story I'm condemned to tell.

Perhaps telling it will reveal what really happened.

Sorting Mail   3

Tiny had said, "Now you have a story to tell." The post office, after I had arranged the space more to my liking, offered me a forum to do just that but never with a hat on. I'll explain.

The long building, serving as a post office and our home, stretched out, starting with the three bay garage where I have been for years now, building a birch bark canoe with a lot of help from Danny and Cooley, two friends I had met on my snowstorm Jeep-odyssey to Thief Lake. Attached to the garage was the house, a three-bedroom affair whose kitchen was split into an eat-in breakfast and lunch spot for the family set off by a long bar with stools, the coffee stand we operated when the store and post office were open, nine hours a day Monday through Saturday starting and ending within an hour either side of the mail truck arrival, morning and afternoon.

Morgan claimed one bedroom as a painting studio, and we had a private dining room behind the kitchen which at its forward end was separated by a serving counter with a roll-up window-cover from the array of tables in the large main room that housed a cafe, store, and the post office. Beyond the cafe and store, the mail room served as my domain. It was divided from the store proper by banks of post office boxes flanking a dutch door that doubled as the postmaster's entry and, by swinging in place a cast iron grill work, a "general delivery" window.

On a hook on the top part of that door I hung my hat, the visor I wore when conducting official post office business (sorting and boxing envelopes, mainly). During those four hours with my hat on, there was no story telling, at least on my part.

Anyone wanting to hear the old story would come early for coffee. Surprisingly, there were, even after a decade, many who did so, early risers who loved to swill coffee and to proffer theories about Roscoe:

"I swear, Roscoe is still alive," Danny would say waiting for his steaming cup to cool. "I caught sight of him from my deer stand last November."

Uncle Joki who usually came in with Danny two days a week disagreed. "That can't be. Though it took twenty years after that escapade that killed Mary, the windigo finally caught up with 'um."

Danny could not be dissuaded. "No way. Roscoe is too tough. Maybe he escaped to Canada and is hiding out there. My deer stand is right on the border."

I let Danny and Joki spar over the odd details of their imagining. Having seen Roscoe slide down the ice floe with my own eyes, I could not believe he had survived no matter how strong he was.

"He drownded," Cooley, who sauntered in, said. "And he was devoured bones and all by the sturgeon that lurk in the deeps." Cooley laughed at his own contribution and at the effect it had on Danny and his uncle.

I couldn't help chime in on Danny's stammering. Cooley always had it over his best friend. "He swam under the ice breathing at air pockets and was finally caught by a fisherman in the open who reeled him up through a hole in the ice."

Danny took my bait. "Yeah? Well why didn't the guy

say something, then?"

"I don't know," Cooley said, taking over. "Maybe he thought Roscoe was a big fish and took him home to fry him up."

Danny was speechless with outrage.

"And maybe he gave him a decent burial," Cooley said soothing his friend's ire.

"Some say," Joki recalled, "he was found frozen in an ice floe by the ghost of the man he killed."

Danny was animated again. "Sure and Scummy's spirit took him secretly to the ice plant in Duluth! He's still there today."

Keeping my hat on as I worked on the mail, I confirmed or denied none of these suppositions, but cupped an ear for anything new or interesting. Mostly, it was pure banter. Those morning sessions were often crowded and raucous, giving friends and neighbors a chance to catch up with daily doings around the lake as well as to spin yarns for entertainment. Danny was the most likely to be there, guffawing and jostling. But few took my story of listener in the snow as anything but a conversation piece. And if Morgan was there or came in from her studio, everybody clammed up. She was the last of those ill-fated windigo-chasers alive and wouldn't tolerate any loose talk about what had happened. After all, she'd lost a lover, a sister, and a daughter in the aftermath. How could any of us know that more suffering lay in store for her when the twins reached maturity.

Those who saw the events that centered on Tillie's more seriously, perhaps even a matter of ghosts and spirits, returned for a decaf in the afternoon about the time I was hanging up my visor. Cooley and Tiny were two of those, usually trailing in when something had prodded them awake at three o'clock the previous morning:

Once Tiny spoke softly as if to himself about his vision of a bright oval of light. "It was making a weird sound it was so luminous," he said. "I woke up and had to look out the window to see, but there was nothing."

The snorting of an impossibly large whitetail buck who was standing in his bedroom once scared Cooley out of sleep. Another time he reported waking up screaming. "I had the feeling that my bed lifted up like Roscoe's ice floe. I fell right out of the sack."

Cooley, especially, was cautious about his reports since he had been an eye witness to the events. He'd been near to being dumped along with Roscoe into the icy waters of Thief Lake but gunned his snowmobile away from the scene to barely escape.

In my early years as postmaster-storyteller, Granny Bassett came, maybe once every other week or so. When she came, it wasn't to speculate. Granny knew the ghostly worlds that lay beneath the ice, that swelled under the pine-cone strewn forest floor, that sparkled in the air lighted but not heated by the mid-winter sun. She honored those spirit worlds and understood them. When she appeared at the end of my postal duties, she stood before me as she had long before in the firelight of her cabin when she told me, "You see from afar," but here in the cafe she only assured me in a glance of her understanding of my restored spirit before saying plainly, "I've come to see the twins, Little Bird and Jay," as she called them in English.

The twins—their given names were Dindiisi and Biinishii though they later called each other Shookii and Popcorn—were growing fast and after many of her inspection tours Granny was displeased with what she saw. It wasn't the twins growth or behavior she worried about but our way of raising them. She knew things about them that neither Morgan nor I could know, future things. What she saw in their futures troubled her, but trying to get her to open up about them proved impossible. She knew more than ever before not to interfere in affairs that had been forebode.

Whatever lay before the twins, what blessings and difficulties they would sustain, both Granny and Morgan thought, could not be changed. Though I did not know what either woman saw in the girls' futures, I parted company with Granny and Morgan on that point. Because of my own troubled upbringing and because in my ignorance of "how to," I, as was my wont, had turned to books to bolster my ideas with opinions of those who wrote on child rearing. I had turned to published experts for support. I thought I could with help assure a better future for Dindii and Biini. When they were six, I adopted their own pet names for each other as a way to stay closer to them. Of course, there would be no guarantees, but I was giving it a try.

I did give it a try and thought for almost fifteen years that I was doing a good job. Morgan had always thought otherwise.

The twins were four when Granny died.

Shortly thereafter, Morgan came at me with a book in her hand. "What's this moose shit?" Morgan held a copy of Dodson's *How to Father*.

I had left the book out for Morgan, but she was having none of it. "It's for people like me, fathers."

"Oh, yeah?" She brandished the book like a cudgel, then read from the cover, "Let's see, 'The first truly comprehensive guide for fathers' it says."

"See?" I hoped, despite her gestures and tone that she would be reasonable, and now that Granny was gone, that we could talk about it.

"Oh, but it goes on. Listen. 'for fathers' I repeat . . . 'that every mother should read!' Who says?" She threw the book right at me. "Moose dung! I don't need some pale-faced academic telling me how to raise my kids. Maybe you do, but don't bring that crap around me." She stormed out, striding through the cafe, silencing the jabber that was going on there.

It would do no good to chase after her, to talk about it. Morgan still lived in a world of pain. She had abandoned, first, a sister, then, a child. She knew she had done wrong, but she couldn't look at it rationally. To compensate, she had decided to raise the girls as Granny had brought up her and her twin, or as she remembered the way Granny had cared for them.

"Dindii and Biini need to know Native ways to survive," Morgan claimed. "Nothing else really matters."

For myself, as early as childhood, I had decided to repeat the *sisu*-mantra of the Finns, my mother's people, rather than follow my father's Algonquin ways which even he never adhered to. It was my grandmother, Banook, who sealed that decision by exposing me to Mi'kmaq legends that at the time confused and scared me. She was a good woman but caught me at the wrong time. Immediately after meeting her, I begged my mother to take me back to Florida, after she buried my father in Nova Scotia. I ran from what Morgan now prized, and unlike her, I had never wanted to return.

The carnage at Tillie's might make me a teller of spirit-stories but did not make me a willing believer.

Morgan's Preacher 4

I was pissed, so angry that I stormed through the cafe even though it was the long way around, further than out the back door and through the garage. Maybe that was a good thing. I could easily have smashed Tatty's canoe with its own paddle since it was at the time nothing more than a skeleton of cedar spine and sapling ribs, but I instead stomped through a crowded morning cafe at the post office and slammed the front door so hard, Cooley told me later, that a pair of deer antlers rocked and tumbled off the knotty-pine wall inside. Lucky no one was sitting under them.

Sure, I knew Tatty was reading that Doctor Spock crap, but this new one that he certainly left out for me to see was the living end. "Moose crap" I call it, "Dodson's dung."

I supposed now that Granny was dead, he thought I would heed his phony opinions and puny experts' advice. What did he know? Nothing. Tatty was a stuffed shirt. He was so afraid of turning out like his inebriated father that he wouldn't even take a single drink. Instead, he slurped up the coffee constantly and repeated his tired old stories of what happened at Tillie's. The nerve he has sometimes, leaving a book out "that every mother should read," when he faints for lack of courage when it really counts. Ha! I was a mother—not much of one on the first try, I admit—twenty years before he even discovered the fact. Tatty had no idea.

I flung that door shut with a smash, took two strides to the middle of the road and immediately went down in my tracks.

I dove right onto the pavement. I froze. With a deafening roar something swooped overhead. I felt it could grab me, like a hawk on a mole, and take me into the air. It felt that big! I lost my wits, went down, rolling back toward the post office door. Then, I was nearly trampled by the crowd that flooded out of the post office to see what was going on.

"What the hell?" The whole crowd shouted together. On that one, I was with them.

Lying on my back looking up with all the rest, I now saw what it was. Coming in low on a second pass, just above the tips of the tallest white pines at Tillie's, right over the middle of the road a jet, a small private plane, swooped. It boomed over the little town's main street and suddenly, just over my head, pulled up and again banked out toward the lake. I didn't know if it was the door slamming or the jet breaking a sound barrier, but the noise I had heard stunned me, turning me into a recumbent statue, mouth hanging open, I suppose, gawking like a tourist.

"There goes Preacher Ted," Joki said. "He's the only one I ever heard of owning a jet plane."

I couldn't help myself. "Who? Preacher? What?"

Joki looked down on me and laughed. He extended a hand toward me. I took it, and he helped me up. "I heard about him up in the Falls last year. Some west coast radio preacher who's building a camp over by Orr."

That was my introduction to Teddy G, Preacher Ted as he liked to be called, the G standing for Good which he pronounced "gawd." At the time I said, "Well, he better keep his goddamned plane out of Thief Lake." Of course, he didn't, even after he finished an airstrip at his camp so he didn't have to land at the Falls. Every time he came up to his camp, and that was two or three times a summer, he flew low over Thief Lake. It came to pass, as they say in the Bible, that every time I heard that jet boom overhead, I got so horny that I almost climbed all over Tatty. And that was unusual in those days.

Yes. I took up with Teddy Good and made no secret of it either. Teddy and Tatty. My lover and my husband.

After a long winter or even after a few-weeks absence in summer, the sound of that jet swirled me up into a tingle I couldn't staunch but in one way. I'd have to hike the woodsy trail from town over the hill to Gulbranson's Bay Resort on Big Trout Lake where Teddy G stayed, where he and his rock 'n roll band, *Teddy G and the Saints*, played the bar on the weekends he was in town, where I locked arms with him after the last set and locked legs with him in his cabin deep into the dark of the short summer nights.

Not to compare the two over much, but Teddy G was everything my husband was not: brash, confident, showy, savvy, and known the world over. He was all that in his father's church and on the radio, too, and he was certainly all that in the cabin bunk we shared. That cabin, a split log structure, sat out on Pelican Point all by itself. Preacher liked both the prominence and the privacy.

It probably wouldn't have worked if it had been a full-time thing, but for over ten years, every time he zoomed overhead, before the dawn I'd find his bed. Preacher—what I always called him—was a better lover than he was a minister. We used to laugh about him evangelizing the women first, before reaching into their husbands' pockets.

I didn't care. Not about people at the lake knowing. Not about what he did back on the west coast.

I didn't think it could hurt the girls, either. Maybe both Granny and my conscience were gone. And should anyone say a single word to Biini or Dindii, that S.O.B. would have me to deal with. Everyone at the lake knew that I was capable of murder if I thought killing was needed. Over the years, before and after my absence in Florida, lake people had seen enough of what I could be like to keep their ever-loving traps shut. No one would risk a midnight fire breaking out in their cabin. So, I thought I had a lock on my love life, but, then again, it was only what I thought.

Preacher was my size, about five-foot seven, built sturdily, and limber as an otter. Handsome? To these Native eyes in those depraved days, he was god-like, wavy hair the color of windward shore sand, a not-too-narrow but prominent nose, good forehead and thin, close-cropped brows, clean shaven always, and the ever-loving life of the party.

I liked to watch his fingers move over the guitar frets, long, lithe, and quick. The band he brought with him might have played hymns and such over at his church, but at Gulbranson's it was strictly rock 'n roll. All from the fifties and sixties, no British stuff. No Motown. No Fats or Chubby, either. He rocked around the clock, and when he sang "Sweet Little Sheila" I didn't care a whit about the blue eyes or the pony tail. It was all about "true love will never die." He'd gyrate like Elvis and croon like Avalon. Preacher was a class act. So I thought.

The Friday evening I first spotted his jet, I saw the pilot himself up on Gulbranson's stage. The room was large, built tepee-like but entirely out of knotty pine with jack pine roof poles supporting it all. The great expanse housed the main dining room, a curved bar near the entry, and a roomy bandstand. Windows, the kind they call double-hung, circled the entire place with the jack pine poles resting on posts each side of every window. A virgin timber, white pine trunk twenty feet high held the roof poles in a metal collar high above the center of the room.

By the time I came down the hill nearing the resort, first having put the little ones to bed with a story of *manomin* harvesting, I heard the band, pulsing loud through the screens of the open windows. I slipped in and slid on to a stool at the bar near the door.

There he was, bathed in golden light, a sunburst Stratocaster slung over his shoulder, standing easy at the mic crooning "Pretty Woman" in a slick falsetto. *Comfortable* was the word that came to mind. He loved to be looked at, that was sure. Nothing was forced, all natural seeming. I couldn't help myself as he pushed the song toward its final crescendo singing,

> *But wait. What do I see?*
> *Is she walking back to me?*
> *Yeah, she's walking back to me.*
> *Oh, oh, pretty woman.*

Sliding off the bar stool, I found myself dancing right in front of Preacher as he hammered home the last two syllables of "wo · man." As he intoned "wo" I raised my arms and on "man" brought them down to my sides, thrusting—exactly as he was doing—my pelvis up toward the stage.

Gulbranson would have thrown me out. They didn't serve liquor to Indians and weren't really welcoming to them either, but Preacher immediately said, "Give this woman, this very pretty woman, a drink."

When Al the bartender looked a question at me, I just pointed to the half glass my new singer friend had nesting atop his amp. It turned out to be a vodka gimlet, strong and tangy. It became our usual.

That night, I kept it to two usuals and another something that became usual. Preacher rejoiced in the Lord, as he said, but he also rejoiced in the loins, something he admitted in private, something I took inspiration from whenever I could. I had known the spirits of the forest and of the lake. Those usually turned dark in a hurry and caution was the watchword. But the spirit Teddy G brought to me appeared, for a very long time, a bright, daylight spirit, one that could be celebrated on a Sunday morning, preferably in bed. And so we did.

Preacher administered his father's brand of religion, which called for a whole bunch of odd detail, but most obvious was that they celebrated on Saturday. So Sunday morning was in the sack, not in the pulpit. The band played until ten on Fridays and 'til midnight on Saturday.

"The Lord works in mysterious ways," my man liked to say.

It would be a long while before the girls heard anything about my own mysterious ways. After all, Gulbranson's was on the next lake over and wrapped up on a secluded bay. It had always catered to the Minneapolis crowd, moneyed, loose, and tight-lipped. You'd never see one of them at the post office or anywhere near Thief Lake. Any mail sorted in the morning was delivered to Gulbranson's directly on the afternoon truck as it headed out. In person contacts were few and far between.

So even Tatty failed to notice. How could he with his nose stuck in a book or mail sack all the time? He couldn't piece it together even over a whole summer. I had lots of school-days friends and close family to visit. Hardly any of them had telephones at that time, and it wasn't unusual for me to be gone a day or two fishing or hunting with one or another of them. With no weekend mail, my absence from time to time gave the "father" a chance to plan things with the girls, hikes and canoeing and such. He liked that because, I suppose, he could work his Dobson-Spock theories out on the twins when I wasn't looking. I was willing to make that trade.

Keeping a secret, though, in a fairly tight family in a rather close community is a pain. It wasn't long before I began to feel sorry for my poor old dope. In a way, I wanted a clean slate. So, I had decided to let him in on my little secret. I figured I could deal with any consequences. First, though, I wanted Preacher's blessing.

"Why?" he asked. "Are you trying to muck things up? Feeling guilty?"

"No, I'm not trying to screw up anything but you. Still, don't you think he knows anyway?"

Preacher was a master at reading people, even people he'd never met, like Tatty. After a moment considering, he said, "Yes. I think he knows, but does he know he knows? That's the question."

"He'll know he knew when I tell him, then."

"He might hurt you."

It didn't take me a second to nay-say that. "No, for one thing Tatty knows how I can fight. For another, he wouldn't injure me in a hundred years. No matter what, he is peaceable."

Preacher nodded. "Then you be peaceable."

And I was.

Tatty had finished the supper dishes while I read to Biini and Dindii. I closed their bedroom door and the hall door, too, then went to the kitchen where he was leafing through one of his books, sipping his coffee.

"Tatty," I said pulling out a chair across from him, "I have something to tell you."

He lifted those sad green eyes to mine. "Sounds ominous."

"Well, it's sensitive, and I don't want to hurt you."

He closed his book and set down the mug. "Are you leaving me?"

I thought he would cry. "No. I'm not leaving. It isn't that."

He sighed. "You're having an affair, aren't you?"

I wanted to let this out carefully, not to be too blunt. "Listen, Tatty, our marriage has been a good bargain for both of us all the way along. We've both gotten some of the things we wanted, and we have been fairly good to each other."

"Yeah, okay." He moved me along.

"But you know we've never loved with a passion."

He stirred in his chair. "Oh, I don't know about that. How about that time in Granny's cabin? When I first came to the lake?"

I reached for his hand across the oilcloth. "I remember. Few and far between isn't enough for me, Tatty. I love you but . . ."

He pulled his hand from my grasp but did not get up. He sat there. Finally, he said, "What about Dindii and Biini? They will find out. It will hurt them, but I suppose you wouldn't care about that."

Even though I did so care if they were hurt I kept it as peaceable as I could. "Not if you say nothing. They won't even think it much less believe it."

"So, you're not going to bring this guy around, then."

"No, I'm not." I reassured him, "And I am not going to leave you or the girls."

Tatty watched me. He drilled those eyes into my skull, nearly. "I don't like it. It is a shit deal"—this was strong language for Tatty who never swore—"You better think about it for a while."

I said, "Okay," knowing that I had all winter to do just that.

Childhood

Popcorn 1
(Biini)

It was the summer before we started second grade when I started praying for forgiveness.

Everybody said it was an accident, that it wasn't my fault at all. Still, Dindii kept calling me that awful name, "Popcorn."

At first, she kept it to herself, just between us. It didn't take long after Dindii came back to school on the bus with me. Everybody started calling me "Popcorn." Somehow the kids knew I called her, "Shookii." Most didn't know how those names got started.

Dindii thought I got her name from her shaking the fiery pot all over herself, but it wasn't until after she fell off the stool with all those popcorn seeds flying and the oil splashing all flaming up on her that her name started. She was shaking on the floor, flopping around like a fish trying to unhook itself.

I know I ran, but, really, I wasn't running away. I ran for help. Papa was in his office. "Shookii, popcorn," was all I could say, screaming it over and over again.

"What? Popcorn?" He had his hat on and didn't want to be bothered. Maybe because I kept shouting, "Shookii, popcorn," he finally got it. Maybe he smelled the smoke from the kitchen.

I bet she won't forgive me no matter how long or how often I pray. Maybe I'm doing it all wrong. Anyway, sometimes I do get some comfort in knowing that I saved my sister's life.

   Papa found the stove cabinet on fire. He threw the big living room rug over it. He ran down the hall, and came back with a sheet off Dindii's bed. He wrapped her in it very tender. She was still shaking. "Go find your mother," he said to me.
   I ran down to the fishing dock. She wasn't there. Nobody had seen her. I checked Olsen's. "Nope, saw her two days back is all." I ran back. The car doors were all open.
   "Papa, Papa! I can't find her." Dindii was lying on the back seat of our sedan in her sheet, the car motor was running, and Papa was locking up the post office.
   "Jump in, Biini, we've got to get her to the Hibbing Hospital. We're not waiting for Mama."
   I lay on the floor below my sister, who was moaning my new name, "Popcorn." Yes, that and, "You ran. Popcorn. Ran."
   A sheriff met us at the highway—Papa had called—and drove in front of us sixty miles an hour with the siren blaring into Hibbing's downtown. On the ride, Dindii went all quiet, just staring out of reddened, hurt eyes. She stayed silent for three days, finally, coming all the way awake. She was doped up for her pain and really couldn't talk. I was grateful for the silence and was happy that she was alive.
   Some nights, I dream of the fire. I was running, beating on the mail room door with my fists on fire. I saw my arms. They were crusty and wrinkled like marshmallows blackened at a camp fire. The first few times, I woke us both, me and Dindii, with screams.
   It was strange because Dindii was talking much to me

at that time, but she came to my bed and stroked my hair and face.

"The same dream?" She asked. When I nodded, she said, "Remember, it's not real. You'll be all right."

Even after the dreams stopped appearing often, I wasn't okay. That was when I first heard the word *atonement*. Somehow, I knew, I had to atone for what I had done. I decided to say a thousand prayers, three each day, asking for forgiveness. When I turned twelve—after saying over six thousand prayers, not missing a day—I felt I had to join a church to be forgiven. Some people had a small church-in-a-house two miles down the road toward Orr. I hoped they could teach me how to be forgiven. Just in case, I kept right on three times a day, asking.

I didn't see Dindii's scars, even after she went back to school, not for another five months and then only while she was asleep. Dindii didn't like people looking at her, trying to see under her long sleeves or her high collars. And even if she was kind and comforted me for nightmares, she never let me forget my part in the accident. "Popcorn" was all she ever called me, well, until after the blaze at Tillie's. I guess she could have called me worse.

Shookii 1
(Dindii)

This is how it happened to me.

Biini was hungry.

"Make me popcorn," she said and stamped her foot.

"I don't know how," I told her.

"Mama makes it. I saw you watching."

"You want me to build a fire?"

"No," Biini said, "in a pot on the stove."

Biini was right. It was like magic, and I had watched Mama pop corn over the campfire and on the old Spark gas stove lots of times. I guessed I knew how.

I only know what went wrong because I was told. I remember hardly any of it.

Standing on the step stool to reach the burner knobs, I added lots of oil to the pan when it was nice and hot. I'd covered the bottom with kernels already. I guess I spilled some oil over the burner, and when the fire flew up, I must have throwed the pan of water right there over the whole mess to put out the fire. But it spread. Then, I tipped the corn pot over on myself. That's how my arms and front got burned.

My sister just stood there. *That* I remember.

I fell off the stool.

That's when Biini ran. I saw her leave. I was told she went running for help. I never saw it that way.

"Shookii, popcorn. Shookii, popcorn. Shookii, popcorn." She screamed, repeating it over and over. Then she was gone.

Help came, I guess, in time to save me from the burning oil and the kitchen from flames—a cabinet to the side of the stove had started on fire. I know that because it never got painted again. Anything else, I couldn't know. I was on the floor.

Anyway, that's how I became known as Shookii. I shook the pot all over myself, and my name was a reminder of the scars I kept hidden under my long sleeves and collars. My chest was ruined. It looked like a snow tractor ran me over.

Biini gave me this stupid name, not on purpose, I guess, but it stuck faster than my oil-soaked tee shirt stuck to my frying skin. "Shookii."

It solved a problem, at least in summer. We are "identical" twins with similar Ojibwe names, Dindiisi, and Biinishii, which to the whites at Thief Lake, somehow—maybe because they really don't listen, or because they really don't care—sound the same. Look alike; sound alike. We were always being mistook with each other.

How does that make you feel? Dizzy, like you have double vision. You don't feel like yourself. And even after our nicknames stuck, it was a always a problem, outside of summer when I still wore long sleeves all the time. Only in warm weather could people stop, look at my arms, or at my sister's arms, and then know which was the poor little burned girl. Unless it was shot-sleeve weather, they couldn't tell.

I couldn't do nothin' to stop the name, but I stuck my sister with "Popcorn," so she would never forget who was at the root of my burnt body.

I forgave her, but never told her that.

I wanted her to suffer right along with me.

Danny Holds Forth 5

The mail truck was late that Monday morning, so I had yet to don my visor. In the kitchen, I was dishing up breakfast for Biini and my poor little Dindii. I liked using the short form of Biinishii and Dindiisi at that time though everyone but Morgan was calling them Popcorn and Shookii.

Out in the cafe, Danny was holding forth, telling everyone for the umpteenth time since I had become postmaster how he and I met. He usually had pent-up jabbering to loosen after a lonely weekend.

"You remember that snowstorm in '78? Biggest one since 1941!"

Everyone was nodding. The 1978 storm had shut down the state for three full days and, more importantly for the locals, marked the most notorious killing ever in Thief Lake. It was the beginning of the end of Tillie's, which had been closed now for five years, and was the end of the line for both owners, Roscoe Lucci and Jay "Scummy" Martinen, each a son of ore miners of the early 1900s.

Danny was rambling on. "Well, Cooley and me were out fetching Uncle Joki from his sister's house down south and stopped on the way at Bobbie's to get a cinnamon bun and coffee."

Someone chimed in, "You sure you guys split just one bun?" Everyone laughed. Both Cooley and Danny were of ample girths.

Danny shook off the hoot. He was used to it. "Jeez, was that road a mess! Cars in the ditches, rear ends left sticking outta' snowdrifts. Stuck at all angles. Lucky hardly anyone got killed . . ." Danny must have recalled at that moment that Scummy and Roscoe were both killed, although neither died from the storm. He righted himself and said, "Old Tatty here might have frozen if Scummy hadn't come along.

"Anyway, there we were, Cooley and me, enjoying our very own, individual cinnamon buns at the counter"– Danny cast a self-satisfied glance around—"when Nadine (the waitress, ya know) sweeps over with this new-plated bun and this guy." Danny pointed at me. "He looked like a deer in the headlights, couldn't say anything but 'yes' and 'no.'

"Remember that, Tatty?" I nodded. "Lucky Nadine didn't ask, 'Here or to go,' cause 'yes' and 'no' don't fit that one."

No one laughed. They had all heard it before.

"Anyway, when he found his tongue, that was when I got it! 'You're Mary's husband!' We were calling her Mary at that time." The whole crowd bent their gaze to the table and not because they had all heard it before.

No one there needed reminding, least of all me. It was sore knowledge that I had been married to a woman for fifteen years and still didn't know her real name, Morgan. She had fooled everybody. Scummy had cooked that one up right after the windigo chase to protect her from the law. Roscoe was the one who did time for the death of her twin. If she hadn't switched identities, Morgan would have been in prison, too. As it came out to the authorities (Oh, the sheriff was quite suspicious but couldn't prove anything), the co-organizer of the ill-fated windigo hunt had paid the ultimate price. She had frozen to death. They buried Roscoe in Stillwater penitentiary for years and his conspirator, Morgan (really Mary), they buried forever. After a twenty-year absence, Morgan returned and took her name back. No one said a thing. There was too much else to talk about.

Danny, again on an upswing, was crowing. "Me and Cooley were playing this game, 'salt and pepper.' We'd be talking and then say the same thing at the same time. The first one to say 'salt 'n pepper' got a point. I always won."

Cooley shook his head, sadly. "That's because I wasn't really playing."

"Yes, you were."

"No, I wasn't." Cooley didn't see it coming.

"Yes, you were." Danny got ready.

"No, I wasn't." He joined Cooley in his denial.

"Salt 'n pepper!" Danny clapped his hands. "See. I always win."

At that moment, Tiny dragged himself in and plunked himself down at the counter. "You still playing that idiotic game, Danny?" Today, my brother-in-law had an edge to his voice though he managed still to be friendly enough.

Danny screwed up his face, like an idiot, mumbling something out of one side of his mouth. "Got to have some fun," he said. Then he straightened up, face included, and continued on. "I was just telling folks how Tatty and me first met. You know. He was coming for Windsong's delivery."

Mr. Hooper Daniels, Danny to all, had a certain way of stepping in shit without coming up stinky. He was kind enough to everybody, so everyone forgave his foibles in advance.

Windsong was not a name anyone mentioned lightly,

except, this time, Danny. It was too complicated.

Morgan was Windsong's mother, Scummy her father. At the time of the snowstorm, though, when I first came to Thief Lake, no one but Windsong's parents knew that. Folks thought it was Mary who conceived Windsong with Roscoe. Even Roscoe thought that. The two had conceived a child, yes. But the true Mary died pregnant. Roscoe was jailed. Morgan, taking Mary's name, bore her own child, Windsong, and shortly after left town. Granny raised the girl. She never let Roscoe get near the child after his parole. Mainly, that was Tiny's doing. When all this came out at Tillie's in the middle of the snowstorm of the century, the barroom had grown hot as a real hell. Business partners and friends thirty-two years, Scummy and Roscoe fell victim to decades-long protective plots, twenty-year secrets, and outright lies. The outcome was the death of one and the disappearance of the other.

Danny recovered with grace, "And now we have the delightful company of Shookii and Popcorn!"

Dindii and Biini heard their names from the other room and suddenly were paying attention. They both waved at their audience beyond the proscenium of the pass-through separating the kitchen and cafe. Dindii stood, took a bow. Everyone in the cafe clapped with what seemed joy and relief.

Morgan was already in her studio—she didn't take well to the morning gatherings of what she called the clan—so I usually started the coffee service.

"Coffee, Tiny?" I asked.

He nodded and said, "Make it a big one. My boy's kids kept me up all weekend. I need the lift."

"Well, that's a nice grandpa. 'Give them all the attention they need.'" I was quoting one of my authors.

The Nothing That Is Not There 65

I went further, "And give the mothers time off for some Canadian fishing."

Morgan had told me she and Tiny's daughter-in-law, Beane planned a fishing trip north for the weekend. The freezer was newly stocked with walleye fillets to prove their good luck and skill.

"Canada! Hell, that's not why I was babysitting. My daughter-in-law is laid flat with a summer cold. Beanie didn't go nowhere. Too worried about her triple brood catching it. Her hubby, George had to work the weekend and brought the kids to me."

"Well, then." I was confused. "Where did all that walleye come from?" I wondered if Morgan had gone out alone.

"What Morgan took home?" Midway in his question, Tiny slowed his speech as if he had stepped in one of those piles Danny was so fond of and just realized it. "Well, I tell you," he hemmed and hawed, then seemed to decide he was in too deep to stop, "they came from my fish locker. Morgan picked them up Sunday evening."

Suspicion rose immediately, but I decided to let Tiny off the hook and take it up with Morgan later. "Thanks, Tiny. We were getting low on fish. You know how I'm better at climbing rocks than hooking walleye."

Tiny gratefully tipped his cup. He quickly turned to Danny.

I thought I heard the mail truck turning down the hill. I shooed the kids outside to wait for the school bus, took up my visor, opened the office.

As I headed out the door, Danny was yakking to Tiny. "We'd warned him about stopping in ta Tillie's . . ." which was his favorite part of his story. He usually saved it for newcomers, but not having been present for the action, my brother-in-law Tiny was a good enough ear and was acting interested in hearing it. I wondered about that sudden attention, shook my head, and went outside to meet the truck.

Work had always been my salvation for worry and my panacea for grief. It didn't have to be tough physical work to bring relief, either. It just needed to get my mind off my difficulties. And what Tiny had just accidentally told me was enough for me to seek the shelter of work.

Like magic, there was the mail truck and Sandy, the route driver, already stacking the boxes of place-sorted mail—two full cartons for Thief Lake folk and a half carton for the Gulbranson route Sandy would stuff into rural route boxes this afternoon after I final-sorted and ordered it.

"Big load today," I greeted him.

"Monday's always heavy," Sandy replied. "It always picks up in the fall, too."

We chatted just a bit since he was already running late, and I slipped him a doughnut from our pastry case before he went. "See you this afternoon." Sandy collected the outgoing along his stops down to the Virginia, Minnesota regional post office and did a quick turnaround to bring back a light afternoon delivery—most of the packages for general delivery came late in the day.

Already my mind was clear. Intent on my tasks, I focused on throwing mail. Inside, the post office was filling up now, buzzing with folk looking for letters and bills. Morgan had come out of her studio to fill orders at the counter and cash out groceries. The girls had pranced out to the school bus after taking their bows and applause.

I barely needed to think. It seemed that the letters themselves flew from my hands into the right place, nestling behind the little steel doors of the boxes. Thief Lake mail came first. The sooner I threw that load, the faster the crowd would dissipate. Most everyone came to pick up in the morning, very few in the afternoon unless they were expecting a check or a package. It could get close inside the post office when the truck arrived, especially in bad weather.

Finished with the lake mail, I turned to the half carton for the Gulbranson route. Right off, I stopped. The first item was a 10 x 10 flat addressed to *Teddy G and the Saints*, c/o Gulbranson's Resort, RR 3, Big Trout Lake, Minnesota. The sender was a music company in Hollywood, California.

Suddenly, I felt sick. Just as quickly, I knew. Oh, I had known. I just hadn't wanted to admit the truth. Now, I couldn't avoid it, and I was angry.

"Can I get some stamps, Mr. Langille?" One of the fishing-resort helpers from Hibbing was asking.

Her request brought me back to business where I couldn't be mad. "Sure, sure. Here's what we've got." I laid out the first class choices. My work at the window done, I shut the dutch door and finished sorting for Sandy's afternoon run. Then I sat, alone in the office.

Now, there was no doubt in my mind what Morgan had been up to. She had been gone from home too much that summer for me to miss it, but I had preferred to ignore the whole thing. Her absence gave me more weekend time with Dindii and Biini, especially dear after the popcorn-cooking accident. I had thought I needed to avoid confrontation with Morgan, and had hoped her recent waywardness would somehow pass. Now, I saw I had been wrong.

I'd caught her this time and now, I would castigate her.

That evening after choking down a plate of walleye and garden potatoes, I put the kids to bed with a story and came back to the kitchen. I'd closed the bedroom and the hall doors so our discussion wouldn't rile the girls.

Morgan was sitting at the table, stirring her last cup of coffee. She'd no doubt dashed a shot of Kahlua into it while I was gone.

"How was Beanie?" I started right in. "Who caught the most fish?" These sounded like the usual questions. I didn't want to tip my hand until she was deep into lying, even though she'd told some whoppers already.

"They were taking the bait." She kept her answer short and indirect.

"And Beanie?"

"She's just fine." Morgan said. She now seemed alert to my drift and added, "Actually, she took the trophy for biggest and most, too."

I was ready to spring my trap. "Well, that's funny, because Tiny told me that Beanie was laid up with a bad summer cold. George, he said, dumped the kids off at his place for the weekend so they wouldn't catch it before school started."

For the first time in years, Morgan wasn't quick enough to turn a lie.

"Don't bother covering your tracks. Tiny told me you got all that walleye from his fish locker."

I had thrown two jabs, and now I hit her with a roundhouse punch. "So, where did you spend your weekend? Gulbranson's?"

She had to give me a fight even though she was flat on her back in deception.

"What is this? The inquisition?"

"Only when you're lying."

"You just lay off, buster." She yelled.

"You're flat out lying." I insisted.

She couldn't shut her mouth and asked, "About what?"

I looked straight at her. "About visiting Beanie. About fishing with her. About your weekend visits to that Preacher's cabin out on Pelican Point. Stop treating me like a fool."

"Well, you seem to know everything, so why are you asking me?"

I pointed to the hall door, toward the girls' room, "I guess you're slipping around so they won't find out their mother is a tramp, but so help me, if they get wind of this, it will be the last time they sleep under the same roof with you."

She came round the table, right up to my face. "Don't you threaten me, mister-culfister."

I probably shouldn't have said what came next, but I was steaming by then. "I suppose you were out on Pelican Point when Dindii burnt herself. Some mother."

I surprised her. She turned to stone. I didn't back down, not a half-step. I had been right. Now, we were nose to nose both shaking in fury. "Do what you want, but remember what I've said."

Since that phony preacher was in California until spring, she had all winter to think about it.

Papa's Twins 6

The winter following the confrontation with my wayward wife was the most miserable we suffered since I first wintered at Thief Lake. The chill that crept into my marriage also worked frigid fingers into every cranny of the town and chilled recent immigrants to the lake.

September's first rains knocked the leaves to the ground early, all at once. The roads, especially those that ran along the shores of the lake, being dirt and gravel, turned to sodden masses of dead, blackening leaves mixed with mud. Even cautious driving proved treacherous when spinning tires spewed sopping leaf-ooze and sludge over cars following too close, wadding up in the wheel wells and suspension springs. Over-night frost covered the whole mess. Then, morning rains filled the mire all over again. It rained nearly every day.

In the middle of all this came two roughnecks from southern Indiana who having fished the big lakes in Canada as tourists had heard that Olsen's Resort would be up for sale in the spring. They, apparently, planned to get to the owners before the listing. What had been an idea to close a deal, slipping up to the lake quietly, became a fall fiasco witnessed by almost everyone on the lake.

"Have you met the stooges?" Cooley asked me.

I had not. "I'm not sure who you mean. The Three Stooges?"

"Yeah, maybe, but there's just two. I meant Laurel and Hardy."

I was still confused, but Danny helped me out. "The two Indians who want to buy Olsen's."

"Indianans, you fool, not Indians. Don't forget Tatty here is Mi'kmaq.

"Sorry, Tatty. Indian-ianses, I guess."

Cooley slapped his forehead.

I laughed. "Are those their names?"

"Maybe. One is Stanley. Kind of tall and skinny. The big one is Ralph, I think."

I still had not. "No, I haven't had the pleasure."

Danny ran with it. "Well, we, Uncle Joki and me, found them in the ditch. They slid on the leaf-muck right around Halsey's curve and slammed square into the deepest part of the ditch. We needed three trucks to get the car out."

"Anyone hurt?"

Cooley stepped in. "Just the Chevy they were driving. A stump went right through the oil pan. What a stew."

So instead of stealth, impossible after the car wreck, Stan and Ralph used cash, and lots of it, to accomplish their mission. They stayed three days over Olsen's garage across the road from the resort and became reluctant celebrities by the end of the first day. Apparently no one mentioned the incipient transformation of the entire area surrounding the lake into a part of the new Boundary Waters Canoe Area (BWCA) which, along with old man Olsen's approaching 75th birthday, gave him all the reasons he needed to sell. The BWCA was destined to end much of the motor traffic on the nearby wilderness lakes that fed the Thief Lake watershed. Old man Olsen knew it meant the shrinking and slow death of the resorts in the neighborhood, maybe with the exception of Gulbranson's.

After three days, all of which were filled with rain, Laurel and Hardy—everyone called them L & H—bought a used Ford sedan and left town the proud new owners of a motor-launch fishing resort that, they would soon find, was on its way to hard times.

In the second summer of their ownership, Stan and Ralph polished their bar, now empty of customers from Chicago and Milwaukee, with anti-government diatribe and their animosity toward government regulation misplaced on a ranger who had frozen near the narrows the winter after their resort purchase. I guess they didn't realize the man was local and starred on his high school basketball team in its heyday. Sure, their business was down, but trash made L & H two unlikeable people to avoid.

Yes, the southern powerboat crowd went anywhere but the BWCA, but Laurel and Hardy's negative blasts disgusted the locals. The pair had to let go the cook who had served the best fried chicken on the lake for over twenty years. Even the bar stood empty since Stan and Ralph didn't serve Indians. Then they started serving Indians, and that didn't go down easily with the whites. The dock was empty of fishing boats. The bar was a mess. The restaurant closed. Only the cabin trade, an ill-stocked store, and high-octane gas sales were keeping them afloat.

All this was to come, but nobody knew it that first day they left with the deed to the resort, because the weather changed.

An ice storm swept down from Canada, covering everything in a quarter-inch-thick glaze. The storm was followed by a still, hard freeze that kept the ice on the boughs for three days, long enough to break birch limbs and pine branches, leaving behind shattered ice jackets and jagged and stumpy broken boughs.

A fierce windstorm followed, felling the older timber that had managed to keep its icy branches intact, the falling ice sounding like an whole orchestra of ideophones, tinkling down one the frosted forest floor that had hardened in the deep but sunshiny freeze. The wind toppled old-time white pine across the main road and on the lake trails too, making driving impossible. Without snow yet in October, snowmobiles were of no use. Even the few boats that had been left in the water—most were dry-docked to avoid ice damage—couldn't move for a half inch skin of ice locked them in place.

Then, the snows of November isolated the lake. The storms were not notable century-stoppers but came with a frightening frequency, three in the first week, each followed by unseasonable freezes of below zero weather. The second week, starting on Veterans Day, two monsters flew south across the international border and hit Thief Lake with twelve and, then, fourteen inches of wind driven snow which piled in mountains each side of the road. Snowplows operated round the clock. Snowmobiles finally became useful, but they had to stay on shore since the lake ice had yet to set hard and thicken. With the amount of snow cover on the two inch-thick skin, the lake might not freeze all winter, the warm springs and insulating top cover keeping the under layer of ice soft and cavity pocked.

In weather like we were having, tragedy was likely, perhaps, inevitable.

Between the one-footer and the fourteen-inch snow, one of the rangers assigned to the new BWCA, the high school basketball star, headed out to check on the office cabin on the narrows. When he didn't come back, most thought he had hunkered down at the cabin to wait out the storm. But three days later when the weather cleared his partner found no trace of him, at home or cabin. He was just gone.

"Looks like another windigo-chase," Danny said.

Cooley looked at me and covered, again, for Mr. Daniel's gaffs, "Maybe that ranger just up and left for Florida."

Those two had a way with comedy. I laughed, halfway, "That sounds pretty good to me right now. I could be on the beach."

It wasn't Florida. Our new ranger would be found in late spring, or rather his snowmobile in shallow water would be found. Most of the ranger had fallen to the wolves.

His death was peculiar for someone like him who had grown up in the wintry wastes. He certainly knew better than to brave thin ice and certainly should have checked the weather reports before setting out. Danny swore that the man had been hounded by windigos or by the new government-haters, and in his effort to escape them tried to make it across the narrows where the ice was usually thicker. Be that as it may, Cooley reasoned that once drenched, the ranger was quick to freeze. He was covered by the second storm but not deep enough to prevent the timber wolves from finding him. For years, dreams showing him gnawed on, organs eaten, limbs chewed and pulled from their sockets haunted the sleep of many a lake dweller. Peculiar, too—though no one thought about it until years later when a second, then a third ranger disappeared—was the absence of the cause of death.

Danny later said, "He coulda been stabbed. That would never show up."

Cooley had to admit it was true.

Pressing his bad luck, Danny hypothesized once more, "An' he coulda been shot through without the slug hitting anything not eat-able."

"Edible," Cooley corrected, flashing a morose grin. "And it's all edible, cept the bones.

"That's what I said."

"Pepper and salt," Cooley answered.

The ranger's death was suspicious without much suspicion being spent, until the other deaths, which were bona fide murders, came to pass. Each time the town filled with FBI agents. It was a national park, making it a federal case.

During that terrible winter, the waves of storms stopped just after Thanksgiving. Then the deep freeze set in. The unofficial low-temperature record was set then broken, day by day. Twenty degrees below zero at noon, not for a day, not for a week, but for one and a half months, forty-five of the shortest, darkest days and longest nights each side of Christmas. No one could recall an early winter so bitter, so unrelenting.

Even the children, my twins included, were restless

and feeling cooped up. Perhaps we were all depressed. During the big snows, of course, all the town kids were in heaven. Mine knew how to ski, snowshoe, and rock climb. They could tunnel into snowbanks and hollow out a drift to make a cave castle in the snow. When the darkness and the mercury dropped, though, board games and stories they had heard a hundred times before were not enough to soothe tempers and keep a happy family—well, happy.

That was when Morgan got them painting. Most of their paper and the occasional canvas depicted winter scenes. Snowy fields trimmed with high rock walls and dark pines. Maybe snowscapes were fresh in mind.

Morgan reached back to remember the Anishinabe stories her Grandmother had told, including the girl and the windigo story.

"How did the lake get its name, Mama?" Biini wanted to know.

Dindii joined in. "Yes, tell Popcorn the story. She doesn't remember."

"Don't call her that," Morgan said.

"She calls me Shookii. So I call her Popcorn," Dindiisi insisted.

"Tell us, tell us," Biini chanted.

It was a peculiar tale in which a young girl saved her people, losing her life to the evil lake spirits that served a *manidoo* or windigo. It was never clear to me that anything or anybody was stolen, but the story, as Granny Bassett told me in my first days here, concludes with the naming of Thief Lake. Inscrutable as Granny herself. The twins, of course, loved to hear it. And Morgan burnished her recollections of Granny's telling, making horrible *manidoo* faces and growling noise, rising up from haunches, arms raised, fingers spread like talons, reaching for the twins who screamed in fear and joy. It had been at a time like this that I loved Morgan most, for her penchant for native lore and sensibility. Were it that stories alone could fill a Minnesota winter. Even animated telling couldn't ease that savage, dark time.

School was a great help. All during the soggy September, the ice-laden October, snowy November and frigid December, Dindii and Biini dutifully and joyously boarded the bus and traveled the twenty-five miles into Orr for second grade. Dindii missed a few days for medical appointments but she and Biini—both were known by their nicknames at school now, so I joined in using them when Morgan wasn't around—found comfort and interest in attending. That year, they ceased being identical twins, not because of Dindii's burns and grafting scars, not because of the guilt, sorrow, and anger around the kitchen fire itself, and maybe not even so much because of the wedge the burning had driven between them. Call me a needle brain, but I thought the differences I began to see in those two reflected and were caused by the distances Morgan and I found between ourselves and in the way we looked upon each other and on our two girls. If Morgan was there to serve the girls, I was there to protect them.

It was as if Morgan readopted Dindii. Was it the tragedy that had befallen her? Morgan was tragic in her own way but was more like Biini, in that Morgan felt she had caused her sister Mary's fall. Perhaps opposites attract in some way. Maybe Dindii took the place of the real Mary, someone damaged, this time not beyond repair, forming a second chance for Morgan to redeem herself. In any case, Dindii and Morgan became confidants that winter and as time went on became close companions, starting during Dindii's convalescence and continuing years, even up to the reopening of Tillie's Tavern. Well before that time, it was too late for Morgan to again adopt our other twin. She was then both too far off and much too close.

I suppose I took Biini's side, not in defense, but because she had not lost a sister altogether but had diminished in her role as a sister. I was there. I saw clearly that she had saved her adventurous sister, preserved her life by frantic but quick action. It was certain that she felt a weighty sorrow, one that no manner of atonement could lessen, though she took to religious penance to assuage her guilt. I drew Biini close to me to balance the loss she had so undeservedly suffered. As her remorse grew over the years to what I thought might be unhealthy extremes, her dependence on the Bible she used to comfort herself increased. Given what I now know about where her "faith" would lead her, I wish I had intervened much sooner than I did. What else is new?

I couldn't and still cannot deny that I played the same role in Morgan's life, though for years I could not know, except by her outrageous behavior—fist-fighting, dish-smashing, and causing uproars of all kinds—that she suffered hugely. Usually, such acts were so shocking that the sources and motives remained obscure and unquestioned. I suppose, being an only child despised by my father, lonely and afraid, I learned to sympathize with the losers of the world: myself, my wife, and later, my children included. In one way, it was Indian. In another, Finnish. Longtime oppressed, long suffering.

All this is not to say our little family was maudlin. With Morgan's affair with the Preacher in the freezer for the winter, and despite the problems the girls struggled with, we took joy in all the combinations, parent-child, twin sisters, mother and father, of our small clan. How can anyone be blue—except blue with cold—while digging snow caves with seven-year olds, or leading cross country ski excursions to "mountain climb" the wintery crags the glaciers had millenia ago left to scale. We cooked bacon and eggs over a blaze built on the snow?

"Can you make the toast, Dindii?" I asked, not really thinking it through.

Dindii stayed clear of flames. "No, Papa, you do it."

"I've got the pan to handle." Then I realized what I was asking and tried to mend it. "Biini? Can you? And Dindii, you help mama with the cups and plates."

So, Biini and I cooked over the fire and Morgan and Dindii set the stump-table for lunch. No amount of cajoling, no degree of cold would bring Dindii closer to the fire. She sat on a log furthest away.

"Wrap up in my blanket, girl," I said.

"Thank you, Papa." She shared the blanket with Morgan. The new form of our family fell into place that winter.

I had given Morgan my sternest warning. Though she seemed to take it lightly as I expected she might, Morgan acted on it in a serious manner all that interminable winter long. In late spring, though, as soon at that jet buzzed the town, Morgan, like a boozer who's found a hidden bottle, was off again.

Chris-Craft 7

Tatty and had I struck a deal. The summer ended. Preacher had already flown back to California for the winter. Without the temptation pestering me all the time—the dance music, the secluded cabin at Pelican Point, the tangy gimlets, the Sunday morning "sermon on the mount," as Preacher called his love-time howling—without all these, the dark and cold months, though dull, were passable.

I painted snowscapes. Tatty puttered on his birch bark canoe and sorted mail. Biini and Dindii studied their lessons, perfected skiing and snowshoeing, and spent many nights bedded down in Tiny's fish-house bunks. Out there they fished, told each other stories, built snow spirits, and, with Tiny's help, two little igloos. During the spring breakup those two were forever running down to the shore with field glasses, trying to see whose igloo fell through the ice first. Biini marked hers with a green flag, Dindii with a yellow one.

That winter we spent days at a time in Hibbing at the hospital with Dindii who needed skin grafts. The burn scars were hard for me to look at, and the skin grafts, taken from her sides, made that part of her look as bad as her arms and chest had. I worried that her breasts would be misshapen if they ever developed. The doctor said they would come. "You can't stop nature."

Yeah, you can't stop nature. By early May, I had convinced myself that my fling with Teddy G was over.

Absence cooled my jets, but as soon as his jet strafed the town, the Friday of Memorial Day weekend, I was off, panting down the Trout Lake trail on my way to Gulbranson's. I couldn't help it. The twins were canoeing with Tiny. And though Tatty started watching me closely as soon as Preacher's jet flew over, just to see how I behaved, that didn't seem to matter to me. It was as if I watched myself sleepwalk to that woodsy trail, scratching my itch all the way, like floating on a cloud or in a dream, mentally stripping off clothes, his and mine, too, as I stepped through sky-borne fluff. Anyway, that's what I did. I didn't even wait for the music to start that night. It was early afternoon when I knocked on the cabin door.

Preacher wasn't there, but he must have seen me from the dock further out on the point, for he was shouting over the curve of the bay. Once I saw him, I was in a sweat and nearly swam over rather than hike around the bay on land. I forced myself to walk, not run. When I saw him closer up, he looked as radiant as a saint in a triptych.

"Muggsy!" He shouted from the end of the dock. "Come out and meet '*Muggsy!*'"

How he got my nickname started, I don't remember, but he'd always called me that. Now, he grabbed my arm and led me to the stern of the most beautiful boat I had ever seen, even in Florida. He pointed to the large curly, gold, sparkling script that read "*Saint Muggsy,*" and below that in small block letters "Pelican Point, Minn."

I stood like a niche-statue of the Virgin Mary, just taking in the beauty of the thing. I beamed.

Saint Muggsy sported a bowed and tapered wood top punctuated by three spanking-clean glass windshields, protecting each of the passenger compartments that were all upholstered in reddish-brown tucked-leather bench seats and backrests. The sides as well as the decking were of laminated wood strips, flashing their varnish in the sun and looking solid enough to bowl on. The brass hull fittings and the chrome on the front compartment dashboard sparkled as the boat rocked gently in the afternoon breeze. It was a Chris-Craft, built in Michigan.

"Muggsy, meet *Muggsy*. I named her after you."

"How . . . When . . ," I stammered.

"I wanted to surprise you." He took me gently by the shoulders, "Don't think for a minute I take you for granted. In this baby, Baby, we are going to have a blast."

He took me into his arms right there on the dock, and we gyrated, reacquainting ourselves with each other. When he finally peeled himself away, I was fixing to lie right down there on the dock.

"Ready to take a spin?" he said, more of a captain's command than a question. "Step aboard, Matey." He stepped onto the gorgeous wood deck and drew me carefully up to guide me down into the cockpit next to the steering wheel.

"Where's the motor?" I said. At Thief Lake, I had never known a power boat to have anything but an outboard clamped onto its stern. This sleek thing of Preacher's was without that ugly appendage.

"It's an 'M' Hercules inboard." He sat on the deck, spreading his legs wide right beside me, and slid down the back rest, slipping behind the wooden helm which looked just like a larger automobile steering wheel.

Teddy twisted a key in the chrome adorned dashboard. Astern, the Hercules rumbled to life. He cast a line off a little brass boat cleat, and we slid smoothly away from the dock. I slipped my arm over the seat back and smoothed his wavy blonde locks.

He smiled at me and slid his hand up from my knee. "Open that compartment there," he said nodding to an over-sized glove box on my side of the dash. There, I found stowed the fixings for gimlets, including a small insulated bucket of ice.

"Preacher, you sure know how to give a girl a ride!"

"In style, Muggsy, but button that up for a while." Now, at quarter full, well away from the dock past the warning buoys, Teddy jammed a lever up and *Saint Muggsy* took off like the preacher's jet, rising as if to fly, leaving behind the dock, cabin and resort in a high-spray wake. "Full ahead, old girl!"

I nestled next to him, feeling the wind whipping around me, and, sinking into the sun-warmed seats, I found places to warm my hands and things to do with them.

After traveling halfway across Trout Lake, Preacher said, "I'll settle this baby down to a troll while you get to the gimlet-mixing." He cut the engine down to a purr and, throwing one arm behind my shoulders gave me the slyest grin I'd seen in six months. "I had this delivered on the q.t. to have it ready to surprise you as soon as I arrived." His smile widened. "I've got a blanket and a picnic lunch in the stern compartment. Know of any islands we should invade?"

It didn't take much to get the old loins a-itch'n'. I mixed the gimlets on a pull-out tray that slid from under the glove compartment and looked back to spy the picnic basket behind us. We toasted the "best damn love boat on the border lakes," diving headlong into what became a series of nine summers I wouldn't soon forget. "Set your course to That Man Island on the northeast side of the lake, Captain."

"Yes, Ma'am." Teddy was still beaming.
We clicked our glasses. "I'm mighty hungry," I said.

All these small islands up north are uninhabited, although canoe-campers occasionally pitch a tent on one or another. The Man chain of islands, This Man, That Man, Some Man, Half Man, and The Other Man were long, forested, glaciated ridges, poking steeply up through the lake surface, overlapping their lengths to interlace like long fingers along the chain's three mile length. None of the isles were more than three quarters of a mile long, and you could easily swim from one island to another over what had been, before even the Sioux passed through the area, canyons the great glacier had made digging channels through the rock, filling them as it melted. The chain was the ultimate in privacy, and That Man, being shaped somewhat like a gaff, a sheltering hook at the end of the long island, provided a snug little mooring for *Saint Muggsy*. The island's ridge hid us from the open lake and This Man just across the narrow passage sheltered us from prying eyes further on. It was mid-afternoon Friday, and the weekend traffic was yet to pick up. We had the whole chain to ourselves—or so we thought.

Preacher, slipping his bell bottoms off to reveal a Speedo branded "LA," one letter to a buttock, threw up his arms as if from a pulpit, extolling the virtues of God's creation and raising his shirttails above the swimsuit.

"In the beginning, The Lord set the eternal sun in the bluest sky." He swept his arms from side to side as if to embrace the whole of the heavens. "He created the pines to show the way to heaven, the amber waters to sweep us along toward salvation, and," here he lowered his open arms to me, "woman to fulfill the promise of fruitfulness and felicity."

I heard his words but was thinking mostly of the Speedo which began to bulge in front, I thought, and wanted to see, again, what it hid from view—his God-given charms.

Teddy Good wasn't done, though, and his praise ran right into a song of grace. "And good God gave us food!" He exclaimed, "So let's eat!" We spread the blanket over a nice growth of moss, opened the basket and fed each other bites of sandwich and fruit.

We eyed each other as we ate. I mixed us another gimlet for dessert. We stripped and made up for nearly eight months' absence, Preacher expounding his sermon on the mount all the while. Afterwards, we lay on the blanket drying our sweat under the sun watching a lone eagle cruise over the waters between That Man and This.

"Let's take a dip," Preacher said.

"Last one in's a ninny," I shouted, stood, and plunged into the freezing amber-colored water, diving deep along the glacial escarpment. Though he was a California pansy, Preacher followed closely, landing a cannonball right over me. We came together in a chilled embrace. We lasted two minutes in the frigid water.

"Okay, I give. Let's get out," he said.

"I'm ready," I told him, but then I heard something that made me stay put. "That's a little outboard. It's coming this way."

"Well, I'm getting out," Teddy G said, and he swam to the nook of the gaff-shaped marina and grabbed a sturdy twig on an overhanging fir to hoist himself up to shore. He wrapped up in a towel we had left on the branch just as the canoe rounded the point. "Ahoy, mateys." He called.

I was sheltered from view by *Saint Muggsy* but went under anyway. I knew by a singular sound of that outboard that it was Tiny, likely trolling with the girls aboard for walleye that filled the glacial deeps there. His ancient open-top half-horse motor made that distinctive chug like an old washing machine agitating heavy clothes. I had run the motor enough to know the sound well.

I stayed under until I had to breathe, taking a chance each time I surfaced. I had to be as quiet as an otter and as quick too, repositioning to keep *Muggsy* between me and the canoe which I could see the bottom of through the resin-stained water. I heard bits and pieces of Preacher, joshing around with them. I heard something about baptism. Teddy must have known who the girls paddling in the bow were, and Teddy G, as he assured me later, said nothing that would tip our hand. Tiny, idling the small motor, had to know that Preacher was not alone, but the girls likely didn't know that and certainly none could say it was me.

I was chilling rapidly, and it seemed that Preacher wouldn't let them go on their way. He loved an audience, but I was not about to get out in front of my brother and my girls even if it meant freezing to death.

Tiny finally engaged the engine and trolled past, and the threesome disappeared around the tip of This Man, a half mile up.

Preacher held a towel for me when I climbed out and rubbed me down with vigor. Despite my long wintering that year, I was shivering like it was December.

"You'll drown or freeze doing that," Teddy said.

"Better that than frying in the hells of home. Those girls were my twins!"

Preacher nodded. He knew. "I didn't want to hurry them along. That would have been suspicious," he said.

I went to the blanket and donned my clothes. "Let's get back."

"So be it," Preacher said. "Come to the stage tonight. I'll croon some new hymns for you."

With *Muggsy*'s speed, I made it back home hours before Tiny dropped the twins off at the Thief Lake dock. Tatty came in later with them by the time I had supper ready.

My afternoon jaunt, *Saint Muggsy*'s maiden voyage on the northern lakes, turned into a close call. You'd think that I'd straighten up a bit afterwards, but not this girl. As soon as the twins were tucked in bed and the supper dishes done, I was back on the scent of Teddy Good and his Saints. As soon as I sat down at the bar stool nearest the bandstand, Al served up a gimlet without me even ordering. I was off and running once again.

Still, the close call at That Man led me to change one thing: Preacher and I cruised more during the short summer nights than in the long days. We still did picnics, farther up the chain of lakes, further from Thief, but learned to love floating in the middle of Trout under the stars. On those nights surrounded by the glimmer of sky on black waters, we were alone in the expanse of the universe. We skinny dipped, toweled off, and snuggled under blankets in the middle compartment on the bench seat that transformed into a full bed. We were floating through wide galaxies and nebulae of love.

We lay on our backs gazing.

"There's the summer triangle," Preacher said. "The Trinity of the night sky."

"Where?"

He guided my sight. "Almost straight up. See three bright stars in a right triangle? That's Vega, Deneb, and Altair."

"There? That one is *Bineshii Okanin*, the Skeleton Bird's head."

"What say you?" Teddy said.

I swept my arm along the Milky Way. "Its *Ajiijaak*, the Crane flying along the path of the stars, leading all the others through the night sky."

Preacher rose up on an elbow. He looked down on my face. "I didn't know you were an Ojibwe astronomer. You're full of surprises."

I pushed him back down. "Granny taught Mary and me most of the Ojibwe sky when we were kids." I pointed to Polaris in the little dipper. "We have the same name for that one, *Anang Giiwedin* or North Star."

"What's the constellation name? Bear?"

As if to answer, a pair of birds somewhere distant on the black waters quavered their calls to each other. "No, Loon. The northern bird with the stars on his back."

And so we spent the summer teaching each other, among other things, the names of the constellations that swirled in the Trout Lake summer sky.

I never went near Thief Lake in *Saint Muggsy*, but since the Indianians who bought Olsen's Resort were the only ones on the chain of border lakes who stocked the high octane gasoline Preacher preferred to run in the "M" Hercules engine, *Muggsy* became a familiar sight there. The twins were full of news about her.

"I saw the *Saint* today," Biinishii crowed.

Her sister shook her head, looked around to see which of us, me or Tatty, was listening, and since we both were trying for different but related reasons to look any other way than interested, she said, "Big deal. That runabout is always at Olsen's gassing up."

Dindiisi, though, couldn't cow her sister's enthusiasm. "It's the most beautiful boat on all the lakes. *Saint Muggsy* is like the Queen of Heavens and Lakes."

Tatty intervened, thank god. "All right sisters. Play nice."

Biini said, "I am nice. I'm a nice Christian girl, aren't I, Mom?"

She had drawn me in as always. "Yes, you're a very nice girl." I did as little as possible to propagate Biini's interest in Christian ways. I humored Preacher, but I didn't believe any of it. I don't think he did either.

Dindii rolled her eyes. "Maybe, but mostly when parents are around." Now she appealed to parental natures, and looking our way said, "You guys just don't know."

"Let's stop the bickering," Tatty said. He looked at his watch, crossed the room, and put on his visor. That would be the last of his participation. I shooed the girls into the studio and got them drawing rather than talking. Biini drew *Saint Muggsy*, a boat with wings. Dindii sketched a landscape showing Tillie's among the white pines. I pinned those two drawings on my studio wall. For all I know, they are still there, signifying the sharp contrasts in the twins' developing interests.

That summer, my second cavorting the lakes with Preacher, proved, after that first close call, uneventful on the family front, though there was plenty of action out on the nighttime lakes after Gulbranson's bar closed. Sooner than I thought possible, most of the summer was over, and up to that point, Tatty hadn't confronted me about my night absences. I supposed he was giving me all the rope I needed to hang myself.

Youth

Popcorn 2
(Biini)

For most of our childhood, I thought that Shookii, who was only named Dindiisi then, and I were one person. Of course, we were born together. She is just a few minutes older. It seemed that we always woke up and fell asleep at the same time. We ate together and liked the same foods. We got sick at the same times with fevers, colds, and one time the flu. She felt like my left hand. I was her right.

When we were going on seven, all that changed. The fire burned us apart. I saw in a new way afterwards that she was a separate person from me. When I saw her catch fire at the stove that day and go to the floor shaking and squirming, I saw she was in agony, but I felt no pain at all. All I felt was fear. That's when I knew for sure that we were parted souls. Before that, I just hadn't seen that.

That was the most frightening thing about the accident. Sure, my sister's burning was horrible. Her scars were ugly. But the worst of it for me was that suddenly I was nobody. I hadn't lost just half of me. I'd lost everything. I didn't know who I was, and I didn't know how to find out. My parents were set all on Shookii. Though they didn't blame me for the accident, I couldn't break through the hurt to go to them.

When Shookii's life settled down, mine didn't. I wasn't me anymore. Dindii didn't seem lost like I was, but she wasn't her old self, either. She looked almost the same though she always had those long sleeves covering her arms and often wore turtlenecks. But she was closed off to me. I couldn't ask her anything or learn how to be like she was. The kid she used to be, for years, was now shut. I couldn't read her. She gave no signs. She didn't let me in.

People thought I turned to prayer because of guilt. Part of that is true, but the rest was that I had to find out who I was. I needed to be another person than the one I couldn't find anymore. When I looked for me, I found the door to religion standing open.

We took lots of trips to Shookii's doctor. On the way to one appointment one early morning, a couple of miles from our house along the dirt and gravel road to Orr, I noticed for the first time a house a little back from the road. Its front door was open, light was streaming out onto the stoop. "Who lives there?" I asked.

"Someone who likes mosquitoes and rodents," Mama said. "That's why the door is open."

Shookii and Papa laughed. "No, no," Papa said. "It's Old Borg, the Swede, they call him. His real name is Eric Ericksen."

"Then why do they call him Old Borg?" I wondered out loud.

"Because he eats mosquitoes and rats for breakfast." Shookii said.

Papa chuckled. "He is a Swedenborgian. So they call him Borg for short."

"What's a Sweetened Boogian?" I wanted to know.

This time Mama laughed. "Someone who's sweet on religion. A faith-nut."

Papa always wanted to teach us the truth. He came in then. "Well, he seems like a nut, but really he just follows a certain branch of Christianity named after a Swedish mystic. They call it 'The New Church,'" he said.

"Is it just for Swedes? Like Olsens?"

Mama took over, "They'll take anyone they can get."

I thought this Old Borg might be someone to help me become a new person.

That was the beginning of my church-going days, the first step I took to find out who I really was. I started by walking across the road from that house like a thousand times. Then, I'd stand across the road and watch for like hundred hours or two. Finally, I sneaked closer to look through that door that was always open. I plucked up my courage to get near, then to poked my head in. All that took me almost three years. What I found inside was a person who understood me and could help.

Mr. Ericksen had a small congregation. It was mostly his family, kids, grand kids, and a cousin or two with their children. He invited me in and made me feel at home in the bosom of Jesus. I was an Ojibwe kid among Scandinavians, but I felt like one of their tribe.

Looking back now, I think it was the most wonderful time of my life, even though when I was nearly grown up, the Swedenborgs, without meaning to, opened another door that should have remained closed: the entry to Planet Earth's Church of God and its pastor, Teddy Good.

I let Dindii follow her dark, Native religion if that's what it was. She seemed to think it made her smarter somehow, but I knew the Truth. Once in a while she would tell me stuff that were just evil lies—one she told me was that dead people who had murdered others still roamed the lake shores, sometimes as animals such as bears. I refused to listen to her wrongheaded thoughts. If I wasn't her anymore, I had to follow my own path, the true one.

Shookii 2
(Dindii)

I wasn't about to spill the beans because I could never tell if Popcorn was going to upend her can of kernels in front of our parents. I couldn't trust that girl—that was burned into me when she ran out of the kitchen, speeding away from my shaking body and the burning cabinet above the stove—so, why did I ever tell her anything? When someone is as close to you as Biini was to me for our first seven years, you just keep going there even when you know that only bad will come of it.

She kept bringing up *Saint Muggsy*. Why? I don't know, but I suppose it was some sort of religious connection she made in her tiny, empty brain. She seemed to love that boat despite the way Mama had been treading water behind her hull, hiding from us. I didn't try to make her see, but I hadn't held back trying to warn her about what was what. Popcorn wouldn't believe me, anyway, but I washed my scarred arms of responsibility. She was her own person now. She could choose what to believe.

"I wish I had a picture of that boat," Popcorn said. We were in our room after supper the day we had trolled by That Man Island with Uncle Tiny.

"Well, if you had snapped one, you'd have some evidence."

"What? What's that mean?"

"What I mean, Popcorn, is that you could then see whose clothes were piled on that picnic blanket."

As usual, Biini was or acted dumb. "Clothes?"

"Do you think that Preacher Teddy Good was out there swimming alone? Or was preaching to the mosquitoes?"

"I don't know," Popcorn said. "Maybe he was. Maybe he was working on his Sunday sermon."

That girl didn't know anything. "His church meets on Saturday, you idiot."

Popcorn ignored my name-calling. "Well, he might have been fishing."

I wasn't going to draw her a picture. I saw what our mother was wearing at supper that night. It was for sure the same yellow blouse and those blue shorts she had on in the kitchen that had been piled on a blanket under panties and a bra on That Man Island just that afternoon. Why she didn't think to change, I couldn't figure.

"Well, whoever was with him was still in the lake," I said. "'Why?' is the question."

"I didn't see anybody."

I shook my head. "You didn't hear someone bumping the boat, ducking under, or coming up for air?"

"Well, maybe. Yes, why would he hide?"

I corrected Popcorn, "She."

"She who?"

"You tell me," I said. "The one whose clothes were on the blanket."

"Well, if there was someone, though I doubt it, swimming without clothes on, he or she wouldn't want to prance out in front of Uncle Tiny or us, now would he, or," Popcorn added, "she?"

Popcorn made her point. It made her sure. But I knew better. I believed what I saw, not what I couldn't see.

In her little, budding-Christian mind, she couldn't believe evil was in the world—not devils, not windigos, not cheaters or murderers. Even if she had seen the flames of destruction right in front of her face, she wouldn't say so. She was always running away from the truth, hiding from what was really evil. I wasn't going to be the one to set her straight. I tried a few times, though. She really didn't have a clue.

After all that happened years later, I wish I had just outright told her, "It was Ma there with Teddy G, you dummy." But I suppose it wouldn't have made any difference. You can check with Granny on that. You shouldn't try to change things-a-coming. Popcorn didn't believe that, of course.

Tatty and Roscoe 8

The way I was feeling in the heat of the summer I turned fifty years old, with Morgan off once again romancing the preacher of Planet Earth's Church of God, was only degrees away from the sensations I felt on my first trip to Thief Lake in the middle of the snowstorm of the century, even though the difference in Fahrenheit was at least eighty-five degrees. Both times, Morgan had left me. Thirteen years back, she'd traveled north to her Thief Lake relations, and four years ago—long enough for me to realize both that her infidelity was permanent and that she had succeeded in "sheltering" the girls from the knowledge—had beaten bare the Trout Lake path to the California medicine man who was no better than a patent-remedy carnival barker. The most notable difference, because I keep most of my suffering inside, this time was that my hair turned as white as snow at the end of the longest heat wave of the summer.

It happened all in one night—I'm not pretending I wasn't going gray already—and it might go to show just how regimented and habitual my life had become that I did not even realize the change had taken place until Danny took notice when he showed up for early morning coffee. The twins were still sleeping. Morgan kept to her studio or to Pelican Point day and night. She hadn't entered our bedroom in years. So, Danny was the first to see me that day.

I brought the pot to the cafe bar that separated the kitchen from the store and was pouring two big cups for Danny and me. As I set the pot on its warming pad, I noticed Danny standing silent, his mouth hanging open and his eyes wide.

"What's the matter, Danny?" He didn't move a muscle.

"You look like you've seen a ghost," we said simultaneously.

He stared and shook his head, so much aghast that he didn't even say "Salt and pepper."

I smiled and said it myself.

Danny quoted himself, "I said 'like you seen-a,' but look at yourself!"

I glanced down at the shiny steel coffee server and it came home to me. I backtracked quickly to the bedroom bureau that held the mirror. Yes. I *had* seen a ghost and my hair, closely barbered four days back, was nearly snow white. A dream I had dismissed during sleep came swimming up from my subconscious night-brain. I had seen and talked to Roscoe Lucci, the bear man of Thief Lake, disappeared or dead for over a decade!

In that flood of suddenly recalled dream I sat in my garage intently sewing together two patches of birch bark that I had stripped from a wide-girth tree that spring. These would form the hull of the canoe.

I sensed something as quiet as a mosquito lighting on the back of my neck and felt an ethereal presence in the room. Then, as if the mosquito, growing aggressive and hungry buzzed past my ear, I heard a swishing shuffle, a heavy footfall, and a decidedly relieved sigh.

As I turned my head, I saw a man, burly as a bear plopped down on one of four tree stumps I kept in the garage to raise the canoe to a comfortable working height. Despite the summer heat the dream may have pictured winter, but I couldn't tell. This barrel-shaped character wore a hooded cape-like affair of shaggy furs cinched around his bearded cheeks and chin and flowing down over his ample belly and hunched back. It was belted at the waist and hung loose over his knees to just above his deer-hide boots, He sat heavily and shivered. From under his rangy eyebrows he looked up at me, his black rimmed amber irises beameding a sickening yellow light, and he grunted roughly. Roscoe Lucci had returned in the flesh and in fur. That was the dream that stripped my hair of color.

I went back to the coffee bar. By that time, Cooley had come in and Danny was rumbling something lowly to his friend.

As Cooley was turning toward me, away from Danny, he was saying, "Danny tells me you've seen a . . ." He stopped cold, not needing or able to complete his report. Cooley adopted the slack-jawed posture I had left Danny in.

"A ghost." Both Danny and I said.

"Salt and pepper." Danny said. Apparently, he had recovered form his initial shock.

"I have." I told them, deciding what I saw was more important than hair color. "I dreamed Roscoe was with me in the garage."

"He's alive!" Danny crowed. "See, I told you so, Cooley."

"Bozo, it was a dream. Tatty's dream."

More to myself than to my two friends, I said, "I don't know. Maybe I should check the garage."

Cooley said, "Yeah, do that, Tatty. Danny and I will hold down the fort."

The idea of looking for Roscoe—even though I was absolutely sure I had dreamed his presence and that he could not, having died years ago, be there—came to me because the last time I had talked with him was in Granny's garage-storage-barn where he had been hiding out after murdering his best friend, Jay, over at Tillie's. I had been shocked at his presence then, just as I was now at his dream visitation. I had to look.

I followed that stupid impulse and went directly to the garage. I saw no one there, but I felt even more strongly now that I was fully awake that someone had been present. I gazed idiotically at the stump, then traced with my eyes what seemed all too much like bear tracks left on the cool damp of the concrete floor leading from the side door of the garage to the stump. I was about to get a closer look when a stirring on the far side of the canoe interrupted my observation. I stopped short. My spine tingled, and I turned.

"Who were you talking to, Papa?" It was Dindii, my poor little bird.

"Wooh! You startled me." I knelt, looking for her under the raised canoe and saw her beyond it, sitting on a pile of drying bark squares. I opened my arms to her. "I don't think I was saying anything. Come here, Sweetie. Did you hear someone?"

She ducked under the canoe and cuddled into my hug. "You were talking to a bear," she said, "one with yellow eyes. I saw him."

I took Dindii in my arms, perhaps more to comfort myself than her and certainly to avert her gaze from my face which must have been ashen. "Is that what you saw? Were you dreaming?"

"Not now, Papa. I may have, before."

"Before, child?"

"When you came out here the first time. It was still dark out. Before you changed your hair."

Her hand went to my new white growth of hair. "Why did you bleach your hair, Papa?"

I embraced the child, and, caught in an inexplicable conundrum, I did my best to tell the truth.

"I think it has been getting whiter for a while. I had a haircut last week and a fright, Shookii. That might have done it.

You know about scares. I dreamed that an old friend I met at Tillie's long ago was back. I thought he had been dead for over ten years."

"Since I was born?"

"Yes, from that very time."

"You saw him at Tillie's?"

"Yes, the night the sheriff closed it." This was all true but I couldn't tell her the part of the story between Jay's death at Roscoe's hand and his horrid disappearance.

"Did the windigo kill him?"

"Now, who told you that? Mama?"

Dindii, who was to turn eleven at the end of the year, pulled away some to get a look at me and to better register her precocious disgust with my careless treatment of her intelligence. "I have ears, Papa. People talk. I also asked Mama about it, yes."

I had to say so. "Yes, so they all say, Roscoe died with the windigo. They both went down to the bottom of the lake in the middle of the winter. It was just days after you and Popcorn were born."

She furrowed her brows and seemed to be formulating another question.

"Shookii, I think I'll take you back to bed. You should finish your sleep."

I could tell she wasn't satisfied, but she didn't protest. I took her hand leading her back to bed. Biini was still fast asleep.

I listened at the studio door and heard nothing, not even a light snore. Morgan was certainly at Pelican Point, which meant that, since I had quickly become a partner in sheltering the twins from their mother's bad behavior, I'd have to lie to the twins, saying, "She went fishing early this morning."

I tiptoed down the hall, stopping to comb my hair at the bathroom mirror as if another mirror would show a different reflection. The coolness there brought me back to the years-ago chill of Tillie's toilet and my confession to Roscoe of another frightening vision I'd had as I lay unconscious after my car accident on my first trip to the lake.

At Tillie's, I'd gone to pee after checking in with my new medic friend, Scummy, telling him I was all right, no concussion. I entered the bathroom where the door was ajar. That time, too, I felt a presence unseen.

Then someone in the shadows said, "Sometimes I know I am about to die." I right then identified the voice as Roscoe's, and frightened out of my wits since Scummy had warned me the man could be dangerous, I just played along. "What do you do then?"

He followed with what was a hunting-story metaphor about a windigo. The spirit had appeared to Roscoe as a eight point buck which Roscoe watched from his deer stand built in a tree. The hunter, Roscoe, had become the hunted. He dared not move. He didn't even breathe.

"You get that feeling a lot, Roscoe?" I asked when he'd finished.

"Just three times: First, when I saw the windigo the night Mary died. Second, the day I got out of prison and found my woman—someone I thought was my mate—gone. The third was tonight, when I figured out you are married to the woman I believed I loved."

Standing in front of the mirror at home, enveloped by the memory of Roscoe's words, made me shiver, despite the early morning summer heat. My encounter with Roscoe in Tillie's men's room had felt like an invitation to mayhem, but that night turned Roscoe into more of a peculiar friend than a dangerous enemy.

In that moment years before, just recovering from a jarring accident and a near-death freezing, I related to Roscoe visions of my windigo sighting and of the scene of Mary's death, the night she stepped into a pulsing, freezing, white light. I told him of my accident, swerving to avoid a deer so huge that it dwarfed the Jeep I was driving.

"Did it say something to you?" Roscoe had asked.

I faltered and delayed, saying nothing then, but he got it out of me.

"It said my name," Roscoe said. "Didn't it?"

I affirmed his uncanny guess.

"Then," he said, slumping to the wall, "it's getting close."

At home I shook off my reverie before the bathroom mirror. My day was about to start, and no matter what was happening to me, bewitchment, confusion, or insanity, I knew that work would get me through. I took one more look at myself and ducked down the hall back to the kitchen.

Cooley and Danny had finished the whole pot. I brewed another. While it was perking, Cooley worked down his curiosity.

"So, tell me your dream, Tatty," He said. "It must have been a doozy."

"Yeah," chimed in old Hooper Daniels, "What did Roscoe have to say?"

I wasn't ready to go there. The dream was still vivid, but I had to sort it out before telling anyone, whitehaired or not. So, I gave them something that was news to them but long known to me. I admitted to Danny and his friend something that only my brother-in-law, Tiny, knew. That Roscoe and I ended as friends, not as enemies as everyone seemed to think.

"No shit!" Danny said. "I saw him try to kill you."

Cooley said, "If that's friendship, I don't want it."

"No, he only wanted the truth. I knew. I had seen in a vision what happened to Mary, my wife's twin. No one else knew, and Roscoe needed to find out for his own good."

"Or his own bad," Danny said.

"You saw the evil," I told them, "but I learned what you didn't see, his decency. And what you still don't know was that I talked with Roscoe afterward, after he'd escaped on the snowmobile."

"You couldn't have." Cooley said. "We were with you almost all the time."

I brought over the coffee pot and poured three. I took

a deep breath, knowing they would not like what I was about to tell them.

"While you and everyone were at Windsong's funeral, and after you all came back to Granny's cabin, all that time and into the early morning hours when he fired up and stole your Snowcat, Roscoe was camped out in Granny's storage barn, her garage."

Cooley jumped up off his stool. "All that time you knew he was there?"

I nodded.

"And you couldn't tip us off?" Danny said.

"Roscoe and I bonded over the windigo. I knew I should have reported him to the others—he had killed our friend Scummy just the night before—but of all the people at the lake, of all the people in the world, Roscoe and I shared something both frightening and wonderful. We were like war buddies, comrades in arms, almost brothers."

"Well, I'll be darned," they both said.

"Salt 'n' pepper."

I had to get the twins set for breakfast, and the truck would soon arrive with the day's mail. So, I left my two flabbergasted friends at the counter, put on another pot for the crowd that was to come and went down the hall to the girls' room. Morgan had crept in somehow—or maybe had been in the studio all night—and was with the twins. I went back and put on my visor. Work began.

Rednecks and Death   9

Yes, my workday had begun, but I couldn't keep my mind on the tasks. Part of the problem was the constant commentary on my now white pate. The panoply of responses was almost amusing:

"Looks good on you, Tatty."

"Very distinguished."

"Only your hairdresser knows."

"What the hell happened to you?"

"You been sleeping with that gal, Peroxide?"

The onslaught was both terrible and funny, but more than anything else, it was non-stop and totally distracting. I found myself throwing mail all over the place, mostly into the wrong boxes.

"Am I getting Olsen's mail now?" Bobby Oberg said, handing me a sheaf of Olsen Resort bills."

I had switched them up, sure enough; Bobby's newspapers were in Olsen's box.

Somehow, I even tossed a letter to Rev. Theodore G. Good into the garbage but caught the error before the can was emptied.

I told myself, "You've gone haywire, Tatty."

I heard comments from one of the cafe tables, "He's on a bender." Then whispered so I could hear, "No surprise with what's going on."

I was half done. Stopped myself. Emptied all the boxes and resorted everything, paying attention to the mail rather than the echo of what Roscoe had told me in my dream.

Just as he had done on the bar stool at Tillie's, Roscoe rocked side to side and back and forth on his garage stump-chair, pausing and moaning from time to time. "Watch out for murdering rednecks," he'd said. "Keep a close eye on those kids of yours." He went back to his moaning, and when I asked him what he meant, he roundly ignored me. His was one-way communication.

He looked more animal than man, wearing torn and worn furs, even whiskery-looking boots as if he had been caught in the middle of a spring molt. It was all I could do to look at the poor soul, a rack and ruin of a sturdy man from years ago to whom death or an ten Salt 'n' pepper-year disappearance had done no favors. Every time he moved to fix me in his beaming yellow eyes, I had to turn away, they were so wild, so horrid.

Finally, I dared to lock into his gaze. "There's hell fires ahead," he said. "The holy man seeks to burn the child." He fussed with one of his boots, then recast his gaze at me. "One to two and one, Tillie's comes again. More killings in the snow." He squatted off the stump and gazed under the canoe. "Watch for Father: listen." Roscoe rattled off a litany of cataclysms and prophecies, most of which sounded like ravings, none of which made sense. One moment I knew he was insane, the next what he said felt real, more likely than anything in daylight. "Rednecks" and "killings in the snow" connected and touched a nerve in me.

Like any other dream, though, much was murky, all was impossible and prone to evaporation when one tried to grasp it. Of course. It was unreal. I knew that. But, then, I asked myself, how could Dindii have seen him? Did I dream her presence in the garage when I went again to check for Roscoe? What of those moist paw prints on sweating concrete? I surely saw them while wide awake after three-quarters cup of coffee.

I wanted to drop the mail and rush to the garage to check each detail. It even occurred to me that the entire day, perhaps all my years at Thief Lake, maybe the whole of my fifty-year existence was somebody else's dream, not even my own consciousness. I had experienced the feeling before, knocked unconscious in my seminal-snowstorm accident, avoiding the outsized buck. The car crash turned out to be true. I had scars to prove it. It was real, though without sense.

Morgan's grandmother told her when I first arrived, "You see, he knows," referring to a vision I'd reported to her of Windsong's funeral which I had not attended. That same night, Granny said to me, "You see from afar." Well, if I was seeing from afar, like Roscoe had intimated years ago in another garage, I still wanted no part of it. I'd told Granny as much back then. It was all Algonquin mumbo jumbo, I'd thought, and even though I'd made peace with the spirit of my Mi'kmaq father out there on the birch hills overlooking a frozen Thief Lake just as Roscoe and the windigo disappeared, the businessman and now postmaster in me refused to honor my seerage. I didn't want to know what was coming. I wouldn't do anything about it, anyway. And it terrified me that all that stuff, for lack of a better word, seemed dark, portentous of grief and sorrow, murderous and unkind.

I could not, try though I might, ignore it. My hours-old whitened hair prevented me from burying this most recent dream. Even more, my poor little bird needed my help and support. What she saw, although impossible, must be explained carefully. I owed that much to her and more to myself.

All I had at the moment was Dindii. She was the key to my understanding of what Roscoe had said though I resisted putting my faith and her future in the hands of one so young, no matter how mature she'd become in a year.

After the mail truck left and my patrons had emptied their boxes, discovering no further errors, I tossed off my visor and stuffed my new white locks beneath a canvas bucket cap I wore for fishing. I found Dindii in her room alone, her sister having caught a ride on the truck to a meeting down the road with the Swedenborgians.

"Hey there, Sweetie. How's my little bird?"

"Fine."

"Feel like taking a walk with me? I want to show you something, talk about something."

Dindii seemed to have been waiting for me. She bounced off the bed looking willing and eager. "Let's go." She fell in beside me without another word.

I took her along the shoreline moving north, and when we were directly across from the spot I had years before seen Roscoe slip under the water, I grabbed Dindii's hand, and we walked straight up a path that led away from the lake and to a mature stand of birches on the hilltop. Reaching the crest, we paused at a large flat piece of gray glaciated granite. The spacious stone afforded a clearing from which to survey the forest and, through the limbless tall trunks of the birches, the entire lake below. I squatted on the stone. Dindii sat encircling her knees with her always-covered arms.

"I haven't been here since right after you were born, but now I have to show you."

"The lake? The forest?"

"Last time I was up here, both were frozen. I stood here and watched the man, the bear-man you saw this morning, slide down an upturned ice floe into the freezing waters. The ice sheet flipped over, and its bulk jammed shut a huge open space in the lake ice, trapping Roscoe beneath. It sent a knee-high wave of cold-steaming water out over the surface of the frozen lake. When I looked again, after the steam dissipated, there was nothing left of Roscoe. He was gone."

Dindii interrupted. "But I saw him this morning. I heard him, too."

"What did you hear him say?"

She seemed to search for the right words, then carefully announced, "He said, 'Open Tillie's,' at one point."

"In just that way?"

"Not exactly, but I'm sure of what he meant."

"What else?" I asked.

"Something about burning a child."

"Who would do that?" I ignored the clear reference to her burns. It didn't, like most of Roscoe's ravings, fit with the reality. I tried to lead her, but either she had heard or remembered something different than I had.

"I didn't understand but he said, 'From three, two t' one, again.'"

"Did he warn of hell fires ahead?" I asked.

"Yes. I heard that, and he looked right at me when he said it." She did not seem disturbed. "He said 'Rednecks kill in the snow.'"

"What do you think he meant by that?"

"I don't know, Papa, but I've never liked Stan and Ollie very much, you know Laurel and Hardy, and I think he meant them."

I wrapped an arm around her thin shoulders. "I can see your point. Anything else?"

Dindii who after her accident was always serious, sober, and sage said, "Just the most important."

"What's that?"

"He said, 'Watch for Father: listen.'"

"Do you think he meant me?"

She looked up into my face a long time, then pointed behind me. "I think the bear-man meant him."

I slipped my arm off her shoulder and steadied my rise to look behind me, just as I heard a rustling in the birch slash that covered the forest floor. I saw what Dindii could not know was my father, the apparition of my father, one I had seen winters ago, clad in black then, now in birch-white, on that pushed-up and ground-down rock above Thief Lake. Although he did not speak, I heard him say, as he lifted an arm to point at Dindii, "Tend the girl. Keep her near."

Dindiisi rose to her feet and rushed toward the figure, "Grandpa. I hear you." And at that, the ghost of my father dissolved into the paper of birch bark tumbling along the ground in the hot wind that suddenly rose from the lake.

My daughter turned back to me and clasped me in a hug for all she was worth. I patted her dark head and smoothed her hair. "Yes, that was grandpa, my father."

"He was a Mi'kmaq medicine man," she said.

How Dindii knew these things, I couldn't tell. The

weird happenings of this day seemed to fill her with a unworldly knowing. And I was no one to disbelieve she had seen and heard Roscoe speak, just as she had witnessed my father speak silence.

What she gleaned from these encounters, she did not say directly, maybe could not say, but they guided her right then and became readily apparent in the years to follow. Dindii became known as good medicine for Thief Lake though she did not follow in father's footsteps but was, like me, reluctant to fully engage the spirit world better to build solid things.

Right now, though, she seemed to me to be just a frightened child. Dindii sat herself again on the edge of the stone and dangled her legs. She looked up at me, as if to demand some sort of explanation for everything she had seen in the last six hours. I sat crosslegged next to her. We watched each other's face intently. I started where I knew best, in confusion.

"Of course, the man you saw here is not a blood grandfather. Yes, he was my dad, and so is in a way related to you." I stopped to think if this was the best way to begin. Not knowing, I barged on. "Father was a good man, but he was not a good parent to me. He was often demanding and angry. So, when he died—I was just a bit younger than you are now—I did not feel especially sad, but later, when I was grown, I wished I had known him better, that I had learned his ways more than I had."

Dindii placed a hand on my knee. "I suppose you never had a talk with him like we do?"

I felt like laughing but simply agreed, "No, and I wish I had. When he was gone, I knew I was incomplete without him, that we had not been fully father and child."

My daughter kept an expectant look on her face, encouraging me. "I was haunted by his memory, I knew, but until I arrived at Thief Lake I could ignore the ghostly feelings I had from time to time."

"I think I understand, Papa."

"When I came to the lake, I started having visions. Like the vision we just shared. The first was a vision of a huge deer buck, bigger than the Jeep I was driving. On a hairpin turn, it leapt over the roof of my car and sent me into a ditch. I was out cold, had a concussion, I think."

"I've heard Danny and Cooley talk about finding you, your car. You weren't there."

"Jay Martinen, "Scummy," who was your true grandfather, found me first." I didn't have to force myself to add some kind words about Scummy. I took up her resting hand in mine. "Your grandfather was the kindest, gentlest man at the lake."

"The bear man killed him at Tillie's."

It wasn't an accusation, just a matter of fact statement from a child.

"There is no forgiveness for what Roscoe did, but the history is complicated. While I was knocked out in the Jeep, before Jay found me, I witnessed a long vision that told me just how frightened and angry the bear man was. And when I met him, just an hour later, I came to understand more about him than I did about myself. In just a few hours, we became friends forever." I didn't tell her that the forever lasted just two days before Roscoe disappeared.

Dindii took her hand from mine and raised her index finger to me, "That's why you can believe what he says."

"I know. Somehow, through his dramatic death, Roscoe sent me here—to this very same rock though it was covered in snow then—to finish what my father and I had not. That day the vision of my father completed my trip to Thief Lake and formed the occasion to decide to stay here and become a father to you and Popcorn."

Dindii smiled. "And now he's told you to watch out for me."

"And Popcorn, too."

She shook her head. "No, I think that will be up to Mama, and it has to do with Tillie's."

I regarded my young daughter. "Tillie's?" Here I had brought Dindii to explain my visions of Roscoe and, once on the hill, of my father, and I now found myself less knowledgeable than my girl who was still a child. "What does Tillie's have to do with anything?"

"Didn't you really meet everyone there? Even Mama?"

"I did learn she was someone other than who I'd married. Yes."

Dindii sounding very adult continued, "And doesn't this rock here tie everything together: the lake, your fathering, Roscoe, and all that happened at Tillie's?"

I wanted to follow her logic but couldn't. "Maybe."

"Well, Tillie's is not just an old tavern. I think it is a gathering of spirits. First of windigos, like the one told of in the small girl legend and, then, of the one everyone chased."

"I suppose." I hoped she wouldn't continue. She did.

"And didn't Mary's ghost bring everyone back there? And now, even closed for all my life, don't both Roscoe and your father point to Tillie's?"

I shook my head. She seemed to be both in and from

another world, a wunderkind reading stone tablets or making prophecies. I barely recognized her.

Dindii went on as if she must finish. "I think what all this means, your new white hair too, is that whatever we think of them, we have to listen to the spirits that surround us. We need to bring the lake people together again, to a spirit center. That is what Tillie's must be."

"Why not the churches, the Swedenborgians?"

She stood up and looked out on the lake. "No. That's not false, but not true for Theif Lake, either. Look at Teddy G's so-called church! All the bad that is rising here is more than murder in the snow. I feel it is a wrong. Like the theft of childhood. We need to honor someone like the 'small girl' who saved her people from the *manidoo*. We need a homegrown gathering place. One where the lake people's history both Native and white is known."

"What? Make Roscoe and my father saints there?"

She spoke seriously, "No one can be a saint. Not even Granny."

We ended it there. Dindii took my hand, something like *I* was the child, and we headed down the path to the lake.

Somehow, Dindii could make sense of what I thought of as Algonquin mumbo jumbo, forming it into a certain course of action that could save us all. But from what? I wanted hard proof, not superstition. Still, I had then as I had before to admit that the spirit world, at least at the lake, had a power that the everyday life of a postmaster seemed to lack.

On our way back, when we passed Tillie's, neither of us spoke a word, as if in reverence to or in trepidation of the place.

Teens

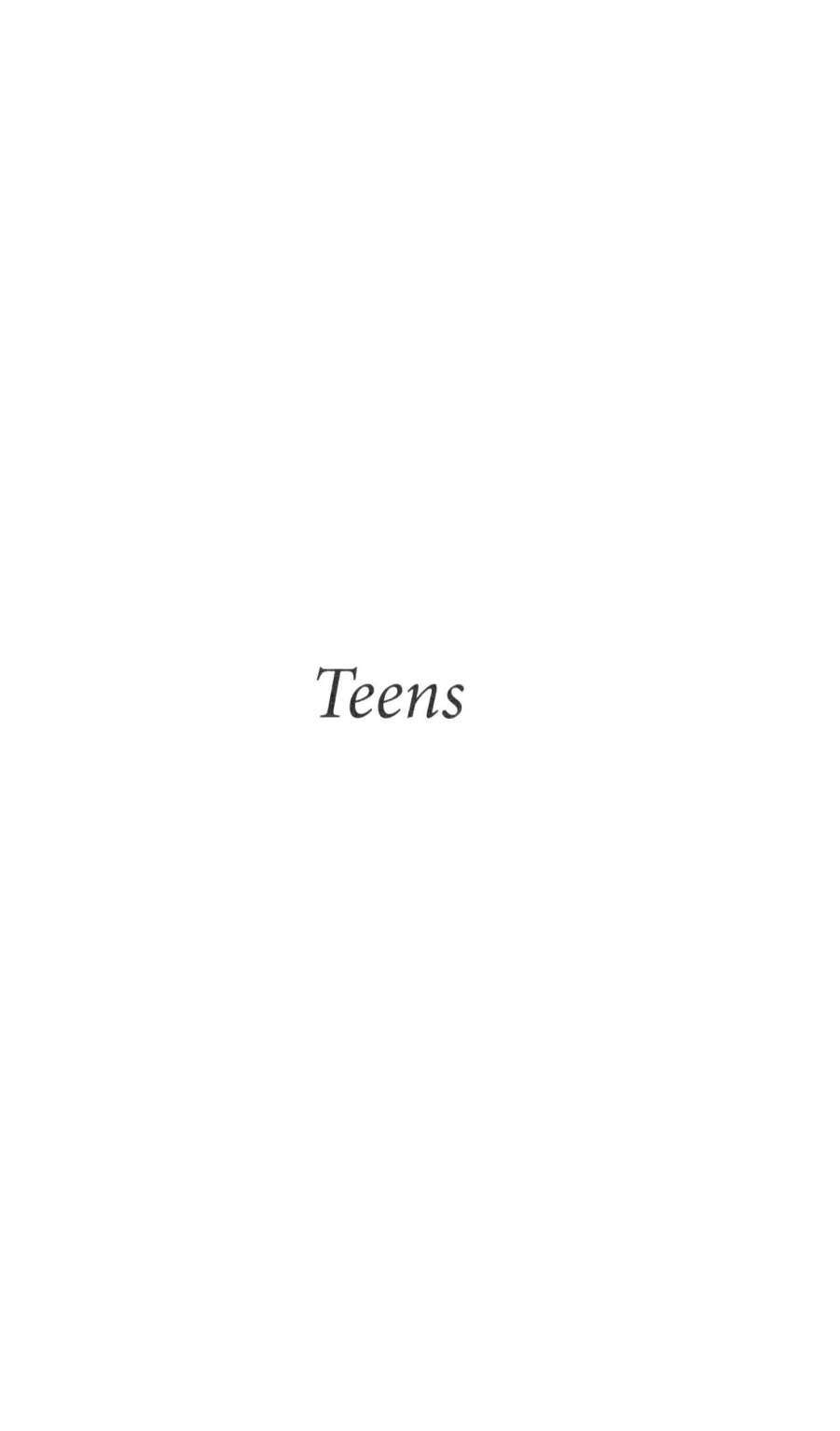

Popcorn 3
(Biini)

When I was little—I'm almost thirteen now—I wrinkled up my nose at just about everything but mostly at stuff I didn't like. It was the smell. Fried cabbage. Poop, whether from dogs, bears, deer, or people, (I hated the outhouses, and there were plenty of them at the lake). Stinkweed that sprang up during July in tall, fuzzy stalks and leaves. What we called "crappy cheese," aka "blue cheese." And anything rotten, from old tree trunks lying flat in the forest, to something forgotten at the back of the refrigerator. Very old bananas were my exception. There was something sweet and rare about their pleasant odor.

There were good things on my nose, too. *Manomen*, wild rice, cooked in a rabbit broth, just uncovered at the table. I remember Grannie's best. Sweet corn in butter, on the cob or in the bowl. The first blades of grass poking up in a mud patch mixed with icy half-melted snow, the freshest thing ever. Pine sap snapping in a winter campfire, loosing a sharp but sweet smoke in the still December air. The smell of Mama: scents of oil paints and rich brushed hair. And of Papa: Castile soap and musky mail bags. It's really hard to describe.

Of all things, the best was the first whiff of Uncle Tiny's fish-house air, bursting out through the door he'd just opened, in a heated rush, both welcoming and distinct. It hit you when you finished your mile-and-a-half walk from shore with your nose frozen clean and ready to smell something familiar. You'd be greeted at the first crack of the door with a deep but perky aroma. It was like the smell of venison gravy mixed with the odor of week-long slept-in wool blankets. It was the way Uncle Tiny smelled always. At times like pretzels and beer in a tavern after the wood floor was just broomed with that pink sweeping compound. Or like the soggy sawdust I loved in a summer ice-house, cool, rich, and slow to tickle the nose. When Uncle Tiny hugged us to his big barrel chest, the fragrance flew up the nose in a friendly way and filled the brain with giggles and squeals. The fish-house scent worked like sunshine, pushing through pine-tree sprigs on boughs, streaming rays in a hundred directions and twining all colors together in different hues.

The power of that fish-house smell lived mostly in the memory of the things that were said and done in that tiny shack. It was nothing like the smell of fish, which were never left in the house but were quickly gutted outside, filleted, wrapped in wax paper, and frozen in tin containers in the snowbanks that surrounded the house. Just a passing whiff of Uncle Tiny still brings back times spent out there, and, for sure, one certain night when I learned something I had known for over five years but had pushed to the back of my mind each time it floated up. It had to do with Shookii and with Mama. That memory is writing in smell on my mind.

I was in the top bunk, drifting along on a cloud of fish-house-smell, feeling comfortable and warm even though I was sleeping in the middle of a lake-sized ice floe in the deeps of a Minnesota winter night. The smell of the birch logs in the stove that were glowing like sunlight through amber and Uncle Tiny's mysterious scent wove a web around me. Its warps and woofs were made of smells and also of the whispering of Uncle Tiny and my sister Shookii.

Their voices danced atop the snaps and pops of the stove wood. Sounds and smells ran together in my mind like a dream at the end of a long-night's sleep.

From the rise and fall of those two voices, one higher, like mine, the other a rumbling of Uncle Tiny's speech, rose a vision so fearsome to me that it startled me fully awake. Even in the dim glow the wood stove made inside the fish-house, I saw clearly that bright, sunny May afternoon when the three of us putted along in a walleye-troll pushed by Uncle Tiny's half-horse engine between This Man and That Man islands. Even more brightly, as if Shookii was shining a lantern on them, I saw the yellow and blue colors of what was now in the dark of the fish house suddenly and unmistakably my mother's clothing. It was tossed carelessly on the blanket of Preacher Teddy Good. I couldn't shed the vision, eyes open or closed, but if I had, I would have still heard the scene that Uncle Tiny and Shookii talked about as if their hushed words rose from the glare of my Mama's piled garments.

Shookii was saying, "Uncle Tiny, I got a question."

"Fire away, Shookii. Uncle Tiny has answers."

"I saw something, and I heard something, too, that day, what five years ago, when you motored and Popcorn and I paddled through the channel between This Man and That. You remember?"

The long silence that followed was louder than his words that came, it seemed, a full minute later. "I know the time you mean."

Sister continued. "It's about the clothes on the blanket. I saw shadows of someone finning, hiding behind that fancy cruiser the minister pilots every summer. A silhouette played out across the sand at the bottom of that cove." Shookii made a peculiar sound, like she was about to cry or sneeze or cough all at once but then said, "Mama wore those clothes that evening while she was serving dinner."

Uncle Tiny made a grumbling sound way down in his throat. "Sounds like you got it figured."

I slowly lifted my head, bringing my eyes between the thin mattress and the guard rail so I could see those two. Tiny had his back to me, but I saw Shookii screw up her face and wrinkle her nose like she'd just entered an outhouse that hadn't had a lime treatment in months.

"I had it figured, sure, but I never could puzzle out why she didn't change clothes when she got home. Why?"

I shut my eyes just as Tiny cast a glance over his shoulder. "Did you and Biini talk about this?"

"I laid it out, but she never got it, or she wouldn't admit it. You know how she is, 'all purity and light,' like they say in the Gospels."

I nearly shouted at them right then when they both chuckled. If there's one thing I can't stand it's people belittling the Word of God. But I kept my peace as the Lord taught me.

Uncle Tiny went on. "No, I guess she wouldn't listen to any blasphemy about sister Morgan, would she?"

Shookii looked up at the bunk I was in, but by then I had pulled my face away from the edge back into the shadows of the bedding, so she couldn't really know that I was watching and listening. She must have believed I was still sleeping, so she continued, "I don't think she could handle it. No, she couldn't, at least back then. But I don't care so much about that, Uncle, I just want to know 'why.' Why was she so obvious? Almost like she wanted to be caught like that."

There was an even longer silence than before. In that quiet, I realized that I knew the answer. The sinner always wants to be found out. Transgression must be made known, or forgiveness cannot follow. Mama couldn't tell us or Papa she was caught in a devil's web of sin that would send her to hell because she loved us all so much. But still she wanted to confess, and that was why she wore those yellow shorts and the blue blouse she knew we had seen from our canoe.

Uncle Tiny finally answered.

"Your Mama always wanted to be good, but it was her sister that got all the decency in this life. She was the sweetest thing. I ain't been so hot on beneficence myself, but I don't lie about it. As much as I love my sister, she is weak with wildness. *That* she can't change no matter what."

"Is that why she ran away after our real Mama was born?" Shookii asked.

"She hides the truth of her spirit, but sometimes it shines through, like when she came back after nearly twenty years, like when she gave you dinner in her shucked clothes. She knew you would see, that you had seen. That's why she did it, like an acknowledgment."

"I don't understand."

"She knew Biini wouldn't see. She knew you would. I think she was opening a pathway with you, not for you to go wrong, but so you could understand that you could love her and that you didn't have to act like her. You follow her. Not in a bad way. I think she sees a path out of trouble through you, someone who can ride the woman's way without falling into hurt or evil deeds. Me, you, and Morgan, we three aren't Christian"—he was right about that on all sides—"but I think your Mama sees redemption in you, in you being both like and unlike her."

There was even a longer silence, maybe it lasted all night, because those were the last words I remember, but the buzzing in my brain was so loud that I couldn't hear anything else, anyway. I had no idea what Uncle Tiny meant. Mama loved me as much as she loved Shookii. She wanted us both to be like her. So, what Uncle Tiny told my sister just had to be wrong. He'd said it just to pacify her, poor thing.

I knew better. I knew The Truth. Mama had to be released from her cycle of sin and lying. I no longer had to pray for my own forgiveness—I was still praying three times a day—but I did have to pray for my mother's deliverance from evil, and if that didn't work, I knew exactly what to do.

Shookii 3
(Dindii)

I couldn't wait for the big freeze. The excitement I felt wasn't for my birthday coming up. When the ice was thick enough to walk on—in some years as late as Christmas time—the prickly tension anticipating the setting-in of the fish houses out on the lake was almost too much to bear. That feeling, not the excitement of birthdays or Christmas, brought on all the wonder and joy of winter.

Uncle Tiny was the tribal elder designated to bless the ice, which he did by building and burning a huge bonfire over the deepest part of the lake where the ice tended to be the thinnest. How many hours it took that fire to melt through the ice, finally being snuffed out by its own melt water, told us all how thick and strong the ice sheet was. Just drilling a hole and measuring wasn't good enough. Of course, Uncle Tiny knew when it was safe enough to haul out the birch, pine, and fir limbs that he or my cousin George had felled the previous year. If there was enough snow to help skid the logs out of the forest, that was a good thing, but the most important thing was the cold.

After the lake had thinly skinned over with ice—the years that the snow was late and the subzero temperatures were early created the most beautiful, crystal clear sheet across the miles of open lake—it took a "good freeze," measuring near zero, for five days and five nights to deepen the skin to Uncle Tiny's satisfaction. That and another measure he claimed to check: that a frozen beaver pelt would stand stiff all day in the sun, were "my guides to safety," he said.

Once Thief Lake had Tiny's okay, everyone dragged their ice houses out on thick-plank skids. In the old days, Tiny told me, they used horses and sometimes a knotted rope pulled by both the men and the women to drag the houses out and set them on the ice. The plank-skids melded into the lake's surface by the end of fishing season and would be sacrificed or fished out in the spring thaw after the houses that sat on them came off the lake on the next year's timbers. The houses and skids were set aside for the following season.

Uncle Tiny wasn't always the first one out there, but the careful people, both Native and white, waited until the bonfire to begin their winter labor. The guys who had taken over Olsen's Resort the summer before thought they would jump my uncle's claim to the best spot and dragged their shack out there before Tiny's bonfire. Maybe they didn't know. Maybe they didn't ask anyone, but there'd been no stiff beaver pelts in the sunshine at the lake yet that year. The ice held long enough for those two bumpkins, as Uncle Tiny called them, to get their Chevy truck off the lake, but no sooner had they made shore than the house broke through and during the night sank two feet lower on one corner before freezing solid into the ice sheet by daybreak. Those guys had to saw open a new door to the house on the upper end and fished in a canted shack for the rest of the season.

They fell to fist fighting out on the ice over their own stupidity. That must have been a sight to see, broken noses. Blood on the snow. Wrestling until they gasped. I never went into Olsen's, but I know everybody joked about those two rubes banging their heads on their fish-house rafters all winter. Even afterward, that stubborn pair never asked the lake people for advice, because, like everyone said, they already knew everything that was worth knowing. If they hadn't turned Redneck-mean, it would've all been funny.

The winter I was to turn thirteen the freeze set in early. I'd become a woman that year and despite my worries over the scarring on my chest, my breasts were developing and were as beautiful as could be. Well, anyway, that year the lake sheeted up early. You could tell it was going to happen because the first frost came in mid-August and the skies remained clear a week after Indian Summer. Then the temperature dropped fast. By the middle of September, ice skinned the lake, and it was only halfway to Halloween that uncle Tiny and cousin George began hauling timber out on the lake. The cold gripped the lake something fierce, and George's beaver pelts stood at attention day in and day out. At the highest, the temperature was zero in the middle of the afternoon.

I remember that year for lots of reasons, one being how comical it was to watch the trucks skid along on the ice. Snow was yet to fall and to get traction needed a steady foot on the gas. Single, dual, and even triple spinouts were the order of the day. The young, new to driving, vied for the most revolutions, and some choreographed up to three trucks at once staying as close as possible without smashing into one another as they spun. There was just one fender bender: Stan and Ollie of Olsen's Resort were those fools of the day, of course.

Uncle Tiny took his first trip out, trailing a sand spreader he had "borrowed" from his job at the County. The sand turned the ice brown on the trail he made but the lake glittered and was still beautiful in its other parts. We had a fine Halloween bonfire, the earliest of any in my life. It took nearly three hours to melt through the ice.

The next day, it snowed eight inches, plenty to allow the skidding-out of the fish houses. Most memorable for me that season was our first night in Tiny's fish-house. It was mid-November, close to my thirteenth birthday, and I felt that I had joined the adult community that spring, giving me the right to put to a real test some hard questions I'd held privately a long time. Not being a kid anymore, I deserved to know.

I waited until Popcorn was out of the way. Not that I was hiding anything, but I didn't want her interrupting me with her Swedenborgian claptrap or her Pollyannaish singsong. You couldn't discuss anything serious around her, except her version of religion. So, when she went to bed early, as she always did either to say her ever-loving prayers or to review in her mind the poetry she was so fond of writing—and she was, I admit, not a bad poet, either, better than Papa—I took the chance to question my uncle.

I started by feeding a couple quarter-logs to the fire, something usually reserved to Uncle Tiny but tonight, setting the scene for an adult conversation. As I swung the stove door shut, I looked at my uncle—I have to admit, a little like a child but with an adult's seriousness—saying, "Uncle Tiny, I got a question."

He understood the tone of my approach right off, likely because I'd fed the stove like a grownup would.

He used my Native name to punctuate my tone. "Shoot, Dindii. Uncle Tiny has answers."

"You remember that day you took us fishing along the Man chain about six years ago?"

Tiny thought a moment and asked, "That time you tied into that five pound walleye?"

"No. It was the year after that. First time we saw *Saint Muggsy*."

My uncle didn't often frown, but he screwed his face up real twisty. "Yeah, what about it?"

I didn't care that he sounded a bit defensive. I was determined to get his take on this event. "Well, I saw something; I heard something, too, that day when we trolled through the channel between This Man and That."

"I remember," he said, looking back at the bunks, probably to see if Popcorn was still awake. He reached for the wood pile and like he felt a chill in the little room added another birch quarter to the fire, getting a real good blaze going. Then he watched the flames for a while before closing the stove door.

"I think I know what you're getting at, Dindii."

I could see the scene from years back like it had unfolded just this past summer. "When we came around the bend to the little harbor, Preacher Ted was standing on a blanket toweling off on shore."

Tiny nodded. "I remember."

"My question is about the clothes I saw on the blanket and about who was in the water, bumping the hull beneath that fancy cruiser the minister started speeding around in that summer." I almost started to cry, feeling a bit beside myself. I hadn't realized how tough it would be to talk about.

"Okay. You've got my attention."

"Mama wore those same clothes that evening while she was serving us dinner."

Now I thought Uncle Tiny was about to cry. He made a glubbing sound way down in his throat. "Sounds like you got it figured."

"I had it figured, except for why. Why didn't she change into something else when she got home?"

My uncle looked over to the bunks again. Then he asked, "Did you and Biini talk about this?"

"I did, but she never got it or wouldn't admit it."

Uncle Tiny lifted one corner of his mouth, looking like a sly fox at that moment. "Popcorn wants to be 'all purity and light,' like they say in the Gospels."

It wasn't really funny, but I couldn't help but chuckle a bit. Everybody seemed to think Popcorn was a real born-again believer. Most did not approve a whole lot.

"No, she wouldn't blaspheme her Mama, would she?" Tiny said.

Now I looked up at the bunk and thought I caught movement there, but Popcorn was lost in the shadows and, if she was listening, didn't let on. Just in case, I lowered my voice a bit. "I don't think she could handle it. No, she couldn't, at least back then. But I don't care so much about that, Uncle, I just want to know 'why.' Why did Mama make it so obvious?"

There was an even longer silence than before. In that quiet, I realized that I knew the answer:

Mama was sharing a secret with me. She was hoping I could save her from herself. If I had been feeling grown up before, now I knew better what adulthood was about.

Tiny's answers to my questions weren't as important to me as my right to ask him as an equal. My uncle cared deeply about private talks, and he honored my questions as if they meant the world to him. I figured that Popcorn was listening, but since she was pretending to be asleep, I could count on silence from her. Let her think what she would.

I suppose we believe what we want to believe. I didn't think that my uncle knew it all, but I liked at least part of what he told me: that my mother needed me on her side, especially now that I was a woman, no longer a child. He might have guessed at it, but Tiny was no fool and left it open and up to me to follow if I would. I decided I would help Mama if I could, but like any other grownup, I would have to get something for what I was willing to give. Uncle Tiny opened that one up for me as well.

The last thing he said to me before I climbed up into the bunk with Popcorn was the most important.

"Your mama hides more from herself than she does from others. Your Papa knows as well as you and I do what goes on out at Pelican Point because she didn't hide it from him. But one of those things she hides from herself is what Tillie's means to her. We all know that she will never be at rest until she allows that place to reopen and follow its due course. Everything that matters to her is somehow tied to that place: her sister's death, the birth of your mother, Windsong, and the murder of your grandfather, Jay. She thinks keeping the tavern closed pushes her ghosts of the past back, but until she faces them right there, she won't be quite whole."

I don't know what Popcorn was thinking when I climbed up and pushed her over to make room— she might have been asleep by that time though she was probably busy hatching some poetic plan to save someone's soul, likely mine or Mama's—but I was making a decision, cooking up a plan of my own to get Tillie's Tavern open once again so we could all face whatever the future held for us.

The next morning in keeping with my new, grownup station while Tiny was out taking his morning pee and smoke, I poured a coffee from the pot he had perked and got dressed for walking.

I slipped out the door and walked behind the fish-house to tell my Uncle I was going. I didn't want to leave mysteriously, but neither did I want to face my sister.

"I'm walking in, Uncle."

He puffed on his smoke and opened his arms to the beauty of the morning. "An early walk clears the spirit," he said. "Take a few fish with you." He handed me one of the tins he kept stashed in the snowbank.

I took the fish and quickly turned to the path leading to shore. My uncle was right. The fresh air got my mind working and my spirit clean. I headed straight toward Tillie's.

I left the main path before I hit shore and, since no one went to the tavern in those days, wallowed through a quarter mile of drifts to get there, wishing with each step, like galloping through mud, that I had not been so eager and forgotten my snowshoes at the fish house. Once at the tavern, I hoisted myself up the snow-laden front steps and tried to spy anything I could through a knothole in a board covering the corner window. Inside it was dusky with only a few slits of light let in by ill-fitting or warped boards nailed over adjacent windows, glancing off a mirror behind what had been a polished wooden bar now darkly dusty. Vague shapes, like furniture covered with sheets or canvas showed in the mirror but like the story of Tillie's itself, the images were murky and hard to see. In that moment, I was startled by movement, by a figure seemingly to throw off a blanket and stump toward my peep hole.

I pulled back and took my eye away from the spy hole.

I had to quickly cover both my eyes with my deerskin choppers to keep the just-risen sunlight glancing off snow from blinding me. Easing those rough mitten covers off my peepers a bit at a time, in half a minute, I could see again. It could have been the new sunlight or a flicker of flame, which was impossible, but for just a moment, a yellow beam fled through my peephole and seemed to bounce against birch trunks, ricocheting off into the dark of the pine forest.

I couldn't be sure of what I'd seen, so flashed with sunshine were my eyes. Suddenly shivering, I turned back down the stair guiding myself through nearly shut eyelids around to the shadowy side of the tavern. All the lower story windows were boarded up at the front, but around the corner on the long west side of the building, second-story windows were unboarded. I gazed up, thinking of scaling a tree growing close to that side but changed my mind when I saw that blanket-clad figure at one of the windows at the far end, just turning away. This time I was sure. I watched the person, or whatever it was, draw away suddenly, but did not see it reappear. I waited, breathing hard. Nothing stirred. I let the scare quiet down. Then, something else caught my attention in the morning light.

Below the second-story windows I saw a weather-beaten old mural depicting a huge bottle of beer and next to it a poem or part of a poem that had been carefully, at one time, painted across the length of the siding:

> If you're feeling sad ► ¤ ¤ ¤ ◄
> Stop ► ¤ ¤ ¤ ◄ Tillie's t' tip a few.
> Your friends around ► ¤ ¤ ¤ ◄
> Your blues ► ¤ ¤ ¤ ◄
> ► ¤ ¤ ¤ ◄ from sadness and► ¤ ¤ ¤ ◄
> To ► ¤ ¤ ¤ ◄time with our► ¤ ¤ ¤ ◄

The weathering of twelve winters and the lack of care of the building before that made the entire poem faint, and many of the words, especially at the line ends where the afternoon sun baked the siding most had peeled off or faded and were hardly visible. Still, as if I knew it was important, I read what was there and, when I got home, wrote it in my school notebook. That poem and whatever or whoever I had seen inside Tillie's—I had kept glancing back as I left but there was no reappearance—was all I had to go on for the time being. I had to wait to find out what it meant, and without getting laughed at, I certainly couldn't ask anyone at the lake about it. I'd have to find out on my own.

That I could do.

Heaven's Gates   10

Looking from where I am now at things I did and the ways I thought—I really don't know what this place is, except it isn't at the lake though I can clearly see everything at Thief and Trout lakes, and it isn't my choice, either—I can only guess how I might have handled my life differently, better, I suppose, and certainly in less troublesome ways. Still, you can take but one path in life, no matter what you think the result will be, and that course more likely than not won't be your safest bet.

When I first saw that dandy preacher up on the bandstand, doing the jive, setting and flexing those alluring hips just so, I felt more alive than I had in decades. After that night, the music danced in my spirit even at age fifty with menopause beginning. Everyday I woke humming or singing and wanting to dance. I was like a girl again, seventeen, and ready to go all night and the next day, too. I enjoyed everything much more, even my droll times with Tatty and my duty-bound chores with the household and the twins. I had finally been freed of a horrid past that was full of death, ghosts, small-town rivalries, and wrong-headed, gossipy opinions.

I was at a distance, finally, from the old goings-on at Tillie's: the windigo chase when I was not yet eighteen, my sister's frozen death that very same night, and, from what came much later but was connected so closely to Mary's freezing: Jay's bottle-goring and Roscoe's watery descent, though his body was never found, to the bottom of the lake. As a result of that deliberate act of insanity, going in search of the mystical and carnivorous windigo, I lost a sister and a child. Then, two decades later, I lost both again. I spent twenty years in hiding, a self-imposed exile from the only home I had known, Granny's cabin at Thief Lake. Still feeling like I was on the run, I returned to take up my mothering of Windsong too late. She was a lost daughter that I abandoned. I was to watch her die, like sister Mary, whom I had kept alive in my soul for the past twenty years. Windsong gave up her own life birthing her twins, Biinishii and Dindiisi. And I was wrong yet again when I thought I could repay all the trouble I'd caused by staying with my granddaughters, conniving to make my husband stay, too, to make sure the girls' lives turned out well, at least better than mine. What did I know?

I can say it now: It would have been better for us all, Windsong, Tatty, the twins, and even for the memories of Jay Martinen and his partner-friend, Roscoe, if I had stayed in Florida instead of trying to patch things up back at the lake. What is so odd to me is that my husband who did not want to stay in "that god-forsaken refrigerator" has thrived there and has even done a bit of good for the town and for the twins as well. I never would have guessed. It makes me look all the worse.

I wonder. Am I, or, correctly, was I that bad? No, not awful, but troubled for sure. Even with a fresh start in Florida after Mary's killing in the windigo chase, I couldn't keep the mayhem of my soul from spilling over the lip of my behavior-bowl. Usually, I had cause. The earth is wondrous but unfair. When one of my dandy teachers at FSU in Tallahassee groped my left cheek during an "after-class conference," I blew like a Gulf coast hurricane. Realizing that I was not about to turn and offer the other cheek to him, he grabbed his crummy old briefcase from the desk and, spewing papers out of it, ran for the hall door when I started to yell at the top of my lungs. He tripped over his bell bottoms, strewing even more student work, a chewed-on pencil, and a half-eaten sandwich in the hall.

I followed the bastard all the way to his car, knocked him down, and emptied everything that was left in his crappy case right over his head. I suppose that should have been enough, but it was insufficient for me, I'll say. I jumped on the hood of his puny Renault Dauphine and kicked in his windshield. He just sat on the ground like he'd been struck by lightning. Enough? Not for me! I hopped on the roof and jumped down on the skimpy little trunk lid, kicking out the rear window. I landed a good one, left-footed no less, that smashed the safety glass in a spray of shimmering beads into the back seat. I was having too much fun to stop there, and finding myself on the parking lot pavement, I pried up a landscaping stone—they told me later that it weighed thirty pounds—and beat every side window in—there were four to a side which made it more fun and more expensive to replace, too—finally dumping the stone in the middle of the driver's seat.

I went too far, I know. The dude was hustled out of there before the next semester, but not before I paid for the damages. The dean didn't think that sparing the car body was sufficient restraint even under the circumstances which everyone understood but pretended not to believe. I spent a year on probation at the school but still graduated. I'm never looking for trouble. It just seems to find me.

The advent of Teddy Good's worship of me allowed me to leave all my bad acting behind, at least for a while, though I suppose just cavorting with him was not behaving well. Anyway, he knew nothing of my past, and he didn't care about it if he did. With Preacher, I was free of the ghosts and horrors of my past, from my complicated identity having lost half of myself when my twin Mary turned to ice. So, to my mind, under the influence of Teddy G, I became a new person, restored fully as a whole being, instead of what I had felt like: that half-chewed ham sandwich stuffed in a leather case, my bread drying out and my insides rotting.

For years after the twins began to walk and to talk in sentences I could understand, my interest in raising them grew cooler just at my husband began to warm up to the task, finding his inspiration in those bullshit baby books and their pansy-assed philosophy. When Granny died, severing the last tie I had with a stable, meaningful upbringing, I lost most of my energy for being a wonderful parent. Oh, I loved those girls, no doubt about that, but the work, all that work of being there every day, every minute, fully at attention was too much for me. As Biini and Dindii grew, I shrank. Living in a family as the grown-up seemed to me like doing time in prison. I felt like I was dying. The more I shrank from my duties—how I detest that word. I never wanted to do chores—the more interested Tatty became in being a model parent. I began to hate him for it. And who was to blame? Me. I set it all up, and I was going to let it all fall, too.

Was it Tatty's fault? He turned to the kids and away

from me. I suppose I wouldn't have been so lonely and couldn't have felt so isolated if he he'd had time for me, like it was when we were in Florida. Then, of course, I couldn't have cared less. I was the only one around for him to care about. And since he didn't care much for himself at that time, that was okay by him.

I think I was envious of my own kin, my granddaughters. Maybe I didn't have anything extra in me to give. Mary'd had all that—she died in my place, giving everything—and no caring was leftover for me. Somehow, I thought everything should come naturally, without thinking, just knowing what to do, but the only thing that seemed to come naturally to me was making trouble for myself and those close to me. Some people just can't help it. Anguish and anger follow some of us like faithful but currish dogs, yapping and nipping until you want to scream and kick them. I had to get away. I couldn't leave the lake, so I just stepped outside my skin and became another person, Teddy Good's mistress.

I wasn't hiding from my past, though. When I walked over to Pelican Point, the old Morgan—the windigo chaser, crazy runner, the troubled one—just stayed behind, and I entered through the gates of paradise to an entirely new world, whole, sure, and happy. There was no way I was going to give that up. No way possible.

Sometimes I felt so good that I thought of staying at Gulbranson's or of flying out on the jet to California with Teddy Good to become a convert to his father's religion. I wasn't that far gone. I had sense enough to know that life would not continue for me away from the lake. As it was, it didn't continue even staying at the lake.

One thing was certain: I had to shelter my kids. That

was a given. Even as they grew into their teens, they needed me, and I was going to be there for them as much as my ghosts would let me, no matter what, even if Tatty tried to stop me. I was careful and vigilant. After that close call at That Man Island, I stayed away from every place the twins might turn up to see me in the company of Preacher. I never brought gifts or mementos home from Gulbranson's, and I always had an alibi. Tatty was helpful in that department, too. He didn't want to cover for me, but sometimes it was that or just tell the kids the truth. Neither of us wanted that.

They say you can't stop tongues wagging, but it only took one incident for me to quash that theory. After a jealous bitch I'd gone to high school with who lived on the Gulbranson Road threatened to expose me, saying she was about to have a chat with Biini and Dindii, I put that old-said-saw to shame. She and I had a night meeting on the woodsy path above Pelican Point. I thrashed her good where it wouldn't show much and pushed her off a not-too-high cliff, breaking her leg on the way down. I climbed below and stuck my face just above hers as she lay moaning on the rocks, saying, "I'll go get you some help, but if you ever gab about me to anyone, I'll kill you. Understand?"

She just moaned. "Understand!" I shouted.

She turned an awful shade of pale and said, "Yeah, I get it."

"Good." And I went, taking my time, to phone the boat house where the dock boys hung out at night, drinking beer.

When someone answered, I told him, "I heard someone scream and start moaning down near the beach under Pulpit Peak at the point."

It was Tony, the head dock boy. "Probably a drunk, passing out," he said. "Who's this, anyway?"

"Just a passerby who doesn't want to get tangled up in a mess. You're right about drunks, boy, but you don't want to leave someone who might be a guest out there 'til morning, do you?"

I had him, and he knew it. He called to the others, "Hey, shut up. We got work to do." The boys must have dragged their feet because Big Boy added, "I've got an idea. This sounds like it could be an adventure. Charlie, get the flashlights. Jimmy, grab a six pack."

Back on the phone, he asked, "Come on, who's this?"

I almost laughed because the first thing to come to mind was, "A good Samaritan," which was all I said. Preacher would be proud of me referring to the Bible.

Teddy Good filled me in the next night. "Did you hear about our neighbor?"

I posed as innocent as could be, knowing the head dock boy wouldn't recognize my voice and wouldn't rat me out if he did. He'd better not. "No," I answered Preacher, "What happened?"

"The boys at the boathouse heard someone screaming down at Pulpit Peak Beach last night. They thought it would be a Gulbranson guest. Turns out it was that old bag Sadie who lives half a mile down the road."

"What was she doing out at the beach?"

"Must have been drunk. She fell off that low cliff onto the beach. Broke her leg."

I played it up. "You don't say?"

"The dock boys dropped her twice on the way in. Now, her hip's broken, too."

"Ouch. Poor old Sadie."

I had come to Teddy through heaven's gate but was still acting like the devil. Sadie did not return. To this day, she is still limping around Hibbing, keeping her mouth shut. If I had to, I'd do it again.

Other than a few dark spots like that, my association with Teddy G was goodness and light. He treated me like a sainted lady—and Preacher sure knew how to treat a lady—praising me, keeping me in gimlets, riding the lakes and my bones day or night, and entertaining me from the bandstand on weekends, something that was very public—to the Minneapolis crowd—but had very private significance. He might be singing "Sweet Little Sheila" to the audience, but it was all for me, and I knew it.

All that might be true, but as anyone who grows up at the lake knows, seasons change and it's mostly to winter, it seems. Somewhere in that Good Book—I'm not a Bible-thumper by any means and I don't care to call up chapters and verses either—it says something like:

> There is a season, turn, turn, turn
> And a time to every purpose under Heaven
> A time to build up, a time to break down
> A time to dance, a time to mourn

It doesn't make the best poetry, but when *Teddy Good and the Saints* sang the song, it sounded just fine. And later, when I started to suspect more than funny business was going on with my great, jet setter boyfriend, I often thought about "a time to break down" and about mourning, too. It took a long time to hit home. It all showed me not for the last time just how wrong I had been about everything.

The Seasons 11

What I miss most about the good old world is the changing of seasons, not the time itself—summer was always my favorite, of course—but the on-the-brink of the shift from one season of the year to the other, for instance, the first moment in spring that the sun touches your brow with a warmth you haven't felt in months, the air still cool but less crisp, a smidgen wetter, fresher. Or while walking a trail newly watered by snow melt you see a couple blades of grass or leaves of strawberry reaching up or spreading out to catch the first gleam from the sun on its ascending path, and all at once you see, as if you'd never noticed before—and why would you? It had been since September and it is now late April—that the trees are fattening their buds like it was all their idea anyway.

The white man's calendar shows four equal oddly shifted seasons. Nobody believes, at least this far north, that the first day of winter is December 21st, although here June 21st is roundly accepted as the first day of summer. If summer started earlier, the lake people would be grateful but also would be looking over their weather-shoulders for a blizzard. The latest snowfall, about two inches, was recorded on June 4th in Mizpah just south of International Falls and not too far from Thief Lake. If you wait until September 21st to see the fall redden the maples and yellow the birch leaves, you'll have missed it. Our first frost comes in mid-August almost every year.

Certainly, winter is the longest season at the lake and in most of Minnesota proper. Here, it is known to last the better part of six months—and can stretch to seven, easily—judging from the piles of boots and parkas hung on hooks by every front and back door around the shoreline. If you pop in to visit any time of day between the middle of October and the beginning of April, you're likely to be greeted by your host, sitting near a wood stove but wearing his fur-trimmed coat, albeit with the hood dangling loose at his back. Most of us keep our long johns on day and night, adding snow pants before we head out the door. The parka is left on much of the day and night, usually unzipped at the front unless one is eating when it is hung over a chair at the table, or unless one is snoozing when it is laid over the blankets and quilts to hold in warmth during sleep.

At the end of long winter, Granny would announce spring cleaning which meant that the whole house, every window and door, would be opened and left that way to air out the accumulation, in clothing, carpets, and nearly everything else that wasn't hard-surfaced, of pine and birch smoke and six-months-worth of sweat in parkas, boot liners, undergarments and knit hats. Then you'd see boiled long johns hung on the line outside to dry and freeze overnight alongside parkas clipped upside down for a good two-day airing. Even after Granny's treatment, I could, blindfolded no less, sniff-out any family member by the endemic smell of their parka which permeated, it seemed, to the bone.

If winter was the longest-lasting season, summer barely flashed its glow on your back and it was gone before you could turn around. And warm does not really describe a Thief Lake summer. We enjoyed some pretty hot days—it was often over sixty-five degrees unless it rained—and if the mercury rose to over seventy, people would be complaining like it was a Finlander's sauna. No, it wasn't the temperature that defined summer even looking at the 120 degree difference from hottest summer day to coldest winter night.

Summer at the lake, means light. Light to bask in sweetness. Light to fish til nearly midnight. Daylight to hike long trails. Sunshine to sparkle on the waves, illuminating the shallows where the youngsters try to hook sunfish and crappies. The splendid sunsets are long in their glory and eternal in their twilights. Equally, crepuscular leisure in mornings fill the lake people with hope enough to last nearly through the darkest months of winter. Summertime, no matter its brevity, was not for sleeping-in. Everyone was stirring by four in the morning, an hour before sunrise. If you were abed late, the light reached down the hall, a giant burning ghost that bred ideas of strangeness and abduction in your mind, telling you to rise and get ready. Sunlight stirred a restlessness that pulsed through a twenty-hour day. We slept deeply but in short stints. Each summer sun-show was lighter than two and a half deep-winter days.

Summers after the advent of Teddy Good's ministry in the area and his direct ministration to me marked the highlights of my days. I rousted the twins, if I could—they were such sleepyheads, especially into their teens—before the sun rose and took them out on Thief Lake to catch breakfast. By the time they were fourteen, they were not just good fisherwomen but great ones. I could count on them to keep the freezer filled without any help from

Tiny's stores or my own efforts. It seemed that they knew the very movements of the walleyes in the lake, altering their course each morning we went out to synchronize with the fish as they circled the lake working the shadowy depths below the shallows for minnows and fry playing tag in sunny waters. As the weather warmed, Dindii and Biini found the edges of the deep holes where the lunkers finned their time away waiting for something to crest the edge of the deeps and, then, a sudden waggle of the tail brought the big fish surging to the outcrop or even beyond, above the surface to snag the unsuspecting but skittish prey. Often that "victim" belonged to one of the twins, jigging her line just so, moving the minnow or worm to look injured or unaware of its danger. Then the water became sky and the walleye breakfast. Their skill and calm excitement filled me with joy.

Mornings are the best time to fish. But mornings are also the best time to tire teenagers to the point that they won't notice a mother's absence so much. By late afternoon nap time, I was dressed for an evening of religious devotion the likes of which I had never known before. And at the height of the summer, *Teddy Good and the Saints* played five nights a week, taking Mondays off for field trips and to check in on the bible camp over at Orr. I didn't miss a one of his concerts unless a twin, and sometimes both, came up with a must-do for me. I worked the fishing angle and did a fair amount of plein-air watercolor with them to fill what they came to call "mommy time" as if they understood, without comprehending my need for "alone time," as I called it.

As the twin's fourteenth summer came round, two occasions gave me pause—though I did not pause—

about all my activity. The first came from Dindii.

"Mama, you know what I'd like to paint next?"

This sounded like a guessing game to me. "A moose antler for the post office."

"Well, yes I would like that, and I know Uncle Tiny has a perfectly matched pair in his warehouse. First, though, I would like to repaint the mural at Tillie's."

I couldn't play dumb. Every time you walked to the town dock, you passed that peeling, rotten mural. I had wished it away a thousand times, and now, here it was in the mouth of my sweet Dindii. "Where did you get that idea?"

She was matter of fact. "It came to me winters ago after the bear man visited the garage."

Now I was stricken. "What? A bear man? Who is that?"

"I don't really know, but he came to warn Papa about trouble." She moved right on—I had to let her continue since I was shocked, unable to talk—like it was a normal conversation. "Anyway, the following winter one time, when I came back from the fish house in early morning, I crossed over the lot to the tavern and looked inside through a knot hole. I saw a blanket covered sofa that reminded me of that bear man I'd seen in the garage.

"Later, I saw the mural."

How to keep Dindii from that unholiest monument-to-insanity, I could not at that moment know. It was sheer luck that had prevented an intrusion of Tillie's into our lives until now. I just knew I had to keep her out. "But why? Why fix the old decrepit thing?"

"I heard the bear man say, "Open Tillie's."

"No!" I nearly screamed it. Dindii didn't even step

back. I couldn't threaten anything. I had to reason with her about unreasonableness. "How could you hear someone who is dead? Roscoe Lucci is long gone, Dindii." I kick myself yet for using his name.

Dindii wasn't interested in names just then and said, "Maybe I dreamed it, but what's wrong with fixing up an old mural? I think it would look nice. Everybody would admire it."

She had a point, but I thought that the impulse would fade, that I could out-wait her.

That was the first cautionary.

Not too long afterward, some time in August, Biini started asking me about the Reverend Good, as she called him. "Is he really a bad man?"

Now I hate to lie, not because it is wrong or a sin or anything, but because it's just too easy to get caught doing it. I prefer to have others, like my dear old postmaster husband, do the fibbing for me. So, I took another tack that didn't require a direct lie. "Who is saying Reverend Good is a bad man?"

Biini was as matter of fact as her sister. "Mr. Ericksen," she said.

"Erickson?" I didn't place the man.

"Old Borg. Reverend Ericksen. *You know.*"

"Oh, the Swedenborgian you are always running to."

Biini frowned. "I do not run to him. I attend the services. I can believe anything I want, but is what he says true? Is Mr. Good not good?"

I still was wriggling like that worm Biini fished with. "Why would I know?"

Biini looked at me in a very peculiar way almost

like she was looking through me at something she remembered that I didn't know about. "I thought you knew him. Don't you?"

I was too deep into this conversation. I plied the small-town excuse. "Oh, Biini, everybody knows Teddy G here—I nearly bit my tongue for using that familiar name—he's a famous television evangelist with a great big church in California and a college out there too. I know him like that."

She let me off the hook as if I were the fish she did not want to catch. "Well, what do you think, then. Is he a bad man?"

I mustered all the sincerity I could—it was not very hard, either, since I had my own gauge of goodness when it came to Preacher—and answered her calmly and carefully, taking her face between my hands and kissing her. "I am quite sure that Reverend Good is a decent man. You can tell Old Borg I said so."

That night, fall fell. The temperature dropped to twenty-five at sunset and stayed right there for ten hours. That sent the trees their annual reminder to drop everything and signaled the sap to run for root-land. Within five days, with the help of continual drops in the mercury, the entire lake basin was painted all colors of the palette from ruby to gold, from fierce red to tawny, from port to blood-tinged yellow. I immersed the girls in the splendor, as if my presence was necessary. We hiked with tripods and brush boxes, set up on bald hills and painted hours on end. I welcomed the diversion until Dindii hiked up and set down her tripod above the lake and a flat granite outcrop.

I heard her telling Biini, "This is where I saw great-grandpa."

"Oh, you did not."

"Ask Papa, then."

"Do you see dead people?"

I kept my nose to my brush work, listening.

"Maybe I do. Don't you pray to a dead man? Anyway, you don't have to believe me."

Biini glowered at her twin. "No I don't. And I will not. I believe in Jesus who is the living God."

As usual that ended any conversation between my kids. Dindii looked to local spirits, hallowed lynx and wolverine rather than churchy specters. I was mother, through Windsong, to spirit chasers who, though they looked exactly alike, pursued ghosts as different from one another a the girls' appearances were alike.

As fast as their talk ended, so did the glories of fall.

Rain swept down from Canada. It was four days, during which every leaf was knocked from its tree, before the sun shone through. A wonderland for artists and old lovers turned barren and gray. Within weeks, snow was falling on frozen ground. Two goods came of it: there would be no painting out of doors, and Teddy Good beat a hasty retreat back to California, taking his bad and his good with him. I would miss the man, of course, but the complexities of our tryst, if that is what you'd call it, were fast coming to the fore, and I needed a break.

So, the seasons changed, had changed, and would continue carrying my two girls along year by year, already across the threshold of adulthood with its disillusionment and pain, and further into late adolescence during which, if it were like mine and sister Mary's had been, they could and likely would inflict agonies on each other, themselves, and what I feared most at that time, upon me. Dindii was to snoop around Tillie's, stirring the ashes of my youth and late return. Biini had begun to cast about in her own way to find greater religious mysteries than those the Swedenborgians had to offer. I feared for them both, and I feared for me.

BWCA 12

I track most of my history nowadays by how old the twins were at any turn of events. They'll be fourteen on their next birthday, but I'm also cognizant of happenings more centered on my work, if one can call it work, since the job of a small town postmaster is a sometime-thing in the view of most of my patrons.

"You know, Tatty, you've got it pretty good."

"How's that, Danny?" I said.

"Well, you work about three hours a day and take home a good paycheck."

Now there is no good to come of arguing with Danny, nor in trying to teach him something he doesn't already know. So, I said, "You've got that right, my friend. I live the life of Riley."

Danny laughed. "Even Riley worked more than you do. Not to criticize, you know."

"Hell," I said, old McKinnon had been dead for his last two years as postmaster, and no one noticed! I've been retired four years. Did you realize that?"

He gave me an odd look and stopped to think about that for a while.

Danny was far from right. The job looked like it was part time, but it was a position, not a job. It occupied me all day and sometimes into the night. First off, a post office, especially in a town the size of Thief Lake, between three and four hundred in winter, is at the center of each and every life in its purview, the high and mighty and the lowest echelons, too. Everyone gets mail. They get it daily. It keeps coming, and going, in a constant hum that pays no mind to the seasons, the weather, or the news, although there is certainly less after fall closures and the departures of summer residents. Only United States holidays and Sundays halt the advance of the mail. And as far as privacy in a small town goes, which isn't very far even amongst the taciturn, despite my best professional behavior, it is awfully difficult not to notice cards and letters passing through the mail slots, boxes, and hands of the sorter. Within a year of accepting the honor and position, all due to the political sway of Morgan's brother, Tiny, I knew who was struggling to pay bills, whose family was keeping in touch, who was buying what fishing lures and tackle from what catalogue, and who was hopelessly or cruelly in love. Being above it all was impossible, though as a man of professional standing, I just never talked about what I knew from handling the mail.

In the kind of winter we endured at the lake, the remote small-town postmaster is the sole federal official regularly on site. After Labor Day, the immigration officers have retreated to Duluth. The customs inspector leaves for ports in Florida. Game wardens, fish counters, and park rangers for the Boundary Waters Canoe Area (BWCA) dwindle in numbers and are seldom seen in town. If a dignitary or investigator comes to town, it is the federal man who gets the call. Even the county sheriff's deputy in this the largest county in Minnesota hardly makes an appearance without there being trouble to account for. As Postmaster of Thief Lake, Minnesota, I was host, first contact, and reluctant guide to politicos,

Alcohol Tobacco and Firearms agents, an occasional Treasury official, just once the Postmaster General, who loved to fish but caught nothing but a cold, and all too often the FBI.

It is this last that has descended on me in force now, my fourteenth year in office. Maybe it is the third-time-is-a-charm axiom, since this is the third unusual death of a BWCA park ranger during the time I've been postmaster. It is somewhat likely that this investigation was, say, "well attended" because this most recent death happened in late fall before the real onset of the big snows of winter. Death visited our town right in the middle of our main street, in an obvious and suspicious manner (the ranger was young and died of poisoning) that brought not one but three agents from the Federal Bureau of Investigation.

They needed lodging of a type that allowed both privacy and public contact as well as comfort in the freezing nights. Much to my dismay, the only choice was to house them at Gulbranson's Resort at the Pelican Point cabin which had all the comforts of winterization, plenty of electricity, private phone service, and at the resort building proper, a large meeting room in which to take statements and conduct other business connected to the investigation.

The show of force was unusual but perhaps centered more politically rather than in accord with justice. Agent DuChien, the lead man, didn't have to remind me, though he certainly did, that this was the third death of a BWCA ranger—all men in their mid to late twenties—in a little more than a decade.

"It is their youth that makes us suspect foul play," he said. "But the area's politics are the main factors."

I played it a bit densely. "What does that have to do with it?"

"There is a lot of hate going around, anti-government anger."

"Not directed at you," I said.

"So far no one has dared. But three dead park rangers in twelve years should tell anyone that there is trouble in fish-city."

I'd learned the local version of that northern Minnesota history. In one way or another every citizen of Thief Lake and, for that matter, in the whole county knew it too. The hallmark of it was interference in the lives of the governed, by the governors. The white curmudgeons at the lake, and there were many, called it by a new name they'd adapted from their studies in grade school: "*annexation*, without representation," government co-opting of citizens' rights.

Those "rights," they maintained, included the freewheeling acquisition of a once-virgin land that had begun even before what were called "the founding fathers." Locally the spirit of so-called independence, which did not include the indigenous folk on either side of the border, began with the *voyageurs*, French fur traders, and continued with wave after wave of youthful fortune hunters and, when the getting was best, by established old-money barons of one sort or another, who chewed through the forests, laid steel rails, stripped the land of and shipped out virgin timber, then pulled back the rocky surface to expose rich iron deposits, seemingly free for the taking by anyone who had the unmitigated gall to wager on a hope and a dream.

The once-famed Seven Iron Men, the cadre of Merritt

brothers, were one group of these. They grasped the opportunity earlier than others to develop rich iron ore deposits that underlay most of the lands directly south of our lake. Never mind that their reach outstretched their grasp. They lacked much of the prime ingredient of American success, money, and having turned to eastern wealth to fund their expansions—to people who had already stripped lands back there a hundred and more years before—fell victim to the legal chicanery of their lenders, and so lost everything, perhaps even hope. The Merritt brothers, though, were local heroes, men who could have succeeded had everyone, including government, played fair. So say the complainers. These same bellyachers, though, hallowed that tight-fisted, supposedly beneficent ruler, Carnegie, no matter his methods and deeds, oddly uplifting the Scot who knew how to wrap avarice in philanthropy, how to disguise controlling with giving.

The latest incursion from the east was not swaddled in business interest but came of government regulation from Washington by way of local heroes: congressmen, ex-governors, supportive state legislators, a US Circuit Court judge and several Presidents, one of whom, Carter, also signed my appointment. Reviewing the history of the move to establish a protective perimeter around the last virgin forest stands, truly pure rivers and lakes, and wildlife-supporting verdure of the region, told me that these men promoting the BWCA were no less presumptuous of their own legacies than the Merritt brothers or the founder of US Steel. Being more politic than the Merritts, though, they were more effective.

DuChien put it tersely: "The Dalkon shield judge

lit the fuse. Twenty years later we had an explosion of ranger-death."

The lead agent referred to outlawing of logging in our neighborhood through the efforts of Miles Lord, the so-called People's Judge of the Minnesota Circuit Court. He was sometimes called "that bastard judge" among our rednecks.

A former Minnesota governor, Orville Freeman, had paved the way to better conserve the wilderness in 1965—the move to protect started at the beginning of the century—while holding tempers in check by moving slowly and listening to, or at least pretending to hear, all sides.

"You know," DuChien said, "if it had been left at the Freeman Directive, all this trouble—strange and unlikely deaths and such—would have likely been avoided."

I stayed non-committal, "You think so?"

"When lumberjacks and truckers started losing jobs in the area, it rubbed people the wrong way," my G-man said.

I recalled a morning table-pounding discussion that Cooley tried to quell. One of the Olsen Resort crew, the guy we called Laurel, was saying, "Okay, ban timber harvesting. But when they start to tell me what size motor I'm going to put on my boats, that's going too far. Next they'll prescribe a brand of toilet paper."

Laurel referred to one of the confusing and more arcane regulations that governed the use of outboard motors in the preserve, something that, according to the partners at Olsen's kept their clientele from booking the kind of vacations they had in the past. Poor L & H were hanging on by the skin of their teeth, if you were to believe their rants.

"It's all in a good cause, my friend," Cooley soothed.

"Sure. Easy for you to say, working for the county and all, but try running a resort here. How can I tell someone from Chicago he can't run his snowmobile across the lake? They just stop coming, and that hurts. Shit, I had to let my cook go and close the restaurant. She was the best, too."

"It's complicated. That's for sure," said Cooley, "but it will all come out in the wash. You'll see." At the time no one knew that Cooley Jokkinen had applied for seasonal work with the BWCA. He was about to trade county snow plowing for federal snowmobiling as a winter-only ranger.

It was Hardy who slammed a fist on the table in answer. "I'll see nothin'! I might be out on my ear. Them government bastards deserve everything they get."

A year-round resident one lake over from Trout chimed in, "Now they're telling me I'm grandfathered in. But they still make lowball offers to try tempting me to get out. I already can't give the cabin to my kids. They'll force me to sell sometime."

Hardy answered, "Yeah, over your dead body. Maybe that's what we need here is a few more corpses."

Cooley must have taken note, but he was not one to back down in a crisis. Even when his life was threatened, he stood tall and firm.

The little chat bordered all sunshine and calm in comparison to the grumbling and frequent vilification of political actors you could hear bandied about. Probably because it was at the post office cafe, threats were curtailed, but outside the door there was serious cause for concern. When the second ranger was found with a head injury that was either a snowmobile mishap or a blow from a branch-wielding assailant, people like old Hardy, unless he was drunk which was often, ceased to rouse the rabble he was a part of, for just a while. Everybody knew the FBI was listening. And now, not four years later, another ranger died. He had ingested poison.

"Was it murder?" I asked DuChien.

The inspector knew better. "I'm gathering facts. The folks in St. Paul will make that determination. Off the record? It looks bad."

"It's terrible."

"The rangers have access to strychnine. They use it on some non-native species that invade the area," DuChien told me.

"Bad stuff, isn't it."

"Very nasty. Painful. Finally, it stops the breath."

"He was asphyxiated?"

"We've ruled out suicide, but murder would be tough to prove. The list of foul-play suspects at the lake is pretty long."

The investigation was long and seemed thorough. The Santa Monica, California branch even interviewed Teddy Good. After an appropriate time, the death was ruled accidental. Nothing much came of all DuChien's effort.

Not a year later, DuChien was back. I learned of it from Shookii who barged into the mail room kicking off snow from her big boots everywhere.

"Papa, that man is back."

"Go out and knock off that snow." She was back in less than a minute. "Slow down, Shookii. What man?"

She took a breath and curled her mouth, looking disgusted with me. "The FBI man, DuChien."

"Now what's happened?" It had been just over a year since DuChien's previous visit.

Shookii was fifteen at that time and had begun taking an interest and an active role in the happenings around the lake. I wasn't surprised that she had heard the news before the postmaster found out. She was, after all, the staff of one at the high school newspaper, *The Trout*.

"He's coming in by snowmobile from Kettle Falls."

"That's odd. And . . ?" I said. Shookii loved news and even more enjoyed dribbling it out a drop at a time.

"A ranger was shot."

"Dead? Shot dead?"

"No, that's the best part. He was left for dead, but bound his own wound. He snowshoed and eventually crawled his way close to the hotel. Someone found him and brought him to the porch on a toboggan."

"Who was that?"

"No one knows. He disappeared after lifting Cooley off the sled."

"Who's at the hotel this time of year?"

"Margaret."

"Well, that was lucky." Margaret had lived on both sides of the border in the wilds over fifty years and was the unofficial doctor of Kettle Falls. She could sew up a hatchet wound, cure fevers with herbs, and had set numerous broken arms and legs over the half century of her residence.

"She saved his life."

"And how do you know all this, Shookii?"

"I was riding Uncle Tiny's snowmobile through the narrows, just for fun, and ran into Mr. DuChien on Evergreen Bay. He was cooking lunch by the shore. The ranger was bundled up on a sled behind the inspector's mobile, sipping a cup of broth. It was Cooley Jokkinen."

"Cooley! Whoever pulled the trigger didn't know who they were dealing with. Old Jokkinen is a tough customer."

"Ya, I shared their lunch with them. Mr. Jokkinen told me he'd gotten off two shots, but his aim was bad because he'd been hit. Deer rifle slug went through his shoulder."

Just as I had marveled at my daughter's prescience up on the table rock, I was now impressed by her presence of mind and logical good sense. "How did you get here ahead of them?"

"Oh, they're going it slow 'cause every time they hit a bump Mr. Jokkinen's shoulder cries out."

"And you raced all the way back here just to tell me?" I said.

"Yes. So you could call an ambulance to bring him into Hibbing hospital."

I was just an actor in Shookii's drama, but I was glad to do her bidding. By the time DuChien and Cooley arrived, the ambulance was well on its way.

"You must have throttled that machine back a notch or two. Shookii's been here nearly an hour. Come in. You should rest inside and warm a bit."

Adolescence

Popcorn 4
(Biini)

It had been three years since I decided that I knew exactly what to do over Mama's sinful ways, and praying, though it helped plenty to soothe the knot in my stomach that tightened every time she disappeared from home, it did not cure her. Prayers are mostly for expressing faith, not for getting what you think you want.

I asked Rev. Ericksen about it. "I've been praying for my mother to mend her ways now for three years. Do you think I should keep it up?"

Mr. Ericksen stroked his long, gray, skimpy whiskers and, as he always seemed to do, smiled as if thinking of something pleasant from his young days. He answered, speaking slowly, in his high-pitched, thin voice. "Your faith has to be in Jesus. If you are sincere, your words can only help, if not your mama, then yourself. Beware of losing faith if your entreaties seem to go unanswered."

"I'm not losing faith in Christ, Reverend. That will never happen. When I was a young girl, I promised to help in any way I could. I'll keep praying, but now that I'm grown some, it's time for me to work in other ways, too."

He seldom seemed worried, but at this he frowned and shook his head. "Be careful, my girl, the devil is afoot. He may be walking the paths along our shores."

"I am careful. I will not fear. For the lord is with me."

The good reverend finished my thought in

benediction: May "goodness and mercy follow you, all the days of your life."

The Ericksens were all sweet, but Reverend was the gentlest of all. I hadn't told him I'd asked Mama about Pastor Good being bad. I didn't tell him that I didn't believe her answer. If Mr. Good was not bad, then Mama had to be. No, that wasn't right. She might have been misled. I just couldn't believe she was evil. Despite her words, though, I knew that Theodore G. Good was the devil, and it was *that* Satan I had to confront. I had a plan.

If I were to follow the Christ who threw the money lenders out of the temple, I would first have to get into the temple of Pastor Good, and I wasn't about to go barging in to Gulbranson's or to sneak along Pulpit Point ridge to the Pelican Point cabin I knew Mama visited frequently. Neither of those places was meant for what I had in mind. It was still winter, so no plan could work until May when things opened up and Teddy Good came back to town.

I started with Papa when he didn't have his visor on yet. He was sipping a morning coffee alone in the cafe. "Papa, I'm bored."

"I'm sorry to hear that, Popcorn." He did not seem interested. "Have you finished your homework?"

"Of course, Papa. That's part of the problem."

"Homework?"

"No, school. I'm fifteen now and since I was five, I've been going to school with the same people, year in and year out. I'm bored with them."

Papa put his cup on its saucer. "That's normal, Popcorn. People like change and variety, but they also like continuity."

"What do you mean?"

"Kind of like having the same thing for breakfast every

morning, say, Cheerios. If you change, to Wheaties, you soon start craving the old O's. Haven't you met any interesting kids now that you're in high school?"

I shook my head slowly. "None of them share my beliefs, really. None are Swedenborgian or even know Jesus."

Papa nodded. "Yes, I remember your standards are high and rather settled."

"Besides, they are all basically like me: kids from the north woods. All they talk about is either hunting, fishing, or hockey."

"You like fishing."

"Papa, I'm good at it, but that doesn't mean it is all I want to talk about. I mean, I would like to meet kids who are different from me. People, maybe even from another country, who speak other languages and such."

He looked at me, not acting surprised, but maybe a little suspicious. "It sounds like you're leading up to something."

"Well, maybe I am. Summer is coming in a while. I wonder if rather than just hanging around Thief Lake all summer, wouldn't it be wonderful to enroll in a summer camp?"

I was leading up to something, of course. I had my sights on the International Summer Camp in Orr which was run by Planet Earth's Church of God and the Reverend Teddy Good. Some said that the campers were from all over the world, but mostly from African nations, and that some of the kids were royalty in their own country. A plain old postmaster's daughter would not ordinarily be admitted, but a Christian daughter of Morgan Langille might be. I didn't think Mama would be eager for me to go, but it might mean I would be out of the way most of the summer and she would only have to deal with Shookii. Still, I approached Papa first.

"Well, that's a novel idea." Papa said. "You could *run* a summer camp for all the outdoor experience you've got."

I pressed my lips together hard. "I'm not looking for a job, Papa. Or to baby sit some speedboat guy's kids. Besides, I am hoping to find a Christian camp."

"I don't think I know of any, but then, that is more your interest than mine."

I was ready. "I know one."

"You do?" Papa said.

"Yes. Planet Earth's Church of God runs an International Summer camp in Orr every year. I think I'd like to apply to get in."

Papa was frowning. He might have been scowling for all I knew about that. He spoke slowly. "Have you put this to your mother, Popcorn?"

I shook my head. "Not exactly."

"What do you mean, 'not exactly'?"

"First, I thought I should ask her if Pastor Good was a good man. Reverend Ericksen thinks he is evil."

Now Papa stood up and put his hands on his hips, towering above me as I sat at the counter. "And what did she tell you?" He set his jaw like he did before giving me and Shookii a lecture.

"More or less, she thought he was a decent man."

Now, Papa crossed his arms and looked down into them, like he was thinking. After what seemed like an hour to me, he said, "Well, I don't have an opinion on that. I know the camp is expensive. I'm not sure you've been exposed to that brand of religion, but if you get your mother's permission, I will support you."

I stood up and hugged him, burying my smile in his chest. "Thank you, Papa. I knew I could count on you. And I already know that there are camp scholarships I can apply for, so the cost won't be much."

Papa wrapped me in his arms. As soon as we ended our hug, he reached over and put his visor on.

I waited two days to see if Papa had talked to Mama about the camp. She didn't say anything to me about it, so I figured they hadn't talked. It would be up to me. I knew from some things Shookii did that it would be best to go to Mama rather than open a "family discussion" at the supper table. When those happened, silence fell like sunset in December, dark and fast. I held off until Mama had finished her latest painting, a spring landscape with a budding birch tree hanging over the foreground. Mama was always in a good mood right away after finishing a canvas.

"Oh, I like this one, Mama. I can't wait 'til spring!"

"I feel the same way, I guess. These thawing landscapes start coming out of my brush about February."

"Remember a little while ago I was asking you about Pastor Good?"

Mama put her palette down. She glared at me. "Not that again."

"Well, I asked because I might be interested in attending summer camp over in Orr when school gets out."

"Sure, but why?"

I went through the reasons I had told Papa.

"Have you spoken to your father about this?"

Why parents have to ask that, I don't know. They should talk with each other more often, in my opinion. Then they wouldn't have to ask over and over again. "I mentioned it, yes."

Again, she asked the same thing as Papa, "And what did he say?"

"Like always, once he understood and warned me, too, he said that he would support me."

"And I suppose he told you to ask me, too."

"Right."

"Why? Why not another camp?"

Beside the international idea, I told her that she had assured me by what she'd said of Pastor Good that his church and camp would be all right.

"Could you help me with my application? I want to apply for a scholarship."

It was as if she were confronting a windigo, she was so tense. "I'll see what I can do," she said stiffly.

Mama and Papa in a rare moment acting together made the announcement at the supper table in the middle of May. Not only was I going to the summer camp in Orr but Planet Earth's Church of God had approved a fully paid summer, including board and a double bunk cabin to share with one of the African queens. It looked to be an exciting time.

I never found out who pushed for it, if anyone, but the invitation included Shookii though she would be in a different cabin.

Shookii had other ideas. "I am not wasting my summer with a bunch of phonies and cranks," she said.

We three groaned in protest.

"It is not my bowl of rabbit stew," Shookii added. "I have plenty to do here. Uncle Tiny is helping me set up a trap line, working up the equipment this summer. Remember, Papa, we were doing a rock climbing trip? I have fishing to do. And I'm attending the Council meetings. I also want to do some painting. Besides, I plan to paddle into Canada for two weeks. Who has time to go to camp?"

Mama tried to soothe things over. "I just hate to see your sisterhood break up for the summer."

Because I knew it to be true, I would say it, rather than let Shookii put it out there.

"If you hadn't noticed over the last five years, we broke up long ago."

Shookii looked steadily at me, then said, "You'll always be my sister, but I'm on my own path, just like you."

Then, we did the dishes together.

Shookii washed. I dried.

Shookii 4
(Dinḍii)

Parents are the most surprised of anyone at what their children do. I wonder if that's because they always think of the kids as infants, toddlers, and youths, even after they grow up. The parents cannot really see it. It is also true though less fro adults outside a immediate family, like my Uncle Tiny or any of the fish counters or rangers, and it is easy for the young girl coming of age who understands this. Knowing this while working on parents and other adults, she can discover a whole lot that adults don't even realize, simply by acting like a child and by asking innocent questions. You wouldn't think so, but grownups talk alot in the presence of a child, or someone they believe is a child. They seem to speak more freely because they think the kid won't understand. Or because she is just part of the background. Invisible.

After I watched Papa go white in the garage, walked with him up Tablerock Hill, and years later, had my conversation with Uncle Tiny in the fish house, I'd started out on a mission. I had plenty to think about. First, Roscoe and what he'd said about opening Tillie's. Then, Papa's ghost-father and what his showing up might mean. Also, why Mama seemed to think Tillie's deserved to be shut even though she was running wild again anyway. Then, about who or what lived in that boarded up bar, and what the verses painted on the building meant. So, I hung around adults more than the other kids of the town did. I pretended to pay no mind but listened intently. I went out to explore company outside the family, the school, and the town of Thief Lake. I was biding my time, keeping my paint brushes ready to restore Tillie's sign, and was piecing together more than facts about the goal of reopening a building. I knew that I actually owned half of it. I went further, planning how it would be used and what it would bring about.

My uncle was my guide, both knowing and being unaware. For a generation, my Uncle Tiny had been at the head of the tribal council. Since he paid attention to others ideas, every tribal leader respected him. He had connections with US government officials and elected folk on both sides of the border. His example showed me how to keep my thoughts to myself while slipping through the traps of opinions in the small circle of people around Thief Lake. It seemed from what I saw Uncle Tiny doing that the best way to go where you wanted was both to ask and to have likeable reasons that it would be good for others, not to mention oneself.

So, I wanted Tillie's to reopen. Why was that good for the town? As a bar, it wouldn't add anything to the community, seeing as how both Gulbranson's and Olsen's dispensed enough liquor to keep the drinkers pickled and staggering. No, Tillie's wouldn't become what it had been, a hangout for the troubled, misled, and the misunderstood. I had sounded my uncle out on the chances the county would issue another liquor license, even for light beer. He knew the ropes.

"Why don't the smaller resorts have bars?" I'd asked him.

"Too much trouble."

I creased my forehead on that one, wondering. "What

kind of trouble?"

Tiny was very patient, not like most adults who would say, "You wouldn't understand."

He said, "Getting a liquor license is expensive and takes time. You have to kowtow to people. Mostly, the resorts just want to rent boats and cabins and be left alone otherwise. Booze is easy enough to find anyway and tends to bring trouble to those who dispense it."

"Did Tillie's have a license? And what's kowtow?"

"Tillie's had one. I think it was the first one issued in the town. But it was long ago cancelled. It went when the place was shut. And kowtow means 'bow to' in Chinese."

"Would Tillie's need approval to reopen?" I wondered.

"Not unless it served food or beer. It could make a great community center," he said.

I didn't spring on it right then, but I knew I had my in. A child talking about opening Tillie's as anything, including a gathering place for lake folk, would seem strange to most people, but if someone like a tribal elder mentioned it, people would think, "Yeah."

I hoped to feed my uncle's ideas through Papa who would mention it to Mama and so on. Actually, Mama herself had told me, she was the trustee of the place and would have to be involved, whether or not she was in favor of the idea (which I knew she would not be). In the last place, I and Biini would have to approve. I would start working on my sister who might be more help than she realized. For sure, keeping part of the building for Lutheran prayer meetings and Bible study would be something she could support.

If all went well, it would be Biini, not me, who would bring it up with the parents. With Tiny in support, I might be able to look like I was holding out, and, then, finally say yes to the religion, if tribal affairs could also be housed in the building. Also, I could probably get support for the restoration of the old sign as an historical memento going way back to the beginnings of the settlement as a wilderness retreat for both newcomer whites and for the Native people who had already been there for centuries.

It was the BWCA that really helped my ideas form. It brought money into the town, beyond just getting by or welfare for the lake folk. The wilderness area also sheltered the woods, lakes, and rivers from the greed of rich. That pleased the original inhabitants.

So, I made it a point to get to know the rangers, conservation officers, and when they came to sort out trouble, even the FBI agents. The federal people wouldn't necessarily help me in my plan, but they might be good to know. Papa was supportive. They all worked for the same employer.

The day I took off on Tiny's snowmobile, with a full tank of gas and a finely tuned engine, I had no idea I would run into either a ranger or an agent. A quarter of the way to the Kettle Falls Hotel, though, I saw a wisp of smoke from a campfire out on the ice and, like we are all supposed to do in the north country, decided to see if someone needed help. The two men I found hunkering over the fire were Agent DuChien and Cooley Jokkinen, the chief winter ranger for the western part of the BWCA which bordered Thief and Trout Lakes. Papa had invited these men to meals at one time or another. They knew me. I certainly knew them, since I listened carefully around the supper table.

As I approached on Tiny's machine, I noticed that one of the men stood up, bringing a rifle to ready but holding it still. I didn't like the look of it and stopped a hundred yards away, stepping off the snowmobile and unwrapping my face, taking off my reflective glasses.

"It's Shookii Langille, Tatty's, the postmaster's kid."

"Agent DuChien, FBI," the man said, waving me on.

DuChien set his rifle in a triangular cradle of sticks away from the fire. When I got close and stopped the engine, he said, "Can't be too careful as you can see looking at Cooley, but welcome Dindii." He had learned my given name around the supper table.

"What's going on? Hi, Mr. Jokkinen." I noticed he was on a gurney-type sled and didn't rise when I dismounted my own ride. "Are you okay?"

He laughed hoarsely then winced, reaching for his left arm. "Just a little shot up. You should see the other guy."

"No joking, now, Cooley," DuChien said. "You laugh at your own stories, and you know how that hurts!"

Cooley turned to me, "Come have some federal soup, girl. It'll warm you up."

DuChien unpacked a campstool from the sled and set it up near the fire. "Chicken noodle is my specialty, mine and Mr. Campbell's."

I sat. "What happened Mr. Jokkinen? How did you get shot?"

"Poacher, likely. Seems so since he left deer innards behind. Well into the Area," he said, which indicated the BWCA where no hunting was allowed. "I made it to the hotel with a good samaritan's help, and Margaret patched me up."

DuChien shook his head. "Here is a true woodsman. He makes it sound like he took a bus to Kettle Falls. No such luck."

Over lunch, the two of them told me much of the story, DuChien filling in for Mr. Jokkinen's ever changing account:

He was knocked down by the shot that went right through his arm and lodged in a birch tree.

The masked poacher approached, and Jokkinen played dead, but was ready to pull the trigger on his 45 if the man raised the rifle. No, the guy turned and took off on Cooley's snowmobile. Jokkinen got off two parting shots but missed both times as he couldn't shoot at a distance one-handed.

He had to bind his wound with his T-shirt that he tore up and to apply a tourniquet he carried in his backpack. "I marked the birch with my own blood and took coordinates."

"You applied sound police methods," DuChien said.

"Thanks." Cooley replied. "Then, I set off toward KF (he meant Kettle Falls) about six miles away, I figured.

Mr. Jokkinen had told DuChien about it, so when Cooley went to sleep in the middle of a sentence, lying on his gurney, DuChien told me more of the story by the campfire. "The tale changes each time he tells it. I'd say he goes from victim to hero in a hurry."

I hoped to hear the whole story, but they had to move along. I thought I could hear the rest at the post office while we were waiting for the ambulance Agent DuChien sent me ahead to call, but there wasn't enough time. I'd have to wait, and I was getting a slew of new crime words, too. Words are the journalist's stock in trade.

After Cooley left by ambulance from the post office, DuChien got Papa to call his phone tree to form a posse to track the stolen snowmobile which they found ditched in the pine rough just the other side of a plowed snowbank about two miles away from the shooting scene. The tracks told the searchers that another snowmobile had been there, perhaps with two men or one real hefty man as told by the depth of the track imprint. Might have had another deer carcasses tied on behind. Snow had fallen in the area which brought out the plow along the lone frozen gravel road that was kept clear in winter. So the search party figured the second snowmobile took the road and dodged detection, especially, since the plow covered over any reentry to the woods. There had been a fair number of other tracks, too, which made detection next to impossible.

So the perpetrator couldn't be followed further. That left the identity of the culprit uncertain.

The search party returned to the shooting scene, thanks to Cooley's coordinates of the site. DuChien dug into the birch that Cooley had marked.

"Whoever shot Jokkinen," DuChien later told Papa—I was there listening—"came back and dug the slug out."

"So, we won't know, will we?" Papa said.

"The slug was gone, but he didn't get this shell casing," he said lifting a plastic bag aloft. This will narrow things down. We'll find him. Even the Mounties are on the case."

I was on it, too.

Cooley Jokkinen 13

Shookii was pestering me for a ride to Hibbing hospital.

"I want to write up Cooley's story for the school paper," she told me. "Can I catch a ride with Sandy on the truck?"

Even though I had my work hat on, I paused, to frown at her. "No, Shookii. And it's Mr. Jokkinen to you. Remember, the truck is on government business. Anyway, they wouldn't let you visit in the hospital without a parent."

"Can you drive me, then?"

I didn't let the girls drive, even in the confines of the lake or out on the ice as other teens' parents did. There were too many crazy people zooming around out there both summer and winter, and I didn't want them to take those chances. Piloting a snowmobile was all right for a fifteen year-old, but even then I worried every minute. Saying no to a solo visit, though, limited me. She had trapped me into driving her. I had to nod to her request.

"Great. When can we go? Tomorrow?"

That would be Wednesday, the lightest mail day of the week, and with a day's notice I could announce the change: Pick up Wed. PM mail Thursday AM. "Okay. Look for me after school." Sandy would stow the light afternoon mail sack in my office.

"Thank you, Papa. I hear Coo . . . Mr. Jokkinen is

getting better."

Her sentiments were real, but I thought she wanted to hear the story of his trauma again, now that he'd had time to embellish it. Cooley Jokkinen was a storyteller, and Shookii wanted to get the scoop before everyone had heard the tale. I had other reasons to listen in. I wanted to try Cooley's testimony against a theory I had about the shooting. As good a yarn spinner as Cooley Jokkinen was, I felt I could winnow the embellishments from the seeds of truth without Cooley catching on.

Shookii wheeled a cart with a huge tape recorder out of the school's front door, with my help loaded it into the trunk, and lugged it into the hospital room. When we arrived, we found Danny there, visiting.

"Looks like this is official business," Danny carped.

Shookii smiled. "For the North County High School *Trout*. This is news, Mr. Daniels."

She plugged in the contraption, cued the tape, and set an RCA microphone that looked like it had been donated to the school for a 1940s musical film right in front of Cooley on the roll-around bed table.

"Just tell it to the mic," Shookii said. "And, please, everybody, remain as quiet and still as possible." She counted down from five, then, saying, "'Poacher's Aim' as told by Ranger Cooley Jokkinen." She pointed a finger at Cooley and nodded:

"I'd been lying in the snow behind a downed white pine trunk, watching this guy from the top of a knoll. I'd stowed my Skidoo behind a brush pile in the little valley behind me. I had killed my engine as soon as I heard the rifle report.

"By the time I huffed up the hill, the poacher was so intent on gutting the whitetail doe he'd shot that he hadn't noticed my approach. He must have known someone was in the area because every once in a while he stopped, looked around as if expecting an interruption, reached toward his rifle propped against a birch tree, then, shrugging, returned to his work which was a god-awful disaster. This guy did not know what he was doing and was certainly not a woodsman, He hadn't turned the deer right to do the gutting and took the heart and liver out right in the field!"

"What a putz," Danny said.

Shookii stopped the tape. She didn't have to warn him. Cooley did that for her. "Listen Danny, this is my story. I earned the telling with the slug through the arm."

"Okay, okay. I just think the guy was a fool."

Cooley resumed:

"The putz"—he gave Danny a satisfied look—"had piled the entrails, including the heart and liver, he'd scraped out between him and the deer's body. I guessed that blood and guts had seeped into the snow and under the knees of his snow gear because I saw him stop and heard him swear. His voice was muffled, and I didn't recognize it. He rose, brushed his pant's knees, and dragged the carcass to a fresh spot to finish, leaving the pile steaming three feet away in the snow. He finished making his mess and dragged the deer another foot or so then wrapped the carcass in some burlap from his pack.

"I shoulda waited to stand up and confront him until he hefted the doe onto his shoulders, but I didn't think ahead enough. I had unsnapped the holster flap of my 45 caliber, pulled out the pistol, and waved the gun around.

"'Hey, there fella,' I said, standing up on the little hill, 'need some help?' I suppose that wasn't the right thing to say. Maybe I should have yelled, 'Stop in the name of the law!' He could see the badge on my windbreaker plain as day. When he scooped up his rifle that the shiny star must have been a tempting target. I must have moved when he went for the rifle which was right there (telling you how much of a fool I am)"—Danny's mouth popped open then, but under Cooley's glare it snapped shut with a flapping sound—"but," Cooley continued, "he got off the first shot. It felt like an ore train running over my arm, huge and hot. The slug pushed me back to the birch trunk behind, and I must have slumped down into the snow. Lucky I hadn't released the safety on the 45 'cause I fell on it face down. Next thing I know, I feel this guy standing over me. He is saying, 'Son of a bitch ranger!'"

Cooley looked at Shookii then at me, shrugging. "Sorry," he said, then went on.

"I played dead or he thought he'd hit my heart. Either way, he let me lie without blasting me again. I might have got off a shot at that point, which at close range would have hurt better'n a deer slug, but, then again, I might not have hit him.

"The poacher must have seen my tracks coming from the other side of the rise and spotted my Skidoo in the bracken. Since I'd left the key in the ignition (another smooth move by yours truly) he brought it down the hill to the carcass and tied the deer on the back. My arm was throbbing, and though lightheaded, I was coming to my senses. I rolled onto my back to fire just as he started out. Now, I'm a marksman, but I'd taken a thirty-aught-six round in my shooting arm, was arching over my backpack, firing supine-like which no one practices especially with a pack on his back. My first shot went over his head. He gunned my Skidoo full throttle. My second shot was closer—I think it hit the deer which I hope scared the bejesus out of that dirty poacher-turd. In half a minute, he was gone. In two, I couldn't even hear my Skidoo in the distance.

"So, there I was. Likely, bleeding to death. My only transportation stolen. Let me tell you, it got mighty quiet out there in the woods with nothing but a pile of guts and a bloody tree trunk for company. I said to myself, 'All right, Jokkinen, either you lie here and die, or you bind up your wound and head for the nearest first aid station. Take your pick, my friend.' I listened to my father who often reminded me, 'Only dead fish go with the flow.'"

Danny couldn't hold it in. "Just show me that dude, and I'll plug both his arms and his forehead, too!"

"Jesus, Danny," Cooley said, "just wait til I'm finished."

Danny waded in deeper, "You're already Finnish, Jokkinen!"

Shookii kept the reels moving but waved for silence.

Cooley, shaking his head, went on:

"It took me a while and a lot of grunting and groaning, but I wriggled out of my backpack and found my first aid supplies. Not much for a bullet wound, but I did have a tourniquet. I stripped down, took off my longsleeve T-shirt and ripped the sleeve into strips. I smeared some salve around the wound with my makeshift bandages and bound the whole thing—doing this mostly one-handed was a real trick, but my friend the birch trunk helped hold things in place while I applied pressure with the tourniquet. I redressed and ate half my egg salad sandwich from the pack. I had half a mind but no stomach to eat the deer heart and liver my shooter left behind. I wrapped them in the plastic my sandwich came from and tied them into a sort of hammock, If I could light a fire later, I'd cook the meat up. I hung the makeshift bag from my pack. The Minnesota air would keep my dinner refrigerated.

"It might have taken an hour to dress the wound and get ready. It could have been longer but I knew I better start out soon if I wanted to make Kettle Falls by sunset, around 5:30 that day. By the sun, it was already toward noon. Sleeping in the woods that night was not an option.

"I took a compass reading. The road ran a mile from my friendly birch tree, but before it reached Kettle Falls it would have wound around eight and a half miles. The distance wasn't so much more considering the benefit of walking on a flat solid surface, but I didn't want to run into my poacher friend who could easily finish the job he started. He knew I was armed, but better to let him think me dead. He wouldn't be looking for me in that case.

"The Falls were three ridges away, across four ponds which would be frozen solid by now and over two lakes which were fairly sheltered but might not be too safe to walk across their middles. I decided to keep near the shores, where the cover of pines and cedar was closer if need be. If I broke through the ice at any point near shore, at least I wouldn't go under, just knee or waist high. It would be more work to cut over the ridges but a whole lot shorter than following the shores and portages all the way along. At the beginning I was feeling like it would be a piece of cake, a Sara Lee frozen cake I supposed, to make fairly short work of my walk.

"I found a game trail not too far along and, following it, kept moving in more or less the right direction. Trapping as well as hunting was disallowed in the area, but that didn't stop some of the locals from setting snares or traps. With snowshoes on, I wasn't likely to snap a wolf trap on my ankle, but I hadn't gone a half mile along the trail when I tripped on a snare and went down. I hit my wounded side a good one but snow cover cushioned my fall a bit. I heard my own voice echo from the next ridge. I'd let out quite a howl.

"Sitting on a snow-drifted stump, I checked my dressing. It was more than damp but I didn't want to change it just yet. Getting some miles in was more important. I snugged the tourniquet just a bit, not too tight, and rested while I ate a peanut butter cookie I'd picked up at Lahti's Bakery in Orr early that morning. I started out again paying closer attention to the path. It took a little more energy to lift my steps up higher, but that balanced the saved effort and time it would take to recover from another fall. I made the first ridge an hour after I'd started out. Not too bad, considering.

"I didn't pause at the top. Instead I stepped down laterally on my webbed soles to test the incline and to take shelter from sight behind. I listened for any sign of a motor, and peeked back. Even from up the hill, I couldn't see my starting point. I did see some of my tracks in the distance, And just as I noticed I'd left a trail dotted with blood, mine or the deer's, I heard something that chilled my bones. 'Was that a howl?' I heard something but too indistinctly to tell. If I had known a wolf couple had just finished an appetizer of offal at the poacher's table, I might have moved a bit faster, though there is no outrunning wolves on a scent. Anyway, I couldn't know I was being tracked by a poacher or wolves. Either would be bad."

Cooley shifted in bed and looked around at us three listeners with an important air and a self-satisfied grin. He sipped his water through a straw down to the bottom of the glass, making a slurping gurgle. Then he shifted in bed again and resumed:

"Moving down the slope sideways worked me up a sweat. Going down is not as easy as it might seem. A sapling or two saved me from sliding down when the snow avalanched a little beneath my step. I grabbed out for a branch with my good arm to stop a fall. Still, moving downslope is quicker than climbing up, and within ten minutes, I arrived at the shore of the first pond. I listened again before breaking out of the woods, and stepped gingerly through the frozen reed bed at the shore. There was no sign of water around the cattail stems. The ice on the pond beyond was more than thick enough to support me. Hearing no report of an engine, I went across the open width of the glorified pothole as fast as I could move. Now on a flat surface, I could tell just how worn out I was getting. 'Should I rest?' I wondered. 'No, Cooley, keep moving for now.'"

"Yeah, keep movin' is right!" Danny was back on tape. "Are you sure wolves were following ya? I'm not sayin', you know, but imagination plays tricks out there in the big freeze. Specially, if you're hurting."

I said nothing, of course. If Cooley didn't say something, Shookii would. So, I would let Danny take the heat.

"Just shut your trap and listen. You'll find out," our

storyteller said.

Cooley continued:

"I picked up the game trail on the other side and moved back into the forest working my way toward the next pond, about a quarter mile, following a little seeping creek that ran between the two. I made myself a promise to stop at the bottom of the next ridge, lake side, to build a bit of a fire, redress my wound, and roast up the deer's heart. My arm was throbbing and stopping would do me good.

"I've been alone out in the wild plenty. This was a lot different. Even without a machine to get me from point A to point B, I usually wouldn't worry. Maybe because I was out there injured for the first time in my life, I started thinking of what could come to pass. I thought of that story of the man in the Yukon, out in seventy-five degree below zero weather. He would be all right if nothing happened. But something did happen and only his dog finished the journey. I didn't even have a dog. It hadn't been too many years ago that another ranger had lay buried, half eaten, all winter long, and I couldn't shake either of those stories from my mind. Now, thinking back, like Danny said, it was the wound that was working on me, sapping my strength and bending me down.

"I'll say one thing, whistling doesn't help, and singing takes too much breath.

"I found an opening wide enough to build a good blaze in but close enough to some fallen timber that would furnish good fuel. I was careful not to build my fire under a snow laden tree like the story-man had. It took twenty minutes to gather, light, and feed a little cooking fire. I took a couple of trips to the edge of the meadow to drag dry wood back to my fire using my good arm. If I was going to strip to my skin, I wanted glowing coals built up. I used a wire gizmo from my pack to hold the heart and the liver I'd sliced up, turning the small slabs of organs from one side to the next."

"Worst-er sauce woulda come in handy," Danny joked.

"Worcestershire, dummy."

"That's what I said, "Worcaster. Sure."

"Listen!" Cooley said.

"I had just bit into my first slice of liver when the wolf broke through the cedars at the edge of the meadow. She was small, like forty pounds or so, but looked huge the way they do when they are bristled up. And I knew very well that she had a mate nearby, likely slinking up behind me. I didn't look. That's exactly what they want. If you look around for the other one, the first one will spring.

"There I was. My shootin' iron in the pack, one armed, and half naked, facing a she-wolf and sensing a much larger one at my back. Lucky I had the fire going. No wild animal wants to approach a fire. They can't understand it. They, and rightly so, fear it. So, I slowly, oh so slowly reached out to my little pile of twigs and branches, pulling a few out of the bunch to set on the little blaze. The fire perked up right off, and the female took a step back, now about thirty feet away, still only three or four bounds from my throat. I pulled and fed again, staying close as I could to the flames as they leapt up.

I took up a piece of liver with my knife and tossed it to the left of the she-wolf, being careful to aim away and further back. When she went for it, I did the same, tossing another piece over my bad shoulder where I thought the male might be. When I heard him move, I reached over for my pack. It took some doing, but I was able to get my 45 out and make sure it was ready to fire. Then, with the two pieces of the liver I had left I did my tossing trick again. These morsels were cooked, but I hoped they would be appetizing to my two friends. When the female went for the second piece, I tossed the other back toward her mate and counted three, turned, and fired.

"I figured on getting the male. If I got off a good shot, his mate would leave me."

At that moment the duty nurse came in. "I'm sorry, but Mr. Jokkinen has some shots coming and also needs his rest. I'll have to ask you, and your equipment, to leave for now. You can come back tomorrow if he is still here."

Shookii complained. "We are just at the best part!"

"Oh, you mean when the wolves fight over the deer heart?" The nurse said.

My young reporter looked a bit confused. "No, Cooley, Mr. Jokkinen I mean, cut the liver up and tossed half of it to each wolf."

The nurse looked at Cooley, raising her eyebrow. Apparently Cooley had told it several different ways, already. "Believe me, the story will be much better tomorrow," she said. "Now, everybody out. You too, Mr. Daniels."

Despite being interrupted, Cooley sighed and looked a bit relieved. Storytelling can be hard work.

Rapprochement 14

The twins' separation became stark and official the May after Cooley Jokkinen was shot. It had been a long time coming, and I knew enough about sisterhood, teenagers, and family control to realize that there was little to be done. My sister and onetime namesake, Mary, and I might have achieved a rapprochement had she lived. We were both carrying children. Neither of us had thoughts of leaving the lake. We were still hanging with each other, though our interests were totally different, except for having boyfriends, the fathers of our babies, that kept us together. Then she didn't live. So, the hope I had left for my twins went toward wishing them lives long enough to reunite.

I shouldn't say little could be done. Nothing is more like it. Oh, I tried. Tatty tried. But only trees can be pruned to shape, not people, and certainly not kids.

Once Biini set her heart on attending Teddy Good's summer camp, she was unapproachable. Something in that girl had changed over the winter, and it wasn't good. I knew that after some time. I know that now, but at the time I still had hopes that once at camp among all those foreign students, African princes and princesses, she would clamor for the simplicity of the Swedenborgians who in their way were bad enough for the unity of our family and my kids' sisterhood. I should have known, yeah. I should have known about Biini and about Teddy, too. Even Christian believers go wild at times, and they know how to keep it on the down low, a lesson Biini learned from me. I suppose it's my fault.

Dindii was another matter. Even after she started writing for the Bois Forte Council Newsletter, even after she did what I never wanted her to do—reopening the godawful rat trap of a tavern, Tillie's—even when she became, really, a mover and shaker in both the white and Native communities, she was open to me. I didn't like everything she was doing, but I admired it all and helped in ways both obvious and not to be acknowledged. When Dindii started braiding her hair in a Native way, so did I. When she made and began to wear deerskin vests that bore Native symbols painted on front and back, I asked her to make me one. With Dindii, I attended the community meetings, powwows, and business meetings about the property.

I couldn't save my own sister's life, but because Dindii and I were close, of similar aspect and shape, looked as much alike as a middle-aged grandmother and a teenaged grandchild could, and cleaved both to Native ideas and dress, I was able to save a sister's life, Dindii's. She should have been there at Tillie's the night before the grand opening. She had planned to be there in the second story meeting room off the kitchen. The meeting notice said that she would be upstairs at Tillie's, heading the dedication discussion. She wasn't. It was me. That night—it seemed on the spur of the moment—she stayed with some elders at the reservation and planned to drive back home in the morning. She phoned to ask me to fill in for her. I agreed to convene the meeting.

I died for her.

Had I not been upstairs after the meeting at Tillie's the night of the conflagration, history would have repeated itself in fire rather than ice. A twin would have burned before the eyes of her sister. I don't know if my girls will reunify, but, like I said, I have hope, even beyond my grave.

I arrived early that evening with supplies for the meeting and the ingredients for a celebratory rabbit stew Granny had taught me to make. A favorite of the twins. The stew had to cook hours. Someone had to make coffee and fill a tray with *bagaan*, bread made from local hazelnuts. I'd brought a small bag of dried blueberries and a half-pint of maple syrup to drizzle over everything and to sweeten the coffee. I brought Dindii's notes and agenda. There were to be six, and we'd meet around the table upstairs in the kitchen that stood over the famous Tillie's sign that Dindii had repainted during the previous year.

I had not only given in to her but had helped her repaint the mural and letter the poem which she insisted on keeping even though she'd added thunderbirds and Native florals to cover what she had blocked out, the huge beer bottle. She skillfully painted blooming vines twining with the poem's lettering which she had rewritten with help from Tatty who told her his story of first encountering the jingle the night the twins were born. At that time when the twins were just taking their first breaths, he was strapped to a sled after Jay Martinen rescued him from his car accident:

> If you're feeling sad *and blue*,
> Stop *in at* Tillie's t' tip a few.
> Your friends around *you*

> Your blues *in brew*
> *Will turn* from sadness and *from rue*
> To *jolly* times with our *three-two*.

Dindii insisted that the peeled-off words her father supplied be italicized and of a different color from those that had survived weathering, as a way of reminding her of the way she found the sign and what it came to mean to her: history, mystery, and welcome.

I brought in my goodies, taking them up the stairs that led up to the kitchen of what had been the apartment of Roscoe's and Jay's bartender. The narrow staircase ran between walls and had been a storage space for bottle boxes and cleaning supplies. Sixteen years back, during the snowstorm of the century when I came to gather up my husband from the crazies at the tavern, I had scaled those steps, threading my way up between crates, boxes, and mops to get away from the lunacy that was reigning below. I'd left Roscoe in a heap on the floor—I knew I had snapped his collarbone with my flying kick, and that Jay would have to set it because there was no other choice in the middle of the storm—and I'd left Tatty on the floor, too, where Roscoe had tackled him trying to make him listen to his raving windigo story. I had other things on my mind than their decades-old madness and lies. Windsong back at the cabin under Granny's care now was bleeding out her last, having delivered the twins in hard labor. I'd need Tatty with me. Granny had sent me, both to spare me the death scene and to rescue him from Tillie's, where no good could prevail. I waited for him upstairs in Tillie's kitchen.

That night, although the place had been part of the

remodel the tribal council had funded, not much had changed since I'd sat there a decade and a half before: a new countertop and sink had been installed, but the wall-mounted faucet still dripped, and the tile splash had been patched, not redone, with ill-matching tile.

I started the coffee, laid out my breads and snacks, and put the stew on to slow cook. It would be hours until it was ready to store. The afternoon sun that had for years bleached and peeled Tillie's sign was low and shone between the pine tree limbs straight into the kitchen. I turned the table, moving it to the center, allowing for my chair at the window end to preside over the six coming to meet. I stood beside my seat, looking out as the coffee perked, watching for nothing in particular but seeing the pine sprigs shredding the sunshine into rays that rippled over the panes of the storm windows and interior sashes in an ever-wheeling and changing pattern that telegraphed from my sordid past a message that I could not understand.

It led me to remember Tatty's words about the twins' birth when he dragged himself up those stairs that night, bandaged head and all:

In the ensuing minutes Tatty'd learned that the woman he had married was someone he hadn't fully known. With Jay and Roscoe both having filled his head with their versions of the story, he was confused and shaken, in addition to lacking sleep and being injured plenty. I let him know what I thought he could handle, and he pieced it together from there.

I'd evaded the law by taking my sister's name. Morgan, the reckless sister, had died as far as the sheriff was concerned. He jailed Roscoe the living perpetrator of the fatal windigo chase. A year later, just months after Windsong was born, I left her with Granny and skedaddled. I wouldn't wait for Roscoe to be released from prison to find out what he'd do, but after his sentence was served, Jay somehow kept him in the dark, repeating the lie that Windsong was Roscoe's daughter, not his own. On that we were wrong. Roscoe knew! He just didn't let on. Then that night when I came for Tatty, the lie came out. Roscoe couldn't handle it being public. He killed the liar, his best friend, medic, and partner, Jay.

Now, sixteen years later, I stood at the same kitchen window mesmerized by the flickering sunbeams cutting through Tatty's ancient words like shadows of blades cutting up syllables from beyond their whirl, "I don't want to go forward on half-truths. Maybe it doesn't matter anyway, but I don't understand why."

The man couldn't content himself with knowing a thing. He always had to know the reasons behind it. I just wanted to live life, wayward and confusing as it could be, to feel everything existence presented. I didn't want to know why. I craved the experience, not the explanation. Not Tatty, though. And I suppose that craving to know why served him well enough. Since that night sixteen winters before, he'd become well-liked at the lake, seemed compassionate, organized, and helpful, all things that I had a hard time with. On the other hand, having had no patience for explanations and reasoning, I got to live more fully. At least I thought I did.

One of the exceptions to my devil-may-care attitude it seems to me was my support of and behavior around Dindii's project. Not only the painting which had been completed a half year before, but also with her drive to reopen Tillie's as a tribal meeting place. Even at sixteen, she could have handled the opposition and complexities of the action, but for once I felt I had to curb my natural instincts and avoid shrugging off a responsibility that was clear as day, especially since both Dindii and Biini could talk of nothing else. Being the only trustee of the place, I was forced to participate.

An open battle emerged from late night meetings at Olsen's resort bar. After years of muttering behind the backs of the powers that operated the BWCA, and after the cry of "tribal interference" in the lives and livelihoods of the white residents at the lake, Laurel and Hardy came out vehemently against Tillie's reopening, their verbal pistols blazing. They had the support of at least some of the white community.

"The council already has meeting places at the reservation. Why do you need another place, and why here?" What was unspoken was the anger and jealousy about Native fishing and gathering rights (no limits, fish netting allowed, no restrictions on movement over borders or trapping—mostly not true) that L & H and company claimed sapped resources of the hospitality and summer vacation business among the resort owners. "We are caught between the rock of the BWCA and the hard place of Native rights," they claimed.

That Tillie's would not serve liquor, not even Minnesota-light 3.2 beer, did not appease these folks. They threatened court action and, after that didn't work, violence. None of it deterred Dindii. She stood up to all comers, parents, neighbors, and even convinced her sister, who in trust owned half of the building, by planning a shared use of the space, dedicating part of it to Christian worship, another to Native gatherings.

"We don't want another religion preached there," Biini told her sister, referring by "we" to herself and her erstwhile spiritual guide, none other than my lover and friend, Teddy Good. Since she attended summer camp, he'd lorded over her religious training, or retraining, and held sway, through her, on questions of property in which he was well schooled by an acquisitive father and by an even greedier nature. Had I known what was really going on right then, I would have taken a deer rifle to the bastard. I did not know how deep his influence had sunk.

Dindii, though, was ready. "Popcorn, this is a civic place for us. It is not a sacred place for Natives. You can consecrate your part. You are half owner." Her arguments were like the wind. They couldn't be contained, because they went right around you. Apparently, she convinced Biini and through her won over her new guru, too.

Even the licensing and permitting went Dindii's way once an insurance company was found for the place. She straddled the line between Native rights and government regulations without making new enemies, flowing like spring water in a brook. It was a sight to see. I was happy. Tatty was proud.

That evening, the meeting went late. There was last minute bickering about the order of speakers, who would cut the ribbon, and myriad bullshit which I handled smoothly for Dindii. I could see why she avoided it all. In fits and starts we proceeded, with occasional breaks for me to stir up the stew at the stove. What's a mother to do? The *conflab* broke up around eleven. By that time the encampment down at the beer garden had calmed, the drumming had ended, and the campers had gone to bed.

I cleaned up after the small group, washing dishes, stacking the documents we had reviewed for Dindii in a handy pile for her to look through in the morning, and gave the kitchen a good sweep. Afterward, I gave the stew a try and took it off the heat. I switched off the light and for a couple minutes stood at the window of my reverie once again. The stars were out, dimmed by the growing egg-shaped moon but still twinkling in a clear March sky. Nothing but the earth itself was moving, rotating past the faces of sun, moon, planets, and stars as it has done from the time it was born. The imperceptible spin of the planet overlaid a sense of comfort on my mind softer and deeper than any feeling I had experienced in decades. I perched on the corner of the old kitchen table, looking past my reflection on the glass at the pine-rimmed meadow below, now filled with tents and bark-covered wigwams, populated by those sleeping through the night oblivious to the movement of the earth that they rode through the dreamy heavens. I felt good. Contentment welled up in me on the vapors of Granny's rabbit stew. I saw an end to an anxiety that had sprung up nearly forty years before when I seconded Roscoe's proposal to chase a December-evening windigo from Tillie's meadow beer garden to the depths of the forest where Mary stepped into a freezing vortex of light to keep me from it. It seemed at that moment that with the reopening of Tillie's all the past could be laid to rest.

At the window my late night rumination was ruined by something odd I heard, something like a rush of warm air pulsing near the stairwell. I looked to the stove. Nothing there but the stew. But I'd distinctly heard a muffled pop. I went into the room adjacent to the kitchen, which was directly over the entrance to the barroom. Thinking the sound came from down front of the building toward the beer garden, I looked out the window. Again, nothing moved below. No sound came from there. What I saw at the window was only my own image projected over a dusky pine stand illuminated by the soon to be set moon. The woman I saw in the glass appeared both defined by surprise and wavering like a dream. Amongst the darkling white pine trunks then, I thought I saw two figures retreating from Tillie's, one holding a lighted emergency flare. Then a loud rumble sounded downstairs that shook the entire second floor. The sound drew me away from that front window to the kitchen again. I looked at the kitchen door that opened over the stair landing. It looked as if sunlight was seeping under the door which was impossible, both because there were no windows in the stairwell and because it was well after midnight. I strode through the kitchen to the stair door, grabbed the door knob. It singed my hand. I backed up a step and whether from surprise or anger kicked the door. At that moment, the window in the kitchen blew out and with a roar like a hungry windigo, a mouth of flame rushed up the stairs, knocking me down and lighting me like a torch!

What are you supposed to do? "Don't run," I remembered. "Stop, drop, and roll," came to my mind. I was already down, but rolled until I hit a table leg and then the sink cabinet. I was coughing fiercely. I crawled on my hands and knees back to the bedroom and once in, slammed the door on the firestorm. I crawled, to the window, opening over the porch of Tillie's barroom.

Lying on the floor I tried to raise the window but had no purchase to slide up the sash. It might have been locked. I looked for anything to break a pane but the room was empty. Nothing was there. Still wheezing and coughing smoke in and out of a windpipe that could only rasp, I rolled on to my back, kicking the window until the glass shattered. I wriggled around and looked over the sill. I saw, loping like a deer through snowdrifts, a single figure dodging from pine trunk to pine trunk away from the place. I tried to call out to him but only croaked a nearly inaudible, low, "Help!"

I tried to raise myself to stand at the sill where I could jump out, but I came only onto my knees. Below I saw my brother, Tiny, jerking up his jeans and zipping them. I couldn't call to him, but it seemed he saw me at the shattered window. There I listened to the last sound I was to hear in that world, drawing me back to the night my sister died, "Ruhsk, ruhsk," grating in my ears. It was the windigo all those years before, calling Roscoe's name "Ruhsk, ruhsk." Then, inferno.

They say I died in that room, asphyxiated, cut and bloody, half charred once the bedroom door let go and the room engulfed in flame. Tiny handed a dead woman through the broken window sash to safety.

Who was carrying the flare, who was dancing from behind the pines, who had set the blaze and why, I couldn't know.

The *Trout* 15

At the post office there was talk of nothing else but what some were calling Cooley Jokkinen's "accident." Those who in private said, "The only good ranger is a dead ranger," did not believe the poacher story that was circulating, saying, "I bet Jokkinen was the poacher. Likely, shot his own self to cover the theft of the Skidoo and the deer."

Laurel, half-owner of Olsen's Resort took the lead in spreading that story. When he tried it out at the post office, Danny came roaring to Cooley's defense, grabbing the little man by the collar and lifting him up against the wall where Laurel squirmed like a pinned spider.

"He nearly died out there, you lousy turd. You take that back!" Danny yelled into the resort owner's face.

As postmaster, I had to intervene. "Danny, put the man down. Listen everybody, this is still the post office, and I expect everyone here to treat it and each other with respect. If you want to argue, take it outside and off the property."

The flurry was quelled, for the time being, but you didn't have to go far to hear nasty talk and hot accusations. I worried. Proud as I was of Dindii for publishing the story, I worried that she might face some of the animosity that seemed to inflame the community. After the North County High School *Trout* published her account of Cooley's story in two installments and it was picked up by the *Hibbing Daily Tribune* and *The Duluth Herald*, which had circulation that covered the whole region, my concern grew acute. I saw later that I was worried about the wrong twin. Dindii was public about her ambitions, and that seemed to insulate her from troubles coming from the redneck crowd who were used to working only in shadow with threat and innuendo. Even after the tribal council hired her to write for the newsletter and her ideas about turning Tillie's into a local meeting center came out, her opponents treated her with caution and respect. Imagine the adverse reaction should an adult attack a teenage writer and a Native one, too. That would do no good for their cause.

After seeing the headlines in issues coming through the mail, I sent for a copy of the articles in the larger papers. BWCA Ranger Shot was the *Tribune* lead. A week later the feature section carried Cooley's tale, "A Story of Survival: as told to Dindiisi Langille and the *Tribune*." At supper I presented Dindii with the copies. We read the feature together, noting some of the changes Cooley had adapted from what we'd heard, making the story more exciting, notably this section:

It was back in '79 that another ranger had lain buried all winter long, half eaten by wolves, and I couldn't shake that fact from my mind. I thought what if I couldn't make it to help? Would I be barely alive when a wolf started gnawing on my arm? Maybe it was the wound that was working on me, sapping my strength and bending me down into fantasy. I'll say one thing, whistling doesn't help, and singing takes too much breath.

I found a clearing to build a good blaze, one close to

some fallen timber that would furnish good fuel. I was careful not to build my fire under a snow laden tree like the to-build-a-fire man had. It took lots of huffin' and puffin' to gather, light, and feed a little cooking fire. I took a couple of trips to the edge of the meadow to drag burnables back to my fire using my good arm. If I was going to strip to my skin to dress my wound, I wanted a nice refractory built up. I took the wire gizmo from my pack to hold the heart and the liver I'd sliced up, over the coals, turning the small slabs of the organs from one side to the next with my knife. I was feeling pretty cheery there, but I chilled when something stirred.

You seldom know when wolves are passing. They are silent animals, except for their baying on the hunt or howling hellos in the night. I sensed them, though. The slightest sound, even with the crackling fire, told me to watch out, to slowly look up from my work.

I was about to bite into my first slice of liver when there she was. Like she'd appeared out of a puff of smoke. The female wolf broke through the cedars at the edge of the meadow and began ranging on what was to be a circular path. She was small, like thirty pounds or so, but looked huge the way they do when they are bristled up.

As she moved toward the right, her mate came into sight from my left. He was huge, it seemed, twice as big as she, and nearly black. The two wolves moved slowly around, each keeping both eyes on me and on the fire. They made two rounds tightening their circle at each turn.

I didn't move or follow them by turning my head. That's exactly what they want. If you look around for one the other will spring.

There I was. My shootin' iron in the pack, one armed, and half naked, facing a circling wolf couple. Even if they had finished off the poacher's leavings, they wouldn't hesitate to go for another kill. I was their wounded buck.

Now, I had the fire going. No wild animal likes to approach a fire. They can't understand it. They fear it, and rightly so. I slowly, oh so slowly reached out to my little pile of twigs and branches, pulling a few out of the bunch to set on my little blaze. The fire perked up right off, and the female took a step back, now about thirty feet away, still only three or four bounds from my throat. I pulled and fed again, staying close as I could to the flames as they leapt up. I expected to hear the male's bound at any second. He would be the one coming in first.

I took up a piece of partly cooked liver with my knife and tossed it to the left of the she-wolf, being careful to aim away and further back. When she went for it, I did the same, tossing another piece back over my wounded side, where I thought the male would be. When I heard him move, I reached for my pack. It took some doing, but I was able to get my .45 out and make sure it was ready to fire.

The wolves, after devouring what I had thrown to them, resumed their circulating and tightening. Then, with the two pieces of liver I had left I did my tossing trick again. These morsels were cooked through, but I hoped they would be appetizing to my two friends. I waited for them to come around, one on each side of me where I could see them both.

Sitting, I shuffled my feet to get a better purchase on my firing position. One foot was asleep and scuffed the a burning branch bringing the whole fire down into a pile of ashes. It didn't go out, but died down to near nothing.

With no fire to worry him, the male leapt immediately right toward me. I had less than a second to aim and fire. In midair the slug hit him square in the chest and pushed him off course. He fell right on the ash pit, already dead.

The female hit me low, chomping down on my leg that was still numbed. I pulled the hammer back and took careful aim, opposite handed, at her mid spine. When the slug hit, her grip on my leg loosed right away. She bounded off into the woods. I must have missed the nerves, maybe shattered a vertebrae, but she was gone.

"Look how they've changed the story," Dindii said.

I checked the headline again. "They must have interviewed him, it says as told to you and the paper."

Dindii sighed. "Mr. Jokkinen likes to build up his tales. That's for sure."

"You're the one becoming famous," I said.

She smiled widely but pooh-poohed the accomplishment, "You mean Mr. Jokkinen is getting notorious, don't you?"

"You're modest," I said. "After all, the council isn't hiring him for the newsletter. They want you."

"He's a Finn." She seemed to halt there, remembering I suppose, that I'm half Finnish. Then she added, "Only Natives work at the council."

Now I smiled. Dindii had become an accomplished disputant. "You argue well, my dear."

"I learned from a master," she said.

Dindiisi's abilities to hold her own quelled some of my worry. She would be of age soon and was already moving about the adult world with confidence and ease.

My concerns should have been showered over her twin.

It wasn't long after Christmas that year that Biini began asking about camp. Though I told her I would support her in it, I wasn't all that much in favor. I believed, given the circumstances, that Morgan would prevent it. Once again I was wrong. Long about April, as Dindii was busy with her writing for the *Trout* and the council newsletter, Morgan came to me.

"I know we haven't talked about it, but you know, I guess, that Biini wants to go to summer camp in Orr."

I must have been frowning.

"You don't approve, right?" She said.

I nodded. "I don't want to hold her back, but I'd rather she do something else. Still, she wants an 'International' experience, and I suppose we can scrape together the money."

Morgan pursed her lips, thinking, it seemed.

"I helped Biini with her application for a camp scholarship."

I could only guess what she meant by "helped," but I avoided mentioning the name of Mr. Good. "That was nice."

"It's been approved. She can go free of charge. Dindii is also invited."

I was surprised at this last. "I doubt she'll go. She is busy."

"I won't make her, but I'd rather they both be there together," Morgan said.

I wanted to ask, "Safety in numbers?" I held back.

"So, we should let them know. Tonight at supper?"

"Fine," I said, but knew it was anything but fine. Somehow it seemed that Morgan despite getting Dindii invited along was cutting the family in two, taking one of the twins over to her side. I was watching carefully for Dindii, and Morgan was helping Biini. We hoped that even split up our supervision of their new directions would be enough to keep them on safe tracks.

After the summer it was plain that neither of us knew how wrong we'd been.

Grown-Up

Popcorn 5
(Biini)

I wasn't wrong about the world opening to me once I left Mr. Ericksen's ministry at his Swedenborgian church for the camp of Planet Earth's Church of God. I told my little old man preacher simply that I was going to camp for the summer. Later so much had happened, so much had changed, that when I returned, I just didn't think about going back to the little church with the Ericksens. I didn't think of anything else besides what had come to be.

Over the years, when Pastor Ericksen read about John's baptism of Jesus, I tried to visualize the dove flying above Christ's head and the halo of the godhead descending on him, but I could never get the feeling or the sight of it. It sounded wonderful but very far away and very long ago, not like something that would happen even in the summer in northern Minnesota. Then, after only a month at the camp, Teddy G, as he wanted to be called, opened my eyes to see the glory of salvation, the feeling and the sight of it all, right then and right there. That was July, half way to my sixteenth birthday, when I found the way. The sacrificial road to Mama's salvation.

I had gone to camp on a mission to save my mother. It was I who was saved, but I entered a secret communion with Mama—she was not to know it from me—and a life filled with the wonder and glory of sacrifice, somewhat like Jesus giving himself for all others. It happened slowly over the first month at camp, and then it came on all at once with my baptism.

Shookii didn't come. I hardly thought she would, and I was relieved that she didn't. She was busy with her writing and with the painting at Tillie's. Those were the important things to her, and I was glad that she was so involved. Both Papa and Mama were pleased with her. That made room for me to follow my own path.

Since Shookii didn't want to be at camp, I at first had a cabin to myself. Then after a few days a new camper, a girl two years older, who had attended previous summers, arrived. She had flown for two days from Ghana in Africa—I had to look it up on the world map—to reach us in northern Minnesota. All I was told about her beforehand was that she was an African princess called Yaa, that she was escaping the brutal summer heat of the equator, and that Planet Earth's Church had a large following in her country.

I loved her from the moment I saw her. I'd just returned from two hours of prayer and meditation in chapel, and there she was in her bunk, fast asleep, in the middle of the day. Wrapped in white sheets, wearing colored beads in her braided hair, she, even in sleep, was radiant. I loved her more when up at daybreak the next morning after sleeping peacefully for eighteen hours, she woke me, sitting on my bunk, by stroking my forehead and singing a hymn in a peculiar English accent.

"Good morning, Biinishii. I am Yaa."

She was gloriously beautiful. I had never seen such dark and glowing skin, such silken and curly hair, such luminescent eyes, golden trimmed setting off chestnut brown irises. All Yaa's features were rounded. There was nothing angular about her although she was tall and her feet long with pink toenails against her coffee-color rounded toes. She glowed in humors, too. Yaa was a delight. She shone the light of salvation everywhere she looked, and right then she was looking at me. She was poetry incarnate.

"We shall be great friends, sisters in faith, Biinishii."

I was just waking up, but to something glorious. "If we are to be sisters, call me Popcorn," I said.

"Popcorn?"

I told her only that it was a private, family name for me. "My twin sister first used it," I said.

"Well then, when we are alone you can call me Mframa as my parents do. It means wind in our language. Otherwise, I am Yaa."

"Popcorn. Wind. What names!" We were already close, and from that first moment and throughout the summer we were inseparable. She trained me for and served during my baptism. We worked the dining room together, setting places and serving the large bowls of food to each table. We sailed on the same boat and became quite fast racers. We canoed together, sang campfire songs in harmony with our distinctive accents, and when we were in bed told stories of childhood and of our families. We were so different, yet we seemed more alike to me than Shookii and I. Being with Yaa, I never felt homesick or alone.

Of course, I was less than forty miles from home, and Yaa was half a continent plus an ocean away from hers. It meant that on Parent's Day, Independence Day, Yaa, having no visitors from home, was part of my family's visitation. So, she met Shookii.

I don't believe that jealousy is a sin, but I know it

is not something that is helpful. I tried not to show my annoyance when Yaa and Shookii took up with each other and were together during much of the Parent Day visit. I tried to tell myself that Shookii was just making sure that Yaa felt part of some family since hers was so far off. Later in the afternoon, though, those two drifted away and disappeared for almost an hour. Papa and Mama used the time to fill me in on Thief Lake news and asked me a thousand questions about camp. Neither mentioned Reverend Good, not once, and both told me how pleased they were that I had such a wonderful cabin mate and constant companion in Yaa.

"She seems like a big sister to you." Papa said.

I told him that she was now a faith-sister, someone I would always be a part of. "She is wise for her age," I said.

Mama said, "Well, that makes me glad. You have someone to learn from and share with."

"Yes," I replied, "Yaa guides me. She has been baptized and wants me to be, too." Neither of them really knew much about baptism, but they both seem to approve.

"It might be good," Mama said.

And Papa nodded.

Late that evening after all the visitors had gone, Yaa and I were in our cabin studying for tomorrow's liturgy. She was to give the benediction. Not being baptized yet, I would simply watch and listen. Yaa read her part with me acting as her congregation. When she had read it perfectly six times, she put her book down.

"Mframa," I said looking at her now as a sister rather than a congregant, "Mframa, what did you and Shookii do when you two went off together?"

Yaa noted my whiny tone and smiled thinly. She sat down next to me.

"Whether you always like it or not, you and Shookii are bound to each other, as twins. If I am to know you well, I must also be acquainted with your twin, and less so, with your mother and father."

"So what did you learn?"

Yaa reached for my hand and caressed it. "Let your feelings be. You have nothing to fear from me." She looked steadily into my eyes. "Like your sister, you are steadfast and strong. Though you are the private one, she living outside herself, you will both do much in the world. You are of great faith, believing without having to see. Shookii looks for truth only in what she can touch and sense."

"Is this what you talked of for an hour?" I said.

She squeezed my hand and let it go. "Mostly I spoke of your baptism."

"Tell me about that." Baptism was something I truly wanted.

"Did you come here to save your mother?"

"Did Shookii tell you that?"

She shook her head, her braided beads tumbled from side to side. "No, she didn't, but I am right, aren't I?"

"Yes." I said.

"When you are baptized into Planet Earth's Church of God, you will fulfill that purpose. Your mother will be released from her bondage." She searched my face and added, "None of your mission here did I share with your sister. I only said that you would be a different person when you returned home."

"I will be?" I said.

"If you open yourself to baptism, yes. I know from

my experience what it will do."

"Then, Mframa I want to be baptized."

"Be patient, Popcorn. I will instruct you, and you will pass through the ritual."

I had to ask for more, "And what else did you two discuss?"

"Only her plans to reopen Tillie's. Is that its name?"

"Yes. I think she had a vision about it."

"You have an ambitious and clear-headed sister. She will do great things. If she were African, she would be a princess."

"And I? " I asked, "Then so would I.

No, my dear, you would be a priestess."

The next night, Yaa brought me to a corner of the main grounds that I had never seen before. In a grove of trees a hundred yards or so from our chapel, a white fabric tent in the shape of a cross stood.

"It's always lighted, day and night," Yaa said as we walked around the perimeter.

"It is shaped like a small cathedral," I said. Lights, flickering like candles, cast wavering waves of light on the thin canvas, something like sun through stained glass windows. "It is beautiful."

"This is where you will be baptized, Biinishii Langille."

She used my full name. It sounded serious and formal in my ears.

"Come," she said, "I will show you."

On the right side transept of the tent, Yaa found an opening, drew back the canvas flap, and gestured me in with a sweeping motion. I entered, moving toward a white-cloth-covered altar separated and sheltered from beyond with a another white curtain which made the tent feel smaller than it had looked from outside.

Yaa went forward holding back the altar curtain. "There is the font." She pointed.

The pool ran the length of the tent, leaving just three feet or so for passing all around and, like the tent itself, was cross shaped. At the short, top end of the pool, I suppose in the apse of this "church," a fountain gurgled, feeding the font. The water was deepest there and gradually grew shallower the further one went toward the base of that cross.

We walked around the pool, as Yaa instructed me. "You will enter from the shallow foot of the pool. I will be with you and will bring you to the center of the transept. There you will join the baptist for the ceremony. I will leave you there, take the stair to the right to the altar where I will pray, and after immersing you, he will carry you, as if out of the river Jordan, up the steps to the left, behind that screen there. She pointed as she described the movements, drawing my attention to the approach, the baptismal area, the stairs where white towels were hung at the top of a railing, both before the altar area and the screened area across from and opposite to the altar.

"What then?" I wanted to know.

"You will be cleansed and experience rapture."

"And you?" I asked.

"I will come to you, bringing you a new white, hooded robe, and we will walk in silence back to our cabin. Only once inside again may we speak."

During the week following our visit to the baptismal font, we studied the liturgy of baptism, and Yaa talked me through most of the ceremony.

"They say in Ghana, 'Follow your nose,' which means something like your expression 'go with the flow.' Don't be surprised at anything." She continued, quoting from Corinthians: "Old things have passed away, all things have become new."

Yaa's directions were clear but her explanations were mysterious. "You will begin wetting the hems of your robe, but I will take it up before the water comes too high."

"You will be there?" I asked.

"We will walk the water together, side by side, but you will proceed finally and I will follow carrying your garments. You must choose the way to go."

"I would follow you," I said.

"No, You must proceed alone. Your baptist will repeat John's words to you, '*I* need to be baptized by *you*.' And you must reply, after Matthew, 'Permit it to be so now, for it is fitting,'"

"Why must I say that? And why must I be alone?"

Yaa looked at me a long while. "You must choose. I can bring you so far only, but you must give permission, saying, 'Permit it.'"

Though I did not truly understand this, I trusted Yaa. She would not steer me wrong.

After a week of her instruction, prayer, and study of the Scriptures on the subject, Yaa told me, "You are ready. Today, after sunset you will be baptized."

That evening, she dressed me in a new, gray robe like one she wore. "You wear only the robe," she instructed. She led me from our cabin along back ways, away from the chapel and then down a gentle hill to the rear of the baptistry. We continued around to the front entry, to the long leg of the cross. "Leave your slippers here." She removed hers and waited for me to follow. She parted the flaps of the entry and went before me into the tent, holding the canvas apart.

The light inside was subdued. Not all the candles were lit. The water looked black with golden reflections shimmering from the candlelight over its surface. Yaa took my hand and we walked down the first broad step which was above the water, then down into the pool one step, then another. I pulled my robe up to keep it from touching the surface.

Yaa took my hand drawing it down again, saying nothing. I saw her robe hem floated on the surface, already wet. Then I let mine down, releasing it from my other hand.

Further down we went, little by little, the water rising now to our knees. Further on in the pool, a bare-chested man stood waist deep in the pool directly under the transept. When he said, "It is *I* who need to be baptized by *you*," we halted, and Yaa took my robe from my shoulders as I offered them, as instructed, to her. Then I understood and said, "Permit it to be so now, for it is fitting."

Now, I continued toward the baptist who I recognized by voice and a closer look at his appearance as Reverend Teddy Good. Yaa followed a little behind, my robe draped over her outstretched arms. The preacher stepped back a little and said, "This is my beloved, in whom I am well pleased, Matthew, 3:17," and motioned me to come forward. As I did, Yaa moved to her right along the transept pool to the altar which was fully open to view, the curtain being tied back. I watched her rise out of the water, take the steps up, and lay my gray robe across the altar. I repeated as I was instructed, "That which is born of the spirit is flesh," and heard Reverend Good respond, "And that which is born of the flesh is spirit, John, 3: 6." I had learned it differently among the Swedenborgians, but said it as Yaa instructed in order to be baptized. Then I waded deeper into the pool and came face to face with Teddy G.

He extended his right arm and guided me to it. I floated on my back, while he supported me and drew a cross with water on my forehead saying, "I baptize you in the name of our planet, of the earth, and of the church." He then pushed me gently under the water with his raised hand, and immediately lifted me up with the other. He guided me to the left, up the steps opposite of Yaa at the altar and behind the screen there, taking up two large towels that I'd seen hung there on my first visit.

Once beyond the font, Teddy G dried me with one towel, buffing my skin all up and down until it shone, and guided me down to a wide bench draped with a large white towel. "Lie back now, woman-called-Mary, the baptized name I give to you." He then dried himself and stood over me naked.

This was Mama's release, I knew. This was the rapture.

Shookii 5
(Dindii)

Autumn came early that year as it sometimes does at the end of August. I was finishing the filigree that wove its way around and between letters and words on Tillie's renewed sign. I had blocked out and traced the thunderbird symbol that covered the area that had been occupied by an outsized beer bottle in the original mural. I was painting the bird a copper red with black and white accents and shading. Popcorn insisted on a cross being added at the other end of the mural. There was plenty of space for it, and since she was half owner of the property, I had to humor her. After adding the cross, I came to appreciate the irony of the two symbols living together, separated by a drinking jingle. I supposed Popcorn saw it as a Christian beacon lighting the eagle's way. I saw it as the thunderbird flying high out of reach of over-zealous persecution.

My sister's friend, Yaa, had told me on Parent's Day at the camp that when Popcorn came home from her summer away she would be changed. Yaa was certainly right about that. It looked to me like my sister had come unhinged. She wasn't unhappy, but acted completely out of character, listening to no one, ignoring the slightest imposition of rules, even useful ones like dinner times, and was disappearing frequently for long hours without explanation or excuse. Yes, she was different. She transformed totally from a quiet, prayerful homebody to,

I don't know, a wild-eyed priestess of Planet Earth's Church of God.

I was too busy with my own stuff to be the type to spy or interfere. So, I wasn't exactly aware of what Popcorn was doing, but if Mama had ceased to tread the trail to Gulbranson's Resort, it turned out that her daughter would wear the path down quite regularly, in time, making no secret, to me at least, of where she was headed. Her pal, Yaa, had moved into the cabin on the point with Teddy G, something Mama found out within a day of the church camp session ending for the summer.

That day, I was up on a ladder at Tillie's painting leaves and vines when Mama strode up from the town dock, pumping her fists and swearing out loud. She was so distraught that she started telling me about the encounter before I could really follow her ranting.

"Mama, please, slow down. What did you say?"

She got my hint, smoothed her raven hair back, took a breath, and launched into her story again, quieting down considerably but no less animated. "I thought I'd pay a courtesy call on the Reverend Good since I was down that way fishing," she lied. "I docked at the point and first thing noticed that *Saint Muggsy* wasn't up in her winter berth, yet. It looked like he was extending his stay this year. And that wasn't all.

She stood at the foot of the ladder, looking up at me, her face flushed and arms waving like mad. She couldn't stay still.

"So I went up to the cabin to ask, you know just as a polite neighbor would—lying again—and who should come to the door but that African princess, Yaa. Well, my jaw dropped a mile. I didn't know what to say."

Though I wasn't enjoying my mother's interruption

that much, it seemed funny, at least ironic, that she would come to me with it. I guessed Tiny had been right about her, that she would look to me to save her from herself. I could have quoted Cooley or Danny: "If you don't want to smell the beer, don't hang in the tavern," but she wasn't in the mood for a lesson from me. I came down the ladder and opened my arms to her. It must have been what she needed, for she just fell into them and sobbed and shook for a long, long time. No stranger passing by could have told which was the mother and which the daughter without guessing wrong. It was a role reversal, which would surely lead to trouble.

After a while, she pushed away and grabbed a paint brush saying, "This project won't finish itself, now will it?" She started to add shading to some of the lower lying leaves and said not another word.

Even though Teddy G extended his stay over the next two months after Biini and I started our junior year at North County High, it was plain to see what was going on with Mama and her preacher-lover. In a word, "Nothing." As soon as she'd discovered Yaa at the cabin, she stopped going out to Gulbranson's on the weekends instead, frequenting Olsen's bar where, I guess, they made an exception about serving liquor to Indians.

At the time, I think she believed the Reverend Good had replaced her with that younger acolyte, and in a way that made it easier for her to accept. She had two good eyes. She could see Yaa's rounded parts and her silken skin. She was still mad about it but couldn't compete. Maybe "accept" isn't the right word since she seemed to need the beer and shots to keep total despair at bay.

Over those months, Laurel and Hardy were decent enough to call us when she needed to leave the tavern rather than pass out on the floor. Instead of throwing her out on the sidewalk as they did with other "drunken Indians," they called the only taxi in town, even though it was just a quarter mile walk to the post office. More often, though, it was me who went to fetch her when she was in trouble, helping her to stagger back home.

The Olsen rednecks didn't like me, and I heard plenty of muttering about Tillie's, the "council house," they said I was foisting on their nice white-man town. I guessed they weren't too good to take Indian money at the bar but were too saintly white to otherwise associate with such riffraff. In another time, Mama would have wrecked the place if anyone white had said in her presence the word "Indian" much less connected to "drunken."

But Morgan Langille, my mother, was at that time damaged. Her spirit that fall ran out over tables and floors in overturned beer bottles and dropped brandy shots. Gimlets were out of season. Fortunately, neither the season of despair, nor of brandy or vodka, lasted, and when Mama sobered up just before Halloween, she smelled something in the air that was not beer or booze.

At that time, much of Mama's talk when we were working together was of "that goddamned African queen," though once in a while she spoke of "that cradle-robbing minister." I agreed, though not out loud, with both names. Teddy Good never was on my favorite-persons list, and Yaa had impressed me most in the hour we spent together that summer as a manipulator and verified liar.

During Parent's Day, she'd gotten me away from

Popcorn both to pump me for information and to fill me with her bullshit line about the greatness of Teddy G, her savior.

Yaa had started in, "Why do you think Biinishii wanted to come to our camp? She seems to have liked the Swedenborgians well enough"

Maybe I wanted to shock her. Why should I suspect any mischief on her part? So, I told her what I thought. "She wants to save her mother."

"What do you mean?"

"Well, Mama seems to be romantically involved with your pastor," I said, laying it out in plain English. She acted genuinely surprised.

"With Teddy G?

I nodded, "The very same."

Yaa spent much of the rest of our walk together, defending Teddy G's character and position. "I find it very hard to believe that is true," she said though her tone didn't make her sound all that sure.

I told her, "It's what Popcorn believes that is important. And that is what she thinks, though how she can help the situation by coming to summer camp with the man, I just don't know." Yaa turned quiet then, and we just walked back to the gathering, maintaining an uneasy silence which lasted the rest of the visit.

I'm more like my mama than I want to admit, but I keep much more a close counsel than she ever did. So, when Popcorn came home, having a chance to talk with me in private and pressed me to know what Yaa and I had talked about at Parent's Day, I didn't say much. "She did all of the talking. And mostly about her pastor."

"Did you talk about baptism?"

"Not that I remember," I said. "It's not a thing I'd bring up." Then I added something for her to think about, "I told her that it was Mama who needed saving, rather than you." She seemed to accept that.

I don't like to admit it, but I took advantage of the sisterly closeness Popcorn sought out after her return from camp. I needed her support in my effort to reopen Tillie's, but I also thought that she needed to confide in me. I wasn't altogether right about that, but since we had talked, Popcorn must have felt she could share only some things with me. As it turned out, I was glad she hadn't told me everything—I didn't want to carry that baggage. But she did lay out what had happened when, looking for her, Mama found her visiting Yaa at Pelican Point. That's when the ugly truth surfaced. Popcorn told me about it:

"Mama came down to the cabin. I was there with Yaa, Teddy G being in Orr supervising the winterizing of the camp buildings. Mama didn't even knock. She just flung open the door and burst in.

"'You're coming home with me,' Mama said, 'I don't want you hanging around down here.'

"I didn't know what to say. I felt caught between, and just sat there like a dummy.

"'I said you're going home. Now. Get a move on.'

"I started to get up from the table we'd been sitting at, too ashamed to look at my friend.

"Yaa said, 'You are a woman now. Follow your own nose.'

"Mama at first ignored what Yaa said but then pointed a finger at me. 'You are still a child! You are my child, and you are coming home with me!' Mama yelled.

"She walked right up to me, grabbed my collar, and

with her other hand turned the table over on Yaa who scrambled out from under it and stood. Pointing then at Yaa, Mama said, 'You, African Queen, stay back and leave my child alone.' Mama, one-handed, took my chair and threw it at Yaa, not for a second letting me loose.

"Then," (Popcorn started crying at this point) "Mama dragged me outside and slapped me really hard. She'd never done that before.

"'So, you're a woman now? Not at my house. What's been going on here?' She pulled me down the steps behind her, turned, and slapped me again.

"'What did she mean? You're a woman now! What's that mean?'

"I didn't know what to say. I just blurted it out, 'Teddy G baptized me.'

"Like she didn't know what that meant, she frowned and grabbed my neck like she was going to choke me. 'What? What do you mean?'

"'I, I . . . I laid with him.' And I started to cry."

Now, Popcorn really bawled. It seemed to me that the whole house, maybe the whole church had fallen around her. It was obvious that she was still a child, one who knows with the light of day shining on her that she's gone astray. I felt like the big sister, more than two minutes older, and I comforted her. Then I, too, began to cry.

Choking down my sobs, I asked Popcorn, "What did Mama say?"

"She just said, 'That fuckin' bastard.' Then she pushed me ahead to her boat to bring me back home."

In a family, when something has happened whether to a child or a parent, folks adopt a certain low, grave tone and get secretive. I'd only seen it a couple of times before that day but recognized it right away even at a distance. From Tillie's, I had seen Mama and Popcorn coming up from the dock. They walked past on the road without saying a word, which I thought was strange. Otherwise, they acted pretty normal but serious. Hardy from Olsen's happened to be going down to the landing, passing them, and said something to Mama which got no response. She just walked straight ahead without even looking at the man. That, too, was odd. That got me down the ladder. It was near lunchtime anyway.

By the time I got home Popcorn was locked up in Mama's studio closet. I heard her pounding on the door, crying. At that moment, Mama came out of the studio, closed the door behind her, passing me in the hall, again, without a word, and went right to the garage. She was acting so strange that I was afraid.

I saw her through the kitchen window a minute later. She was carrying the shotgun we use hunting ducks, a 12 gauge. The shell bag was thrown across her shoulder.

I crossed the cafe which was empty at that time and went right to Papa who was still working in his office.

"Mama's walking down the road with the shotgun," was all I said.

"What on earth for?"

"I don't know, but Popcorn is locked in the studio closet."

He flung off his visor. "Something's wrong. Was the breach open?"

Mama was carrying the gun the way we had learned. "Close the breach only when you'll shoot." I nodded, and with that Papa went straight to the studio. His children came first.

Retreat 16

Morgan

I'll give that African queen some credit: she knows when to move it, and quickly. By the time I got Biini home, shoved her into the closet where I keep my paints and canvases locked up, had taken the 12 gauge and shells down from the garage rafters, and rowed my dingy back over to Pelican Point, a couple of hours altogether, Yaa had the dock boy, Tony, who was the only one left on duty for the fall, working like he was evacuating in a fire. *Saint Muggsy* was up in her winter berth though still uncovered, and Tony was pushing a loaded luggage wagon, heaping with stuff, up the walk behind the African queen, running with her arms draped with clothes from the cabin closet. She was getting away clean, but I wasn't after her anyway. I'm not sure I was gunning for Teddy, either, and looking back on it I'm glad he didn't show up. With Yaa in full flight, I figured that Teddy wouldn't be showing his face at Gulbranson's until next season, maybe never.

Okay, what a jilted lover would do when she is fully armed and loaded with no one around differs from what a wronged mother has in mind. Mostly Teddy's crime against Biini was pushing me. I was in the mood for some self expression of the kind I'd enjoyed in college when I had nothing but my feet and paving stones to use as weapons.

I started in the cabin. I gave the bed both barrels for Biini, sending goose down all over the place. I reloaded in front of a shit-grinning portrait of Preacher Good hanging over the fireplace and plugged him right in the kisser. I didn't want to damage the cabin much since Teddy was only renting it from Gulbranson. Then, I saw a framed charcoal of Yaa, which I was sure that Biini had drawn, propped on a table near the space heater. I blasted it good which was to bring on more grief later. Thinking to save the cabin but still looking for revenge, I went back out to *Muggsy*.

I cranked her down to the launching rails, checked for gas, and pushed her into the October waters, tying on behind the little rowboat I'd moored at the dock. I had enough time and gasoline to easily make it to the deepest part of Thief Lake.

August had brought out the color of the forests, but we'd had a lot of cloud cover and rain since, so the lake was skinned over if at all only in the mornings. The big freeze would be coming late that year. Since there was no one to chase me and I was towing my dingy, I took my time getting to the narrows and into Thief. I knew exactly where to go, since Tiny had for years placed his fish house over the deeps, on a line from the town dock to a virgin-timber stand of white pine. "This is one for you, Tiny," I said to the empty air, thinking of *Saint Muggsy* providing shelter for lunkers forty feet below my brother's icehouse.

I let *Muggsy*'s anchor down and tugged at it until I was sure I'd snagged something deep. I took the big gas can, nearly empty now, from the stern compartment, siphoned what was left in the auxiliary tank into it, and hogged it into my skiff. I didn't want to poison the lake or leave telltale signs. I loosed the dingy, keeping it looped to the rear cleat, and went to work: I smashed each of the three windshields, slit the leather seats and backs with a knife Teddy kept handy, and crushed the instruments in the panel one by one with the butt of the shotgun. I dumped the gimlet drawer over the front seat, then starting at the bow, shot two loads through the hull in each of the passenger compartments and a total of four through the engine floor at very close range. I stowed the shotgun and the leftover shells, just three at that point, in the motor housing.

By that time, *Muggsy* was taking on water at a good clip, and I drew over my rowboat and stepped aboard letting the rope loose. I rowed to the *Muggsy*'s bow, reaching over to trip the anchor release. I took a few circuits around Teddy's pride-and-joy as it filled and sank, reeling downward on its anchor chain afore and being dragged down by the weight of its M Hercules inboard aftward. It didn't take five minutes to disappear from sight under the cloud-gray of the soon-to-be-frozen water.

I nosed my boat toward the town dock and started rowing all my tension and problems out with each stroke on the oars. I heard a boom first, then I saw that damned cradle-robbing jet-setter fly low over the lake. If he saw me, he didn't dip his wing but was gone in less than half a minute, likely with his curly haired baby aboard. I just kept working the oars.

About half an hour later, as I was nearing the village dock, I heard another, fiercer boom. Off to my left in the direction of Pelican Point, a shaft of fire shot up above the tree tops. Maybe it was just as well that it happened.

The explosion and fire covered over my fraught activities, and Teddy's hasty departure turned the guilt-compass needle his way, not mine. I'm not one troubled much by remorse, but when I found out what had occurred after I cruised away from Pelican Point, I did feel a bit sad.

There was likely a pin-hole leak in the propane line that eventually filled the cabin with the volatile gas, and about the time I finished with *Saint Muggsy* and had seen Teddy's G's jet buzz the lake, his love-nest cabin had cooled enough for the thermostat to call for the heater to fire up. And fire up it did. After the cabin blew, the gas tank went with it, breaking windows throughout the resort and lighting up some of the trees at the point like match sticks. We all at the lake caught a break—me, especially—because no one was near. Not that I was sure that one of pellets I blasted around the place had hit the cabin's propane line—likely at least one had—but since it was only property, which Teddy's deep-pocketed father wound up paying for, and a few trees nearer the tank, I rested easier. The other stuff, my daughter's "baptism" as she called it, I had yet to deal with and would later that day and, afterward, more than once.

By the time I rowed into Olsen's slip everyone was out at Gulbranson's fighting fire. Not a soul was around. I lifted the gas can from *Muggsy* onto the dock near the premium pump and rowed back around to the town dock to tie up. I walked home through an empty town.

Tatty

Fear of my father restrained me when I was a child. There was not much more than threats needed to keep me, as he called it, "in line." We didn't lock up the boy in my home, and that is what I told Popcorn to calm her.

"I'm sorry Mama did this. I won't let her do it again."

With sisterly care Shookii helped me calm her twin. Popcorn's honesty made things easier. I came to understand what had happened out at the camp, what had set her mother on the rampage, and how Morgan's outrage threw everything more off kilter. It was the hardest story I'd ever had to listen to.

The way Popcorn understood it, her intention was innocent and clear, if, I thought, sorely misplaced. To save her mother, she had sacrificed herself, and though I felt the same rage Morgan had evinced going for the shotgun, I couldn't help but feel that my wife's reaction had as much to do with the sacrifice her own sister had made to save Morgan from her windigo fate as it did with the violation of her daughter by her own lover. How does one feel when he or she every so often needs saving through the loss of another life, or in Biini's case, another's innocence? Still, that was insufficient reason to lock the child in a closet. What else she had done remained to be discovered.

I addressed both the girls, "Look you two, I want you to remember that though you are approaching adulthood, you are not quite there yet. Making mistakes and misjudgments is part of gaining maturity, and there is little I can do to protect you from those. I won't hold your errors against you. We all commit them, sometimes over and over again"—I later wished I had not added the last phrase. "What I can do is invite you to share with me your ideas and plans and your reasons for doing what you will. That includes your mother, too. When she comes back, we'll sit down together, all four, and talk this out."

I felt like I was sticking my finger in a dike after

the ocean had broken through, but weak as my words seemed as soon as I uttered them, I had nothing else to offer. It was not a topic Dr. Spock had covered in his book. As if to punctuate my plea, we heard Teddy G's jet roar overhead. At that moment, we all three seemed relieved. The girls hugged each other. I took them each, then both together, in my arms, as if holding in their childhoods for the very last time. Shortly, we heard the blast. Within five minutes, Danny was at the door, his truck left running outside.

"All hands on deck. That explosion you heard came from Gulbranson's. The woods are on fire! Jump in!"

"You go, Papa. Popcorn and I will stay here or maybe walk down to the dock."

It was something a good citizen could not say no to. I felt all right leaving the twins as long as they were together, so I threw on a helmet and a flak jacket, jumping into Danny's truck cab. The girls waved us on our way.

By the time we arrived, the cabin was a scattered ash field. The trees that still stood were blackened but not aflame. The boat launch and dock were just gone, the debris floating yards out on the cove. There was no sign of bodies, but there was plenty of talk about Teddy G and Yaa. Especially, Yaa, since we all knew that Teddy would have been flying the jet. Whatever had gone on there, he was gone.

"Whada mess," Danny whistled. "Some one was playing with matches."

Danny's firm grasp of the obvious lightened me. I hoped I was alone in my worry about Morgan who Dindii had last reported headed toward the town dock. Maybe she hadn't got to the point. That was my hope, as much for the sake of the twins as for mine.

The devastation at Gulbranson's had all the markings of my wife's worst moments: leading her sister on a fatal windigo chase, smashing a Florida kitchen-full of dishes, picking fist fights on campus in Tallahassee, beating a Renault nearly to death, flinging a foot-jab to break Roscoe's collarbone, and, I suspected, breaking our neighbor Sadie's leg. The mayhem surrounding her was periodical, came up infrequently during high stress times in defense when she felt cornered, but she could also go, even surrounded by her own carnage, through difficult times with the aplomb of a jurist. Then suddenly, without seeming provocation or warning, she could fly into a cataclysmic rage. If she was responsible for the Gulbranson devastation, I could see how it came about. She did have cause for ire, how much anger she loosed was another question.

My old self, the one taught by my father to clam up and say not a thing, played into my silence that day, but so did the careful judgment and official reserve I had learned as a postmaster. Until I knew what part Morgan played, if I was ever to find out, I held my peace, especially, since my daughter was at least on the sidelines of what Danny always called "the mess at the point."

Despite Danny's protests, I walked home, giving myself time to think. What swirled around in my mind, though, was not Popcorn's beguiling or the destruction at Gulbranson's, but the phrase, "I punish children for their parents' sins." Though I didn't know where it came from exactly, I thought it was from the Bible, I understood the import of it, especially in my own case and Morgan's. Certainly, whatever Morgan had done that day, her kids were already suffering. I had stood by for years working to anchor the family, to keep cataclysm at bay. Now, I would make it my business to mitigate these new pains as much as I could. I was ready to do what was needed to comfort and save my family.

Family Meeting 17

Popcorn

To be the troublemaker in a family is a hard thing, especially, when you're not used to making waves. I right away felt that I was naked, stripped, taken by the ear, and paraded down the main street in town. It wasn't the holy kind of nudity I had lately experienced. The shock of discovery rose from my surprise that Mama, for one, had a different view of what I'd done than I did or than Yaa did. Of course, she wouldn't approve, but couldn't she see that I had freed her of her waywardness? That was all I wanted.

Seclusion followed exposure. It was scary to be locked away. Yes, I panicked and pounded on the door, but I remained solitary in a different way, too. Even after Papa released me and I told him all the story, I felt like he backed up a step from me, creating a gulf that would part us always. Although he told Shookii and me that we all mature through mistakes, he never explained how alone that makes a person feel. I was by myself, really, for the first time in my life. Truly separate.

At that instant, my family began to tiptoe around me, just being careful of what, I wasn't sure. One moment it was as if they seemed to whisper—I wondered. Was it about me?—like there was a thick pane of glass between us, dampening sound. Was I sick? On my deathbed?

Suffering a contagious disease? What were they worried about? What were they saying? When I reached out, my sister and parents seemed to recede.

I didn't even like my own company. Who wants to be in the same room with one so morose? And I found I could not pray, not for comfort nor for relief. I couldn't stand my own voice, out loud or in my mind. Repeating penitent or chaste words sounded sanctimonious to me. More and more, I tilted toward silence. Even that was uncomfortable.

There appeared some measure of comfort that day. After Papa left to fight the fire, Shookii and I walked to the town dock, passing Tillie's on the way. That was when I asked Shookii to paint in a cross opposite her thunderbird. Asking seemed like a penance for whatever sins I had committed and, perhaps, for others I was going to engage in. Talking about Tillie's opened to me a future I couldn't wait to live. Anything would be better than the present.

My sister used the occasion to further her cause. I was ready to join her.

"Will you help me reopen the place?" Shookii said.

It was a good time for her to ask. It seemed like something I could look forward to. Something new to work on. Something to clothe myself in, something to bridge that gulf I was already feeling, something to break through the sound barrier. I agreed and that pleased Shookii.

"This opening is partly for me, for us, but it will help Mama, too."

She didn't say how. Taking it on faith, I didn't ask.

"I'm telling you something else. Keep it to yourself," she said.

"What is it?"

"You know our grandfather, our real grandfather, was murdered at Tillie's."

"Jay Martinen. They called him Scummy."

Shookii nodded. She looked serious. "I've seen that man."

"Our grandfather?"

"No. His murderer," Shookii said.

"Where? When? I've always thought that he was dead."

"The first time was seven years ago July. Papa went white that day."

"Is that what happened? Have you seen him since?" I said.

Shookii again nodded. "I saw him inside Tillie's that winter, but I wasn't sure it was him."

"And again?" I asked.

"Yes. I've been around Tillie's a lot for the painting, and I soon knew that someone was staying in the cellar there. It is Roscoe."

"Didn't you tell anyone?" I asked without thinking what I would have done. I immediately decided that she hadn't.

"I've only told you." She took my hand with her scarred one—it was the first time since her burning that she had been so tender. "Now, we have something between us again, something to bind us. The day I saw him in the garage, Roscoe said that we should reopen Tillie's. It is something that will help Mama, help us all. Don't tell anyone."

Put that way, how could I refuse?

When we reached the dock, Mama was rowing up from the resort slip. We caught her skiff and tied it up to the dock. She looked tired.

"You two, together, here to meet me?" She climbed out of the skiff but didn't move toward either of us. Shookii told her about the fire and all.

"Papa and I let Biini out." She smiled, a little crookedly, right at Mama who seemed to ignore both the remark and what was really a smirk.

She walked right by us and then turned, saying, "I'm going to rest a bit. I'll see you at supper." And she just walked off alone, heading for home.

Later, we sat in the family kitchen around our four sided table. Shookii was opposite me, Mama and Papa each on a side. I felt like I was on That Man island with only one friend. I didn't have too much to say. All I wanted was to live another day. I knew that Pastor Good was gone. Everyone had heard the jet. And I was sure that Yaa was with him. They had forsaken me.

Surrounded by my family, sitting under the retractable light dish that was pulled down low over the table, casting shadows over Mama's and Papa's faces but fully illuminating Shookii's and mine, I felt like I was the defendant in a courtroom.

Morgan

The whole thing pissed me off. I was furious and frustrated. Right then I hated Teddy G and, of course, Yaa. I was mad at Tatty, always being permissive, always defending the girls' right to decide, as if they were already adults. For her part, Biini certainly wasn't innocent even if she was only fifteen. She knew better. The only one not on my shit-list was Dindii, though I wondered if she hadn't known all along what was going on. She'd had plenty of time to interview the African princess that summer. Who was on the top of my list? Me.

Oh, I'd been the "guilty" party before. This time would be no different. Heap up the blame, why don't you? "Like mother, like daughter," I could already hear them all saying. Sure, let them ignore a lecherous preacher, a lying conniving African queen, a by-the-babybook pandering dad, and a weak-willed kid who loitered around the-holier-than-thou altar. Of course it was my fault. I'm the mother, for God's sake. Everything is Mama's failure. Well, I won't have it. Bullshit!

I've never backed down, and I won't start now. I'll go face to face, nose to nose with anyone who tries to shun me or mess with me. Remember Sadie? Right. When my sister died, I'd sat with the sheriff breathing fire on my face without blinking, all the time pretending to be her, alive, instead of me, who was supposedly dead. Same when Roscoe went after Jay. I was reluctant to have the truth be told, I admit, but when the time was right I didn't back away.

Authority has no authority with me. It's other people that screw things up. There is no pushing me away. *I'm* the doing the nudging.

Talk all you want about me. So what? Talk's cheap. I won't sit still for knowing looks or lowered voices in my vicinity. I'll take what comes but never take a step back.

I've learned the hard way that when it comes to social interaction, I'm my own best company. I give myself the best advice I get without any second guessing or remorse. I am that I am, you might say.

So, when I rounded the bend coming from Olsen's gas pump and saw my two girls standing on the town dock, I just kept rowing toward them. If they were sent to look for me, I was ready with a story. It wouldn't do to say too much about where I'd been or what I'd been doing. And I didn't care who had let Biini out of the closet, my dear husband or her sister. I knew how to handle it.

When I steered to the dock, they came alongside as I cast up the rope. Biini tied the bow, Dindii the stern, and I stepped out.

I went right to Biini and took her in my arms. "I'm sorry. I was angry with you, but I've got past that. I'm glad they let you out of the closet." I held back my own tears. I placed my hands on Biini's shoulders, standing back and releasing my hug. She was crying.

Dindii mumbled something and tried to smile.

I was done there. Hanging out would only invite interrogation. I didn't want that, yet.

I just said, "I'm going home. I'll make supper for us."

By the time we were sitting in our little kitchen around the supper table, I'd sorted out what I was going to say, only if asked. I'd also decided on exactly what I would not report. Tatty sat across from me, and I knew he would lay out questions and challenges. I was ready. No one knew what I knew. It felt like a courtroom, but I was the jury foreman. I would hold it in until everything they knew was revealed. All I wanted was to get my hands on the goddamned preacher. I knew he was gone, but I had my suspicions about his eventual return. Once that man took a swallow of fine gin, he couldn't stop himself from pouring another. That much I knew. When he came back for more, I swore to myself that I'd act. I kept my own counsel just as much as I needed to.

Tatty

I've spent my life more a bystander than an actor. More an observer than a doer. One of my early family memories frames my penchant quite well:

For a long time I'd refused to see and admit that my father was a drunk. Then on a wet winter Florida evening, he showed me plainly enough. Shuffling into the kitchen through the back door, muttering much too loudly as he made his way around the table, discovering us playing pick-up-sticks on the living room rug, he scoffed at my mother and me.

"Well, isn't this cozy?" He said, swaying over us, "The domestic duo."

He swept an unsteady foot over the pile of sticks, scattering them. I watched, horrified. I let mother take action.

"You're drunk, Peter," mother said.

"The hell I am."

"You're just plain mean. Mean and drunk." Then turning to me, she said, "Look at your father, Tatty, he's drunk, isn't he?"

I could hardly raise my eyes from the ruined pile that had been our game.

"Yeah, T-a-t-t-y," my father stretched out my name, "Tell her. I'm not drunk, now am I? " And when I shook my head inconclusively, he bellowed, "Tell her, now!"

Any words I muttered turned to cotton in my throat. I gagged on my own thoughts.

From that time on, perhaps even well before that occasion, I sought the sidelines, never the midfield. Never mind that my father, revealing the truth that evening, missing a chair, abruptly crashed to the floor and lay there yet the following morning, too drunk even to use the toilet.

Despite notable exceptions—at the tender age of nine, I spoke out firmly against staying in Nova Scotia after my father's burial there, and I stood up to Morgan when opposition was absolutely necessary, as when she began cavorting with Teddy Good—I otherwise stayed out of controversy and confrontation unless it had to do with my daughters.

I'd played the caretaker role with Morgan for years and found the part transferred easily to the twins. Still, raising two girls seldom called for direct action, and I was content to observe and gently guide if anything at all was needed. Otherwise, I stayed away from issues, perhaps to a fault.

This day called for action. I didn't do much but remove hinge pins from the closet door and pull out the door with the help of two pliers, one for me the other for Shookii. I don't call giving comfort an action though I suppose it is. Listening I've always known is something one does actively. So, I suppose I did something, but mostly I just paid attention. And when Popcorn revealed her ordeal with Teddy Good, the baptism and the many visits the preacher had paid to Popcorn and Yaa at their camp cabin in the middle of the night, I met her sobbing story with hugs and acceptance. She was only fifteen.

I thought at the time that the infatuation, if that's what it was, had ended. Good was gone, everyone who could hear knew, and I couldn't fathom a time or a reason he might return. Popcorn, for her part, seemed to want to put it behind her. I was fine with that. Comforting her was enough for me.

When Danny showed up after the explosion, I commended Popcorn to the company of her sister—neither wanted to come along—and rode along with Danny mostly to see what had happened and what was being done. Even if the post office were threatened, I'd not be doing any fire fighting. What I did do was observe, and what I saw filled me with dread at finding Morgan somewhere near.

I was quite sure that she had headed to Pelican Point with our shotgun Shookii saw her carrying. What she did when she arrived, I didn't know, but the devastation was shocking. It bore all the marks of the Morgan Langille meltdowns I had witnessed in college, seen at Tillie's, and visualized with Sadie on the ridge above the cabin. I saw the charred remains of a rustic cabin, blasted apart by the propane tank explosion, and still smoldering; a flotilla of debris thirty yards off shore that represented what was left of the boat lift and dock; but not in evidence, either untouched or ruined, was the pride and joy of the itinerant preacher, his boat, the *Saint Muggsy*. My private conclusion was that Morgan was somewhere out on the water with that Chris-Craft, burning off angst with speed or, more likely, burning the boat in effigy of her failed affair. If she were alive and returned, I would find out. No one else expressed any thought that Morgan may have been present at the "accident." That's what it was to be called, an accident.

After picking through the scene, looking for any sign of Morgan, I told Danny that I would walk home on the trail, the one both Morgan and Popcorn had followed to the Pelican Point cabin.

"I need to clear my brain," I said.

Danny, always ready with a come-back, said, "Well, don't wind up like me, totally erased!"

I slapped his shoulder in response and headed back. I was content to leave the talk of the "accident" to what would become the official story. Eventually, when the shock of the explosion wore off, people began to wonder what had happened to *Saint Muggsy*, which the dock boy, Tony, would swear he had raised on the lift for winter storage. The insurance company asked hard questions. Then again, boats, and fancy ones, too, disappeared both into the vastness of the wilderness and the boathouses of the developed lakes from time to time. None were ever found, as far as anyone knew. I would find out sooner than any where *Saint Muggsy* was hiding. Like much else in Morgan's life, it became a secret I kept when all else went up in flames with my wife on the grand re-opening of Tillie's.

Morgan was fixing supper when I came home.

"Where are the girls?"

Morgan didn't look at me but answered, "Loitering. Down at the dock or maybe at Tillie's. I told them I'd make supper. They'll be along."

I knew better than to push directly with, "What did you do?" So, I asked as politely as I could, "Is the shotgun in the garage?"

"Isn't it always?"

"Shookii told me you had taken it and headed out."

"Don't call her that!" Morgan turned around. "And no. It isn't in the garage." Anticipating my line of thought she added, "It's at the bottom of the lake, if you must know."

I had warmed to my task now and asked, "What have you done?"

Morgan planted her hands on her hips—something she seldom did—and she leaned back on the counter, scowling at me. I thought it was rehearsed, a stance she had planned to take. "Do you know what that goddamned preacher did to our child?" This was the Morgan I knew.

The old cotton throat was back after forty-five years. I could only grimly nod.

"I wanted to give him two doses of duck shot in the chest, that's for sure. By the time I got to his little love nest, though, no one was around. So I shot up the place and took *Saint Muggsy* out for her final voyage. I sent her to the lake bed with her holey bottom, the shotgun, and my well wishes."

It sounded incomplete. "Did you set the cabin afire?"

"Am I an arsonist? No." After thirty-five years, I knew when she was telling the truth.

I nodded. "No, it isn't your style, true."

It was later when the fire marshal detailed his finding that a faulty gas line filled the cabin which exploded when the stove fired up that I pieced together what had happened. Had Morgan intended the "accident," I would have had a hard decision to make. In the meantime, I listened, waited, and watched.

Our get together that evening, around supper, was my opportunity to set our little family on a better course. I acted the court reporter, reading back what had already been testified to, even the most delicate items, but those in gentle terms.

"Let me say something, here," I started. No one even breathed. "We all understand about Biini's baptism and how a misguided minister took advantage of a young, believer. It wasn't his first time." I looked around our little circle. Morgan's eyes were shaded by the lowered light fixture. Popcorn and Shookii watched their hands on the table.

"It is a civil and religious crime, but he is gone now. Let's leave that behind us." No one spoke. "Now, let's agree, no matter how we feel, how angry we may become, that we will always love and support each other. We are a family. We won't lock anyone away. Agree?" We each affirmed my words.

"Good," I continued. "Know that *Saint Muggsy* sunk."

Morgan chimed in here, "Shot full of holes!"

I continued, "Something that will be our family's secret. Agree?" We all did.

I went on. "The 'accident' was just that, an incident with no one to blame." All nodded.

"We go on from here, not as if none of this happened, but go on together because it did happen. We shall love and cherish each other all the more after this reminder that life together is fragile and worth protecting." I reached for Shookii's and Popcorn's hands. Morgan completed a circle, taking the girls' hands on her side.

"We are together, and that's all that matters now."

Shookii

From the day of my accidental burning, I had felt little sympathy for my sister. I felt that through my injuries and scarring I had left Popcorn behind in the cradle of childhood, while I dealt with real and painful adult things: doctor's treatments, the threat of mortality (an idea I felt even before I knew its name), serious social *stigmas* (I had learned that word during this period), and a realization that "things happen" to innocent people, that life is unjust. Popcorn, despite an onslaught of guilt over my burning, was still a child and even more was wrapped in a cocoon of *religiosity* (another word I discovered at that time). Though even our parents may not have realized how far apart we fell until the summer Popcorn went to camp and I stayed at Thief Lake, it became clear to all that June that we were treading different paths.

On the Parent's Day at Popcorn's camp, Yaa's sneaky behavior set me on edge. For the first time in years, I felt protective of my sister and wary of people who might harm her though I had done nothing to safeguard our relationship to that point. When Mama discovered later in October the truth of what Popcorn had fallen into, I was primed to reach for her hand, to try to soothe her pain and to welcome her to an adulthood I'd had years before gotten used to. *Tribulations* paved the way for our *rapprochement* (both words I used in the *Trout* that fall).

As we walked the road which runs past Tillie's

toward the village dock, I comforted her as best I could with words. "Adulthood is scary sometimes," I said to Popcorn, "but it is full of adventure, too." I knew the trauma she had suffered locked in Mama's storage closet not to mention the confusion she was likely to realize in the months ahead as she saw the truth of her misplaced faith in Teddy Good. Although it was temporary—only ten minutes passed from the time Mama left with the shotgun and the time Papa and I pried the door open after unpinning the hinges—her *incarceration* (more nomenclature for a news reporter) left her shaken, feeling weak, and seemingly bewildered. I didn't intend to take advantage of her condition. I thought that involving her in my project, reopening Tillie's, might distract her and open a future to her that had been shut by the close darkness of that closet. I admit it was easier to get her cooperation at that moment than either before Mama's meltdown or than after daily life intruded its insistent demands once again. Whatever the case, Popcorn seemed right then easy to persuade. All I had to do was make room for her inside the building and paint a crucifix on one end of Tillie's sign. Along the way on that project, I would insist on my license as the artist to harmonize the cross and thunderbird using the same colors: coppery red body, black highlights, and ivory-white accents. She even allowed me to wrap the base of the cross with my unifying florals and filigree.

Popcorn and I didn't linger at Tillie's. We stood before the half-finished mural, talking of my plans for a while, then rounded the building to follow a path down to the common dock. That brought us past Tillie's cellar doors. They were the kind set over an angled frame covering the descending stairs, a pair of storm doors keeping the snow and heavy rains from filling the recess. Perhaps Popcorn noticed how hard packed the ground around the opening was or maybe I, feeling closer to my sister now, thought this a good time to take her into my confidence, to tell her about Roscoe, even though I hadn't yet figured out where the story was going to lead as it played out.

"Not long ago I opened those basement doors to see what the foundations were like, something Uncle Tiny recommended." I couldn't blame Popcorn for not being interested in this, but she soon came around when I mentioned Roscoe. "I found that someone had been living down there. There were canned goods and food stuffs in a cold locker. It looked like someone had even been cooking there from at times."

"Who would it be?" Popcorn asked.

"I think it is Roscoe, the bear man."

Popcorn wondered, "Isn't he supposed to be dead? He's the guy who killed our real grandfather, isn't he?"

"Yes and yes." I had told her the story of Roscoe in the garage the day Papa's hair went white.

Popcorn's eyes opened wide with interest. "Do you think he's been living in the cellar all this time?"

I didn't want to tell her everything I suspected. I guess I trusted her only so much. In an effort to get her more on my side, though, I dropped a few details as suppositions: "No. I don't think he is always here, even though if he is alive, he is a real half-owner of the place. Living here full-time would become obvious because Tillie's should have been vacant for many years. Too much activity here would be noticed, eventually. If I were him, I'd have several places to hide, maybe in a high cave in the gorge"

I chose the hardest-to-find spot to which I had followed Roscoe. Since Papa and I had scaled those cliffs up and down practicing rock climbing, I knew it was a place Popcorn would be unlikely to visit. Roscoe was a sometime resident of a particularly difficult-to-access cave.

Then I set Popcorn on a false scent, "He might camp far out in the wilderness along one of the 'canoe only' routes either in Canada or up around the Kettle Falls wilderness." I didn't catch myself in time and added, "Where Cooley was shot."

"So, you think this ghost-of-Roscoe shot Cooley?"

I didn't admit that Roscoe was on my list of suspects in Cooley's shooting. I kept that to myself pending more information. At that time I still had not connected the phrase "our three two" to what Roscoe had said to me in the garage, "three, two t' one, again." I just said, "It's hard to believe, isn't it."

"And it's all too confusing," Popcorn said. "Let's go. We might be able to see the fire from the dock."

As engaged as Popcorn had seemed, she didn't seem to want to pursue Roscoe or Tillie's further just then. What was happening out at Gulbranson's was more important to her. I wanted to be sure that she wouldn't blab about Roscoe at Tillie's later.

"Just one more thing," I said, "don't tell anyone about Roscoe or any of that. Keep it between us two."

She had already turned to the dock trail. She raised one hand in approval but kept right on walking.

I had a strong urge to tell her about Papa's father up on the ridge, but just as Popcorn didn't burden me much with her Christian spirits, I didn't want to tell her more about my visions no matter how real they appeared.

We came to the dock. We couldn't see anything of Pelican Point in the distance, but a thin layer of smoke had spread out our way from that direction. In a few moments after we came to the end of the dock, Mama rowed up in her little skiff, looking to me just as angry as I'd seen her last.

We helped tie off the boat at the dock. I saw, then, that the shotgun was not in the dingy with her. I did not ask her about it. Let Mama say something if she would. I left. Popcorn stayed back to give Mama a hand getting onto the dock.

"Be on time for supper," Mama called to me. I strode off on the trail to Tillie's. Those two took the road.

I was the last to arrive for supper. I had taken a hike past Tillie's up to the gorge overlook where the river ran rampant through a forty-foot deep cleft in the granite that ran two hundred yards long. The current at the bottom of the gorge was so rapid that it seldom froze until the coldest depths of January.

I scanned the cliff opposite the trail for evidence of Roscoe's cave opening that I knew was there. I'd seen Roscoe just disappear into the granite rock face. He was clever as the best of man or beast in the woods, sure-footed, and left as little trace as a ghost. I could not see his entry from this or any angle.

Roscoe's skill in nature had earned him, both among those who thought he was still alive as well as those who figured he must be dead, a reputation as a windigo, a dangerous spirit of the forest, someone who, nothing himself, listened only to the nothing that most folks say is not there. I knew from watching him as closely as I dared, that he listened not as people said but to the nothing that *is* there. His existence or his absence spanned decades, mine and Popcorn's lifetime, went back further than Mama's childhood at the lake, and promised to play a part in local lore longer than I would live.

That day, I saw nothing of him at the gorge. I turned toward home, reluctant and cognizant of what I would find there.

I had no doubt that Papa had pieced everything together after his visit to Pelican Point. He would put out a plan for moving ahead again as a family. That was his philosophy: keep moving ahead. I knew that he understood it all better than any of us. I could trust him to guide the four of us to better times. Mama, for her part, would brag and bluster without admitting anything much. Popcorn would say nothing. I would note everything. After all, I knew there were stories to be told later.

Once home, I was not disappointed.

It was no surprise to me when Papa said, "It is a civil and religious crime, but he" (referring to Teddy Good) "is gone now. Let's leave that behind us." He was the peacemaker and would usually go out of his way to bring everything to rights, unless it meant sacrificing a piece of the family or injuring it in some way. We all agreed to move on, all for our own reasons as well as those Papa expressed.

When he told us the fate of *Saint Muggsy*, Mama's bravado slipped out. She as much as admitted she'd sunk the craft without plainly saying so. She wanted credit even as she avoided censure.

I figured she had something to do with the explosion at Gulbranson's that day, too, but I was willing to go with Papa's account: "The 'accident' was just that, an incident with no one to blame."

Papa would be proven wrong about most of this, but we needed to agree for a time, to be together no matter how briefly. That's all that seemed to matter to us.

As for me, I was burning to write stories for my newspapers—my headline: "Pastor Good Flies Off as Cabin Explodes" wasn't used, of course, but the facts of the story did make print in the tribal newspaper and the *Trout*, too.

Other news coming up soon was more important to me. Headline: "Tillie's Tavern To Be Converted, Spiritual Center Envisioned." I had tons of work to complete at Tillie's before that could happen. The months of relative calm following that day's storm gave me space to accomplish it all, granted, with help from my entire family.

Grand Opening 18

It looked to me for a long time after my wife's blow up over Pastor Good and Popcorn that I had made sound decisions about what to do and what to say regarding both Morgan's and Biini's involvement with Teddy G, his cabin, and his cherished boat. For months following, until two days before the grand opening night at Tillie's, our family seemed as unified and tight knit as I ever remembered it.

Popcorn and Shookii were working if not together then in tandem on the renovation and furnishing of Tillie's. Morgan spent the days the girls were in school, supervising workers at the former tavern, and, with Tiny, advised Shookii on tribal concerns in setting up the interior for meetings and powwows which mostly would be conducted outside on what had been a large beer-garden patio of the tavern. The carpenters removed the ancient bar our local Laurel and Hardy had lost in a bidding war to the Vermillion River Tavern five miles down the road from the lake. They were mighty sore losers, too, claiming backroom dealings aced them out. The bar was installed in its new home the same day, giving the VRT, as it was called "the longest elbow rest" in the township.

Popcorn took charge of two small rooms at the rear of the former barroom, transforming them into a tiny chapel and meeting space that could be used by any of the Christian organizations in the area, Native or not. Among others, the Swedenborgians signed on to use the space.

I was pleased to watch Popcorn come out of her terrible experience with positive energy. Her piety had never overly concerned me, except when she was all too close to Teddy Good, and to see her actively engaged in building something she cared about was gratifying.

Shookii seemed to have energy exceeding the other three of us combined. When she wasn't working at Tillie's, painting walls, cleaning up the carpenters' dust, and polishing the banks of cabinets that had been hidden under the bar, she was writing news articles and editorials as well as promotional pieces on the cultural center coming to Tillie's.

Neither girl, it turned out, was able to devise an unobstructed path to their goals. That was as it would have been for any adult. Shookii had plenty of animosity to deal with in her promotion of a Native center in town. Leading staunch resistance were our local Laurel and Hardy team, which claimed the whole thing was a government plot to further shrink the commercial footprint in the area. They somehow turned every argument for Tillie's renovation and reopening on its head, coming up with the most twisted claims one could imagine, like, "Whatever the Indians get the government has taken from us."

Shookii ran with that one under the headline "Resort Owners Cry *Foul!*" Which included an interview with Olsen's owners and some long-time residents at the lake. I posted part of the interview on the community bulletin board at the post office:

Trout: You've said the Federal government is stealing business from you to give space to the Native tribes around the area. How is that possible?

Olsen's: Listen. For nearly 20 years since logging was outlawed all around here, the government has taken more and more of our freedom and our livelihoods away. We can't run a fishing expedition without a boat and motor which are now mostly outlawed.

Trout: Are there plans to run fishing trips out of the new cultural center?

Olsen's: Not that we know of, but Indians have unrestricted fishing rights. They don't even need to pay for a license. We sure as h . . . do! This is no different than our fight to save the truck portages that the government wanted to get rid of. You think our summer guests want to haul all their gear and canoes, too, on their backs?

Trout: Some say this is about the auction of Tillie's ancient bar now down at the VRT.

Olsen's: That is entirely an unconnected matter, even though the whole thing was a sham, cooked up to look legit. We never had a chance.

Trout: Are you saying the VRT cheated somehow?

Olsen's: There's plenty of fishy business goes on here. All we know is it's not fair to us.

Trout: There has been vandalism at the Tillie's work site. Do you think all the tough talk about the center has brought out the worst in residents?

Olsen's: We had absolutely nothing to do with that. What others do is not our affair. We are talking here about survival. Our partnership and lots of the resort owners here are in big-time debt. We can't afford to lose even one

more customer. If word gets around that Thief Lake has become a haven for outsiders, we might go under.
Trout: Outsiders?
Olsen's: Yeah. Bois Forte Indians, for instance.

How Shookii got our local Laurel and Hardy to go on the record with their diatribes, I'll never understand. She treated the material fairly but they, as they usually did, acted plenty sore when the article came out. They made a lot of noise about being misquoted until the tape recorded interview was played on a local FM station out of tribal headquarters, revealing the duo at their worst. That recording found Laurel saying, "Vandalism? Maybe you asked for it." Hardy came up with, "Shut up, you idiot." After that was aired, they both clammed up.

I was proud of Shookii. She was a careful journalist already and was improving her style with every article.

During those months, there were several times I held my breath and found myself near to praying, too. Insurance investigators visited town twice, both times they wanted to interview Morgan, Tony, the boathouse boy, and a few others in Thief Lake who were noted for sharp observations. An investigator at the Gulbranson's cabin photographed what was left after the explosion, and the other who represented Planet Earth's Church of God, the real owner of *Saint Muggsy*, spent an awful lot of time with Tony, who seemed to be a likely suspect in the theft of the Chris-craft. As it turned out, the boat was insured for $40,000.

The fire marshal ruled the cabin destruction an accident. Gulbranson took the cash and rebuilt the dock but not the cabin. It was too far from the lodge, and too much had gone on in its isolated vicinity. The missing boat was listed as stolen property. It was not found.

I don't know how much either insurer knew about Morgan and Teddy Good. They didn't learn anything more from Morgan, that was sure. According to her account of one interview, she'd told them that Teddy Good was their man. No one else had much to gain considering the trouble of housing an expensive and iconic boat. "You might check some of the buildings at that Camp he runs over in Orr," she told the adjuster.

Though Morgan had done little to conceal her shotgun as she walked down to the dock the morning Teddy and Yaa left, no one had seen her or was willing to *say* they'd seen her. "I took my skiff out fishing," was her story. "I heard an explosion as I was rowing back."

I had seen Morgan slip out of several messes over the years. Her luck had yet to run out. The companies paid their respective insureds and left both Morgan and Tony at peace.

In the middle of those nervous times, November, DuChien came to town for deer hunting. He paid a courtesy call on the other Fed in town, me, meeting up at the cafe with his hunting guide, Cooley. Danny had joined the party, too.

"I'm not letting my friend go alone in the wilderness any more," Danny said.

Cooley said, "I can't argue with that. Especially with a wild shot like DuChien out there."

"Say, Mr. FBI," Danny asked, "whaddya think about our excitement over on Pelican Point?"

DuChien grinned. "It's not in my firehouse, thank God."

"Yeah," Danny persisted, "you might have too many suspects that you know!"

"If there is a crime, destruction of property, theft, attempted murder, or whatever, it will be local, not federal. It didn't happen in the BWCA or national forest either. So," he smiled again, "it's not in my bailiwick."

Danny went on. "The insurance was sniffing around Tony for a while."

Unable to dodge Danny's banter, DuChien gave in. "If I were looking, I'd do more forensics on the gas stove, and I'd find that disappeared Chris-craft. I'd look in the lake. That would be my starting point. I don't think the sheriff is up to a sonar sweep for a fancy boat, but that's what I'd do."

Danny giggled. "Which lake? All of them?"

We had a good laugh on that one. Which lake, indeed. There were dozens, all connected to each other.

Deer season turned out well. DuChien bagged a ten-point buck and Cooley a doe. Danny zeroed out but it was more lack of interest and concentration than shooting skill. He was really around for the ride and to do the cooking. Tiny always brought home venison for everyone, and since the freeze came later than usual in November, he had time to butcher and wrap enough meat for us all.

In December we held a feast in honor of the twins' sixteenth birthday which was replete with tender venison dressed with *manomin*. We held the party in fair December weather at Tillie's former beer garden. On that occasion, I noticed the locked cellar doors and asked Shookii about it.

"Can we take a look?"

She seemed to puzzle on my question a bit, then said, "I don't have the key."

"Isn't it on your Tillie's key chain?" I pointed to it dangling on her rawhide belt.

Now, Shookii and I kept no secrets, but she seemed less than ready to explain. Finally, she said, "Come around the side," and led me to the mural which was finished and looking wonderful under a good coating of lacquer.

As we looked at the mural, Shookii said, "I probably should have told you about the cellar before, but no one besides Popcorn and I know. It's been our secret for months."

"Then, keep it that way," I said.

"No, Papa, I think you should know."

"Okay, but what."

"It's the bear man. Roscoe Lucci."

If I hadn't seen Roscoe in my own garage, I would have refused to believe what Shookii was saying.

She acted as if she were showing me details of the mural, but continued talking about Roscoe. "Three years ago almost to the day, I came here looking at the ruined mural. I peeked inside through a knothole in the boards up the porch stairs and saw something—perhaps, someone, wrapped in a blanket—moving across the room. A couple minutes later when I returned to the mural, I thought I saw Roscoe at that window up there." She pointed to the second story kitchen window above.

"Have you sighted him again? In that cellar?"

"I've spent a lot of time here not just this year, but for a long spell. The cellar wasn't always locked up. Then I went down—Tiny told me once to have a look at the pilings underneath—and found that someone had been living there. Since then, I've watched. I followed the cellar-dweller to the gorge and down a few other trails, too. It is the same man we saw in the garage, Papa. It's Roscoe."

"So, the lock isn't yours? So, you don't have the key?"

"Right. Isn't or wasn't Mr. Lucci an owner of this place?"

"Yes, in partnership with your grandfather, Jay Martinen. When he killed Jay, Roscoe disappeared. I saw him go under the ice that day. We all believed he was dead, and Mama closed Tillie's down."

Shookii nodded. "I know we both thought that what we saw in the garage was a ghost, but he's not. Roscoe is alive. He comes here, maybe lives here sometimes. There are some canned goods stored down there."

People had begun calling out for Dindii. They wanted to cut the cake.

"Coming," she yelled in their direction. That brought our informational tour to a close.

Shookii wasn't territorial about Tillie's. She felt the building and grounds belonged to the community, and she honored Roscoe's ownership even though she and her sister were expending the effort for renovation. Ceding the bear man the cellar seemed to be her compromise on ownership. She seemed to be protecting him, a ghost or a wild man, perhaps both. Her young life was indeed complicated.

Shookii wasn't the only daughter who met difficulties in this new life. Popcorn, too, was working to establish who she was, venturing out into the world. I had concerns about Shookii dealing with the Roscoe story, but I worried too about Popcorn when just two weeks after Teddy Good's departure she began receiving his church's monthly, *The Earth Tomorrow*, and the biweekly newsletter, "Planet News." It was likely that all campers began receiving these in the fall, but I took it a bit more personally. Since they were sent United States mail, though, I had a duty to see they were delivered. As my wronged daughter's father, however, I would just as soon have not turned them over to Popcorn. Morgan wouldn't have. I did.

"Hey, Popcorn, you've got a general delivery," I told her at breakfast. "Stop by to pick it up." I hoped to have a word with her about the mailing from Pastor Good, but all she ever offered and that was when picking up the next copy without my prompting, was, "Don't worry, Papa. It's only mail."

I noted she kept the issues under her bedside table, eventually a short stack of them. It did make me uncomfortable, but I kept my knowledge from Morgan who never went into the girls' room. Morgan might have overreacted. Not long afterward, a more worrisome piece of mail came for Popcorn. It was a first class letter from Yaa whose return address was the same as that on the monthly. Two days later when Popcorn hadn't said anything about it, I asked.

"Sorry, Popcorn, but I couldn't help seeing that Yaa wrote to you. Is she all right?"

Popcorn may have been waiting for my questions. "She just wants me to know that she hasn't forgotten me."

"Well, it is nice to have a friend, but please, Popcorn, be careful. Think." I couldn't say much more until she let me in on her letters.

That was to happen toward Christmas after several exchanges of letters with Yaa. My presort separated local mail from out of state, so I noted the three replies Popcorn had written. I said nothing. Then, after a packet arrived from Yaa the day before solstice, Popcorn came to me at the delivery window.

"Papa, I want to tell you something."

Her tone startled me. I removed my visor and let her into my little office. Indicating a folding chair to her, I sat on my sorting stool. "What is it, Biini?" I said, using her formal name that fit with the seriousness she had brought with her.

"Yaa has invited me to California for Christmas. She even sent me bus fare to Duluth and a plane ticket."

Of all the times I'd tested my childrearing studies, this was the hardest. But I forced myself to hear her out. "What will you do?"

Perhaps she was hoping I'd give her a flat no and solve the conundrum for her. I knew better, though. Restraining her would not work. So, I let my question hang in the air.

She sat a minute quietly, then asked, "What do you think I should do, Papa?"

"Well, you are very busy here with Tillie's, your school studies, and your involvement with the spiritual center. We would certainly miss sharing Christmas with you if you were gone."

Popcorn nodded all along. "I've thought about those things."

"I know you are good friends with Yaa, but wouldn't your visit bring you uncomfortably close to Pastor Good?

Is that something that you want?" I was taking a risk of listening to what I didn't want to hear.

"It is hard to turn down a wonderful trip. And California!" She sat quietly again a minute. "It worries me though. I feel torn, but I don't think I should go without you coming with."

I took her hand. Patted it. "I won't be going to California, Sweetie. Sorry."

"I'm going to write back to tell her I won't be coming. I'm sending the fare and ticket back with my letter."

She rose from her chair and hugged me. "Thank you, Papa."

Right then, I wanted run to Morgan to tell her how right my study of raising children had been. I was glad that I resisted saying anything until asked. Teddy Good's influence wasn't far past.

The grand opening of Tillie's was set for the spring equinox. As the date grew nearer, there was even more excitement and activity on the property, not all of it welcome. Twice windows were smashed with bricks. Then sometime in the middle of the night a fire was set at one corner of the building. To stop the vandalism and attempts at arson, Tiny organized a patrol through the tribal council. Three members took turns watching the property through the night. Tiny set up the sweat lodge and several wigwams in the old beer garden to accommodate the members of the patrol. One wigwam would later house a camp store, the other a kitchen for serving native dishes during the festivities. The presence of sharp eyes brought an end to the vandalism. Or so it seemed.

March weather was decidedly favorable. Spring can be wet. March can be frigid. Late winter storms can bring loads of snow. Still, for a solid week, as people began trickling into town, the weather held just below freezing at night and dry and sunny during the day. It seemed that the climatologists had blessed the event. People were crowded around the two commercial wigwams buying fry bread, hazelnut *bagaan*, dried-blueberry pancakes, and coffee spiked with maple syrup. The store was selling charms, bracelets, dream catchers and all handmade goods, including some deerhide vests that Shookii had hand painted.

The front door porch of Tillie's was draped with painted tarps depicting eagles, lynx, foxes, and wolves. Tiny's son, George, was setting up a microphone stand and speakers to broadcast visiting dignitaries who would say a few words. Tiny would speak, as would Shookii, giving welcome to the council elders and to the spiritual community in general. Old Borg, Mr. Ericksen of the Swedenborgians would be named in Popcorn's speech, but did not want to say anything. George was also supervising the fish smoker and did a brisk business in maplewood smoked trout and whitefish.

The focal point of the ceremonies was the mural that Shookii with a great deal of help from Morgan had finished just six months before. Two weeks prior to the grand opening, Shookii had applied two coats of lacquer to protect the painting from the elements. The weather then had been fair enough to allow the coating to set and cure.

The former beer garden and the area around it began filling the week before the scheduled opening and by

Friday was becoming crowded with all sorts of temporary structures: platform tents and more traditional wigwams covered with birch bark. The early comers fired up the sweat lodge. Those driving campers and vans parked in the small lot at Tillie's and, when that was full, all along the road entering town. The opening was also a boon to the resorts which were not usually even open at that time of year. Most had made efforts to accommodate as many visitors as possible in anything even resembling a winterized room, cabin, or lodge. Only Olsen's remained closed. Our Laurel and Hardy stood on their principles, they said, and "wouldn't participate in the destruction of the town."

Tiny had removed his fish house early in anticipation of being busy for the opening.

"I had to clear the decks for Bird's and Jay's big day," he told me. "Even with your aid they need help. I'm doing the outside stuff, Morgan's doing the inside."

"I sure am happy with all of it," I said.

"Good that Shookii got her driver's license," Tiny said. "Her gadding about doing promotion brought all these people here. Without her articles and appearances we'd have no crowd at all."

I was exceedingly proud of both my girls but especially of Shookii, who seemed to thrive on the project. Her work had brought her into contact with news writers, elected officials, tribal leaders, and on the other side, opposition groups whom she clearly showed she could handle. Just as she had the aplomb to understand the spirit world very early in her teens, she demonstrated acumen maneuvering within the mundane, workaday world of people.

The reopening of Tillie's had taken on huge significance throughout the northland in both white and Native communities. Even the Finnish farmsteaders seemed interested. It was, as Tiny had said, much to do with Shookii's writing and traveling around, talking with everyone she met about the event. Though it was more than a novelty and perhaps because not everyone was favorable to the idea, something about a set of Native teenage twins converting a rather infamous landmark into a socially useful center caught the public's imagination. There was plenty of notice in the Duluth area, and even the *Saint Paul Pioneer Press* carried one of Shookii's articles about the project. It was not so strange that everyone wanted to come.

"Where is Shookii?" I found myself asking Tiny about my own daughter.

"Up at the tribal council. She's visiting some of the elders." He cast a glance around the beer garden and said, "You know, I haven't seen Popcorn either."

"Actually, I haven't seen her since day before yesterday. They'll both be here. You can count on that."

I wasn't even half right. Shookii soon phoned us. She'd decided to stay at Bois Forte, since it had grown too late to drive in daylight. So I knew when to expect Shookii, the next morning.

Popcorn, though, just wasn't there, and no one seemed to know where she was.

Firestorm 19

Tiny

I had lain awake fighting the burning in my groin, listening to the nothing the intense cacophony of the drumming left behind that, by agreement with Thief Lake residents within earshot of Tillie's, had ended at ten-thirty. I knew who would win the battle of the bladder and reluctantly threw off my wool blankets, swept to the side my deer hide door flap of the little wigwam I'd built that week, and tiptoed around the back of my tiny shelter.

The dark silence felt spooky and full of dread. Even the conversations from the clustered tents had hushed, draining from the clear air into the spring-softening ground. Waiting to pee, I looked up following *Ajiijaak*, the Crane flying along the path of the stars which was faded by the setting egg-shaped moon.

I found *Anang Giiwedin*, the north star, at the tail of the loon which told me it was well after midnight. I heard the nothingness that filled space pierced only by the spattering of my urine hitting the pine matting I'd raked up around my wigwam. All alone, it sounded loud. But then toward Tillie's, I heard the silence broken by a whooshing noise coming from inside the bar. Looking that way, out of the corner of my eye, I spotted two people rushing away from the building through the encampment, lighting their way with a hand-held emergency flare.

Behind them was someone dodging around the huge tree trunks bordering the beer-garden. Later I wished I'da taken more note. Was one of them tall and skinny, the other portly, or was one feminine, petite and her partner straight and middle height. Who was the squat dodging bundle? Watching my own business, I hadn't seen clearly and at the time attached little importance to who they were.

I didn't cry out, until the odd sounds from outside and the insistent grumbling inside the building were both overblown by a blast of shattering glass and leaping flame from the kitchen window. At that same window all evening I often glanced up to see my sister, Morgan, sitting with the group at the table and later working at the stove on a stew she was making in a large pot. I hoped she had gone home.

At the blast, I wetted myself, but still hoisted my jeans and zipped up, running through the camp to the barroom entry calling "fire" for all I was worth. My shouts and the explosion roused those asleep in the beer-garden camp who appeared at their tent flaps, and looked toward me, I suppose for instructions. Before I could bellow out any command, I was showered by glass from the front second story window. When I looked up, I saw my sister Morgan at the window mouthing words that would not sound. She was afire. Hers was a silent cry for help. Then, an inferno swept her away from the window.

"All buckets and dishpans to the fire," I shouted, trusting that most of the smart campers had quick access to water. Under my breath, I praised the tribal council for footing the extra bill for hose bibs at two sides of the structure and the pressurized well water system. I saw my son, George, come out of his tent, tightening his belt and slipping into moccasins.

"George, man the far side hose," I called. I ran to the mural side of the building and turned on the spigot. The pressure was good and steady, but probably because George opened the other side spigot to fill buckets the force of my hose soon ran low. Still if the pressure built up again and held, we had a chance, though, Morgan, I worried, might already be lost.

I sprayed up inside the kitchen window with the hose, directing the stream as much as I could within the blown out frame, but much of the flow missed and ran down over the mural Dindii had worked so hard to restore. I set the hose in a tree crotch, aiming it at the building, while I raised one of the painting ladders that was set alongside the mural. I hauled the streaming hose up beside the kitchen window opening and, with pressure now rebounded, doused the coursing flames with what was by then a strong, steady flow. Smoke billowed out the opening as I squirted the flames, but I held firmly to the ladder and hose. I was making progress.

From the top of the ladder I saw something that others, focused on the spectacle of a burning building did not see. At the periphery of the crowd looking up, I recognized Pastor Teddy Good and with him I saw my niece, Biini, grasping Good's jacket sleeve in obvious shock. I was too busy even for that big surprise. I shouted down into the crowd, yelling to some of the men to take the other painter's ladder around to the front to do what I was doing using George's hose on that side. By the time I finished my instructions and looked again for Biini and her "friend," they were gone. I didn't like it, but had too much to do to worry or think much about them.

I handed my hose off to another man and descended, going around to the front. The ladder-and-hose brigade there got going over the porch where George that afternoon had set up a speaker's stand. Flames were still shooting out that window, but we had a chance to limit the fire to just that room and the kitchen if we worked fast. Two men were up the ladder and took turns at the hose. Smoke billowed out with their efforts.

I ran back around the corner to the kitchen side and went up the ladder again. "Douse me with that hose," I told the guy who had spelled me. I tied on a bandanna I carried, over my nose and mouth and drenched it with hose water. "I have to go in. That's the only way we can stop it."

My partner sprayed all around the opening as I climbed through the window frame. I immediately hit the floor where the smoke was less, and reached back up to grasp the hose he handed me. I sprayed around and around, pointed the stream down the stairway through its open door. I coughed roughly. I had trouble breathing well but kept spraying around. The flames in the kitchen and stairwell died down, but the smoke was fierce and thick. I crawled on the floor, dragging the hose toward the front room next to the kitchen. Guiding myself past the stove where Morgan had worked over her stew, I entered the front room where flames were under attack by the other hose. Running out of length on my side, I returned my hose to my window-man and went back to drag the front-window hose into that room. Smoke swirled everywhere but keeping close to the floor and continuing to spray all over to kill the flames, I eventually found Morgan pushed into a heap in the front corner of the room. I took her up carefully and with the help of my man at the front-window ladder lifted her through. I held the hose taut as he crooked his arm around it and wrapped Morgan in an embrace to guard their descent.

I tied the hose at the ladder top and slid down to the ground. By that time the perimeter of Tillie's was crowded. A bucket brigade was bringing more water up from the lake. A team had entered the former barroom on the first floor and attacked the fire at the stairwell.

"Two of you take charge up there," I told the men. Keep spraying everything." I told another pair to scale the roof and open it with their hatchets. "Get the other hose and wet the attic down good." It looked as if we might save the building.

I turned my attention to Morgan. She looked badly burned and was deathly still. "Cut that burnt clothing off, very carefully," I said to three women who had rushed to her side carrying buckets of water. "Dip cloths in the water and lay them over her burns. Keep a blanket on her as much as possible. Cool her and warm her both. Keep new cloths coming, switch them out." The women knew what to do and shooed me away.

"We will care for her. You fight the fire," one said.

Suddenly, Tatty was there.

"She's bad, Tatty," I said.

He knelt beside her. "I think she's alive. Isn't she?" He asked.

"Let us work," the woman-leader said. "Help Tiny. We will care for her."

I grabbed Tatty's arm and dragged him up. "There's nothing we can do to help them but to stay out of their way. Come on."

The fire department volunteers arrived now with

canisters and a pumper truck. They went right to work, spelling those on the roof and the ladders.

Tatty was distraught.

"That could have been Shookii," he said, his hands moving to cover his face. "Morgan was filling in for her."

I put a hand on his shoulder. "If it's the worst, still, Morgan saved a twin from flames," I said.

"Oh God! Is Popcorn in there?" Tatty asked. "No one has seen her today!" He was freaking out.

"Relax. I saw her. She isn't inside."

Tatty immediately wanted to know when and where.

"I was up on the ladder, giving instructions to the crowd, and I saw her down below."

"Thank God," Tatty said.

"I hate to tell you this," I said, "but she was with Teddy Good. Looked too close for my comfort."

"Is that devil here at Thief Lake?"

I tried to reassure my brother-in-law. "It would seem so. I don't know where they went, but I have an idea. We should look at the only place no one here goes. Olsen's."

He was already sprinting in that direction.

On the way over to Olsen's, I told Tatty what I had seen: Two fusee-burning runners, a squat figure dodging behind trees, and my sister, blown into an upstairs corner of Tillie's.

"You didn't recognize those runners?" He asked.

I thought back. "I wonder if the duo was Laurel and Hardy?"

"Well, whomever, it's likely one or the other was the firebug. They carried a torch, didn't they?"

"Yeah, but it might be that no one started this fire. It

might be spontaneous or a bad wiring job. Still now I'm wondering if the pair I saw was Teddy G and Popcorn. They might have circled back into the crowd. Depends."

"On what?" Tatty asked me.

I hated to speculate about my niece but said, "Depends on who's calling the shots, Biini or that bastard Good."

"Let's hope it's Biini. She wouldn't start her own creation on fire."

On the way to Olsen's, DuChien appeared going toward Tillie's. Even before we came up to him he was saying, "I've been looking for you," pointing at Tatty.

It was no time for joking, but Tatty said, "What have I done now?"

DuChien waved off the humor and said, "I just heard where your daughter has been for the last twenty-four hours. Canada. She was with that pathetic preacher, Teddy Good." He pounded a fist into his hand. "He's crossed the line now. Transporting a minor internationally is a Federal offense. I'm going to bust that dude."

I told DuChien where we were headed and what I expected to find there.

"I'll join you." He turned around, and we started off again.

I didn't know the guy behind Olsen's bar. As soon as he saw DuChien's badge, though, he started to spill.

"The owners hired me yesterday. Cash in advance for three day's work. All I needed to do was keep people out and provide for our two guests."

"Show me the register," DuChien demanded.

"Nothin' to show," the clerk said. "They been comin' and goin' without signing in."

"They who?"

"You know. That preacher guy with the camp in Orr. The one who owns the jet airplane."

"Who's here now?" I asked, "and where are the owners?"

"The guy, Preacher Good, left ten minutes ago. Jumped on a snowmobile and roared off." He shrugged. "The owners left before, as soon as they met with the preacherman. First one then left, then the other. Seemed in a hurry."

DuChien turned to Tatty. "Preacher's going back to the Falls. That's where he landed his plane three days back. I'm all over him now." DuChien grabbed the phone behind the bar. He'd impound the jet for evidence, it seemed. "I need a fast machine fully gassed up." The clerk held up his hands, helpless. "Now!" DuChien yelled. The man moved.

Tatty stopped him. "What's the room number?"

"Six," the clerk told us. Then he turned to the garage where the snowmobiles were kept.

I called after DuChien, "Better bring a good guide. Cooley is only five minutes away. I'll call him for you."

"Thanks, Tiny," DuChien said as he followed the clerk to the garage.

"I'd like to go up alone," Taddy said, "but Popcorn might feel better if you came along."

"I will," I told him, "but then I'm going after those two Indiana buskers who own this place. I've got a message to deliver."

"Peace, brother," Tatty said.

I wasn't about to stop. "The peace has been broken. I'll see that Biini is okay, then I've got some trackin' to do."

"All right," Tatty said, "let's go up together."

Tatty knocked on number six. He tapped again, lightly. "Biini, it's Papa. Papa and Uncle Tiny." He turned the knob and the door was unlocked. We went in. Biini was curled up on the bed. She was crying.

"Oh, Papa. Uncle. I'm so sorry."

Tatty went to her, scooping her into his arms and hugging her close. "Popcorn, you are my darling daughter. Don't be sorry or afraid. We'll stay by your side."

I went forward and swept my bandana—dried since the fire—over her tears. I pushed back the hair from her face and said, "We love you, Biini."

"Tell us what happened," Tatty said.

I would stay a while, to get the gist of Biini's story, then I went downstairs to start my search for our local Laurel and Hardy.

Morgan from Beyond 20

Watch out for anyone who says she has the whole story when you start listening to her account of happenings. There's nobody who has the whole megillah. That goes double for anything that has ever happened in Thief Lake. Here people talk a bunch of hooey!

With one exception, though, I've got the story. Yeah, the entire moten gator but for one thing: who lit that fire. Someone did, that's for sure, but being in it, being consumed by it, I couldn't and still can't see who struck the match. The rest is, well, history.

I start with what Dindii saw when she drove up to Tillie's. Never mind how, but I can see it through her eyes. The building looked to her like something a flaming dragon-bird had swooped down on and taken a bite out of, then, had flown away with a mouthful. The second story was a charred wreck with part of the roof caved in on the front room, frameless window holes like sunken eyes weeping smoky tears, and spires of corner posts and wall studs poking the sunny blue sky. Of course, what had been the barroom and was to be the main meeting hall was a smoke-stinking mess, soaked and black-as-sin dirty. Okay, that's the picture.

What Dindii said and did is the real story. As if she had expected exactly what she saw—the near total ruin of two years of planning, construction, and promotion, she stood before the mural and nodded her approval.

"Good work stands the test of time," she said. Maybe Tiny's efforts to head off the kitchen flames with the hose wet and cooled that side of the building enough to preserve the mural. In fact, Dindii's and my work hadn't suffered a bit. Even the lacquer finish went untouched by flame.

Dindii greeted her sister who had been waiting for her arrival with a long embrace. "No crying, sweetheart, now we have more work to do." Biini dried her eyes and smiled on Dindii's gaze.

And go to work she did. Dindii organized a clean up crew to clear the wreckage at the porch and clean up that immediate area. "We are going to celebrate what is still here. We can't open yet, but we can dedicate the center and begin all over again." The headline in the *Duluth News Tribune* would read, "Thief Lake Teens Hallow Community Center Ruins," and restoration gifts immediately started to flow in, care of general delivery, Thief Lake, Minnesota Post Office.

That afternoon, not even a minute later than originally planned, my daughters stepped up the front stair to the porch of Tillie's Thief Lake Community Center to introduce their mission and the first speaker of the day.

Dindii spoke first. "Last night, this place became one even more hallowed than our efforts to restore it could be. Here we lost our mother, our grandmother, and one of our guides. As we work to once again restore this building, it is my hope that it will be renamed after her as the Morgan Langille Community Center.

"We gather here to open this center to the whole town of Thief Lake and to the surrounding area. It will be a little while before we can use the space, but it is already fulfilling its purpose: to bring people of all creeds and faiths together. Your presence here testifies to this. So, as the March sunshine warms us today, join your neighbors and friends in celebrating what you worked hard last night to save. It is your center, and the words of the mural still ring true." She recited:

> "'Stop in at Tillie's t' tip a few.
> Your friends around you
> Your blues in view
> Will turn from sadness and from rue
> To jolly times.'"

She did recite a few different words, but it fit the occasion, and the cheers and applause warmed the spring air even more.

I'm not going to give Tatty all the credit for raising wondrous children, but I cannot see how a mother like I've been—not a good example to myself or anyone else—could bring up even one daughter as righteous as these two. I wish Windsong were alive to see it. And maybe she can. After all, I do, and I was long gone even at the time my brother carried me to the ladder and handed me out the front window that night. The village women were working to save a corpse.

Dead or alive, I approved of Biini's words that day. She spoke after her twin and just as forcefully and optimistically as Dindiisi.

"The hell fire that sent my mother to her eternal reward did its best to destroy this house," Biini said, "but as John (Chapter 14, verses 4-6) quotes our Lord, 'In my

Father's house are many mansions. I go to prepare a place for you.' And maybe we should say 'preserve,' for the rooms I dedicate to you are untouched by flames."

True. The rooms behind the old barroom sustained little damage, that mostly by smoke and water. Biini might have thought it a miracle, but if not that, it was certainly good luck. It was another thing to celebrate.

So, out of the flames that crisped me up, a new spirit and life sprang forth. I can't say I'm not sorry, but better me than one or two of my kids. Now, I've cleared the decks for them.

I'll tell you one thing: Dindii had heard, or thought she'd heard, Roscoe say "From three, two t' one, again," whose meaning she will never know. Well, maybe not "never" but not in her lifetime. I know what he meant. Like a lot of things at the lake, there are two sides to a story and his words were no different. Yeah, he quoted his own words—Roscoe was the originator of Tillie's jingling mural rhyme—"To jolly times, with our three two," which referenced Tillie's on-sale liquor license allowing only light beer, three point two proof alcohol, to be sold on the premises. What he meant speaking to Dindii, though, was in reference to the three survivors of the windigo chase: Jay, me, and himself. Well, there were three for twenty years after Mary's death. Then, there were two after Roscoe stabbed Jay to death. Another sixteen years were to pass before I sizzled in Tillie's fire, and there was just one. Roscoe knew it would happen. Does it mean he set the fire? He was crazy enough.

The morning after the fire, Tatty set out after Roscoe. Dindii by then had told him that Roscoe was alive and often holed up at the gorge when people were crowding his cellar at Tillie's. My brother had also described to Tatty a "squat dodging bundle" who might have easily reminded him of Roscoe hiding behind the white pine trunks surrounding the encampment the night of the fire. With DuChien and Cooley out after Pastor Teddy Good and Tiny tracking down our local Laurel and Hardy, my dear husband—always a few steps behind the action—was the only one who could seek out Roscoe, and maybe was the only man at the lake who believed Roscoe was alive enough to be found. He was certainly the most qualified to approach Roscoe since the bear man had sought Tatty out in the garage, and, as Tatty had years later revealed to Danny and Cooley, they had been close. But let the man tell his own story. I, instead, rather relish relating the sad state of affairs surrounding that bastard Theodore "Teddy" Good, and might as well throw in Laurel's and Hardy's endings while I'm at it. Like I say, don't ask me how, but I know best to let Tatty tell of his encounter with Roscoe.

This is what I know, and it's pretty well complete: FBI agent DuChien had commandeered the 2nd beefiest snowmobile in Olsen's corral. Teddy had the fastest. It had plenty of power for the G-man and Cooley to catch up with their man, following the trail that Preacher Good had taken toward the Falls. Cooley, being more familiar with the terrain and ice conditions, handled the machine. DuChien rode behind telling Cooley how it all had come to this.

"Ever since he 'baptized' Tatty's daughter, taking her virtue for himself, I've kept tabs on this dude," DuChien said, speaking loudly into Cooley's good ear to be heard over the noise of the snowmobile. "They are all the same, no matter how smart or how rich they think they are. Eventually, they make the wrong move."

"Yeah," Cooley yelled. "What was his?"

DuChien leaned closer to Cooley. "He made two big ones. He filed an international flight plan to hide from the sheriff. He wanted to land in Canada to avoid state arrest."

"Sounds smart to me."

DuChien continued. "Maybe, but I have a friend in the TCCA, Canada's FAA. He tipped me."

"Good friend to have. Then what?"

"We'd been watching his church bank accounts. A very large cash withdrawal, $48,000, was made the same day he filed his flight plan."

"That's not a crime, is it?"

"Not if you declare the cash you're carrying. But he declared nothing."

Cooley might have lost the point of the story, but he didn't miss a thing on the trail. He slowed the machine to a stop. "Look there," he said, pointing to the ground.

DuChien followed his sign. "Seems like he's taken to the lake."

"Yeah," Cooley said, "but, 'Longest way round is often times best' remember?"

"'Don't jump over the cuckoo's nest,'" DuChien finished the adage.

Cooley indicated the trail that went out onto the ice, saying, "Here the ice is thick enough, but before he gets to the narrows it will get iffy. He could easily break through."

"Well," DuChien said, "let's catch him first."

Cooley revved the machine. They got underway again.

"Anyway, I follow the money. First it led me to a violation of Federal law so I could apprehend him. Second, I looked for and found where the money went."

Cooley, who was steering the snowmobile up the hill, taking the longer, safer route to the narrows, looked back around grinning. "I'd like to know where that cash is."

"Pastor Good doesn't have it, sorry."

Cooley gunned the machine top end.

"There's nothing illegal about paying cash for a resort hotel, either, unless you're turning it into an underage bordello. He bought Olsen's for $48,000 cash on the barrel head, according to the clerk at Olsen's who witnessed the signing of the bill of sale."

"So, Laurel and Hardy split the proceeds and took off."

"It would seem so, but the clerk noted that Laurel left when Hardy went upstairs to pack. Seems like he took the whole bundle with him. Hardy flew out the door a quarter hour behind, giving chase."

"That's the problem with cash and with partnerships, they both get people to fighting." Cooley said. "Look off to your right." He pointed toward the distant lake shore."

"I see a tiny mote out there is all."

"Yeah, a speck of a preacher. No one else would be out there. If he continues in that direction, he's got trouble. One of the springs feeding the lake comes up right beyond there."

It took DuChien and Cooley nearly a half hour to

reach the point they'd last seen the distant Teddy Good on his snowmobile. What they saw from shore wasn't an open patch of water. A snowmobile track led on toward the narrows, then stopped.

Cooley went slack-jawed. "What the heck? Where'd he go?"

"You think he went under?"

"No chance. It's too warm for that water to freeze back up, but well, you can see for yourself, nothin's here. The track just ends."

Did Pastor Teddy Good join the *Saint Muggsy* in a baptism at Thief Lake. They might be two miles away from each other but, perhaps, are joined in a depth-of-the-lake ceremony. Maybe Teddy had arranged for my barbecuing the previous night and felt he needed cleansing of the spirit. I don't know. Do I care? He's gone.

Once Biini learned of the Reverend Good's weird disappearance, she broke down and told her truth. She couldn't resist his charms or his lies, but she was able to resist his aims. According to Dindii, Teddy wanted Biini to light the fire at Tillie's that night, whether to burn me or Dindii, I don't know. Maybe he was afraid I'd come after him. That was right! But did he not realize her little meeting room and chapel were dear to Biini? She refused, of course.

When he left the hotel, she related, he took Laurel and Hardy with him. Maybe he gave them a couple added thousands to set the blaze. That's not clear. Anyway, that night, Biini went running when the call of fire came round, found the preacher watching the blaze, and was spotted by her uncle clinging to Teddy's sleeves. What she was doing was excoriating the man for what she thought he'd done. She was finnished. It was the last she saw of Good.

And what of our comedy team, Laurel and Hardy?

For a long while, things had not been going swimmingly well for the Indianians. As they had told Dindii in her interview, they were in debt. They were actually just a few payments ahead of foreclosure, and they had been at each other's throats for most of the winter. So when Teddy's cash offer came, the two jumped at the chance to sign a quit claim deed.

Seems that Laurel was just a little ahead of Hardy, though. Rather than stowing the cash in the safe, he stuffed the forty-eight hundreds into his vest pocket and zoomed out of town in his pickup. Anyone in the town would have paid good money to watch those two, like Keystone Cops, roaring down the Thief Lake Road, Hardy in his Camaro chasing, Laurel in the GMC fleeing.

Right behind those clowns came my brother. He caught up to them on Harney's rise overlooking the hollow where Tatty had his accident on the hairpin turn. Gun fire rang out, and Tiny stopped.

Down in the hollow was Laurel's overturned GMC taking shots from Hardy who was hunched behind the open driver's door of his Camaro. Every so often the big man would pop up and take another shot or two. And just as often a rifle shot would hit the door. Hardy must have been hit because he went to the ground then crawled to the rear of the car where he'd be more protected.

By this time, Tiny had hiked the woods down to the hollow with his own rifle. He was close enough to hear what they were yellin' at each other.

"You son of a bitchin' snake, Laurel. You're stealing everything I've got.

"It's payday, Ralph, you pumped up pullet. I earned this dough." He fired and shattered the windsheild.

"That's all you'll get," Laurel said, "a plugged nickel."

They went on that way until Hardy came around the rider's side of the car—he could only hobble and not very fast—to get a shot off behind the upturned truck bed. Somehow, he got two, but he took rifle shot in his huge midsection and went down.

Tiny wasn't about to risk helping though that would be the right thing to do and neither of the partners moved for a long time. Hardy was on the ground, in the open, very still. After some yellin' and loud hollerin', Laurel came out to look. He approached his partner.

"You all right?" Hardy didn't move.

"Tell me ya ain't dead. Come on Ralph."

Now he was standing right over his big partner pointing the rifle down at him. "Speak up, dumb ass," he yelled.

Hardy didn't speak, but he raised his shootin' iron as quick as lightning and put a slug through Laurel's chest. The rifle, too, discharged. The ended their partnership in the worst way.

The former partners shot each other to death. The sheriff counted six pistol slugs through the bed of the truck, three others in Laurel, and four rifle casings from where Laurel was firing. Two others lodged in Hardy's chest and belly.

My brother Tiny was on the scene. He told the town, for years afterward, "If it wasn't blood money to start, it certainly became blood money at the end," he became fond of saying. He'd relieved Laurel of the sheaf of bills which was center-punched with a pistol shot through the It's hard to believe such a poetic ending could come from a not-so-funny comedy team. Tiny might have embellished the story, but one detail is true: he did turn the cash over to the sheriff. He brought DuChien the rifle shells which it turned out matched exactly the one from Cooley's shooting.

It's fate that determined my exit in such company. If I had led a cleaner life, I might have died with Old Borg instead of two fools from south of Fort Wayne, and a bastard California radio evangelist with a penchant for young girls. It seems somehow inappropriate. From where I sit now—wherever that is—there come two blessings: it seems I can finish watching my girls grow to adulthood, and, being alone here, I don't have to jabber with the Olsen's crowd or listen to the blasphemy of a Christian preacher.

I'm content with that.

New Life 21

I had never heard mentioned the name Roscoe Lucci—one of the pivotal characters in Morgan's earlier life—in the first fifteen years of marriage to her. Roscoe and my acquaintance with him at the time I occupied a window seat on an Atlanta-to-Minneapolis flight, was just hours ahead but lay across a gulf of meteorological insanity, back-country hoodoo, and physical collision.

I needed to drive—my first time ever in snow—two hundred miles through what Minnesotans later called the snowstorm of the century. In a few hours, I was to encounter spirits that had haunted Roscoe for decades before our meeting, one of which sent my Jeep into a snow-filled ravine. Once rescued and brought into Roscoe's presence at Tillie's bar, Jay Martinen warned me right off that the man was dangerous. Within the first few hours of that moment, Roscoe confronted me in Tillie's men's room, his first words to me were, "Sometimes I think I'm about to die." Within minutes after saying that he told me, "When I found out who you were, I wanted to kill you."

From those first moments meeting him, until I saw him go under the Thief Lake ice with his windigo-nemesis the very next day, was barely nineteen hours during which he threatened me, as I've said, tackled me on the barroom floor, conducted a twenty-years-too-late inquisition—he played the role of prosecutor, judge, jury, and executioner—savagely attacked and killed my snowbank rescuer, Jay Martinen, and, exerting his supernatural hold on me, used my friendship (odd to call it that, but true) as a shield for his escape. My bonding with Roscoe still strikes me both as more normal and stranger than any single event of those times—perhaps it should be termed a macabre blessing—which concluded with a friendly pact of silence after I met him the following evening in Granny's storage garage. Close up, I saw him next nearly a dozen years later in another garage, my own, before a witness, Shookii, whose clear sight of "the bear man" convinced me that what I took as a vision was real.

All told, I'd spent less than three hours interacting with Roscoe Lucci but even now count him as the most important acquaintance of all I've encountered at Thief Lake. Roscoe revealed his heart and soul before me. I was innocent of his history, then, and could see his injuries and twisted persona as badges of honor.

So, when Morgan died in Tillie's fire and I realized the meaning of his puzzling statement, "from three, two t' one, again," I knew that it was for me to seek him, find him, and confront what he did to Morgan at long last. Both Shookii and Popcorn confirmed that morning that Roscoe hid in a cave under the rim of the Thief Lake gorge.

"Don't go there, Papa," Popcorn begged. "It's too dangerous."

Shookii agreed. "You know what you're doing, but this is the worst time of year. The footing is loose and slippery, and you'd be lucky to even find the cave entry."

I embraced my twins, my motherless orphans, now.

"I have no illusions. I will have ropes and our gear. If he is hiding there, I will find him. Safely. Don't worry."

I couldn't tell them all the why of my decision, that I was the only one who really understood Roscoe. In many senses, having witnessed supernatural events of his life like no one else had, I was Roscoe. "I will come back. You two are not alone. Trust me."

Shookii set her mouth in a tight line of disapproval. "I will trust Granny's word. She said that you 'see from afar.' I hope you've looked."

"I have. I have," I told them. The truth was, though, I was too ensconced in the everyday world anymore to be able to see much beyond my own nose. "I trust Granny, too," I said. That was true.

I loaded the climbing gear I had insisted on buying for Shookii when she started to scale the granite walls that poked up here and there around the lake. I used a toboggan so I could arrive above Roscoe's cave quietly. I had ropes, a saddle, a couple of ice axes and a friction brake. I was hoping to spot the cave entrance from the opposite side of the gorge and track upstream to cross the river where there was yet enough ice.

The gorge is prehistoric, a glaciated split in a granite cliff face about forty feet wide and over two hundred yards long. There is enough feature in the two faces to hold soil which over time had sprouted moss, bushes, and even some cedar trees that sequestered parts of the rock face. I used a pair of birding glasses I'd brought to sweep the opposite wall, concentrating on areas with substantial growth. Above these few hidden places I scanned the top of the cliff for tramped-down snow. I didn't find much, but something I noticed was a series of small protrusions which should have held enough loam to start something growing. Several of the areas seemed worn, trampled. Studying these, I noticed a pattern of handhold-looking crevices and possible footrests traversing some sixty feet of the rock face leading to a well established grove of cedar. This must be the location of the cave entrance, I decided. Above this spot was a stand of second growth white pine most about three feet in diameter. The closest trunk to the dropoff would easily support my weight. I noted the location, set up a tripod of branches on my side for identification, and moved upstream with my load beyond the head of the waterfall where I could cross. I didn't let myself even think about what was to come.

I laid the toboggan across the slowest flow of the snow melt running between what seemed to be solid rock and used it as a bridge to crawl across. Once on the far side, I simply pulled my bridge over behind me. I had to accomplish this three times to get to the far side. The ups and downs and the canted angles the toboggan traversed on my last crossing swept the rope to one side and it started to uncoil into the rivulet I'd just crossed. I grappled with the loops, dislodging my friction brake which tumbled loose and plopped into a rushing torrent below which swept it down toward the head of the falls.

"Now that would have been nice to have," I told the wilderness around me. I decided I could do without it if nothing else went wrong by knotting the rope every so often, fashioning stops to control my descent. After I found the stand of pine I'd seen from across the way and checked its correctness by lining myself up with the branch tripod I'd built on the other side, I rested against the tree trunk and worked on knotting the rope.

I measured three feet of line, spreading the rope wide across my chest and twisted it around itself to make a bulky hand stop. The rope shortened a bit, but I thought it would be plenty long to reach the cedar copse below. I'd already began to doubt my sanity doing this, but I shied away from worry and kept to my work. Once I looped the rope around the large pine I'd chosen, I saw that the rope *was* too short. A three foot diameter trunk used almost ten feet of line to encircle it. I untied from the large pine and moved six or so feet to a fir tree much thinner but more suitable. Now, as I unfurled the line it reached the nearest cedar. I figured I could maneuver from that point. I tugged at the rope. It seemed secure.

I looped the rope through the saddle harness, gathering a length of rope in, and swung out over the forty-foot precipice steadying myself against the wall and not looking down at the raging torrent at the bottom. I began rappelling three feet at a time, allowing the seat harness to slip along the rope from one knot to the next when I grabbed ahold of it to stop. I uncoiled more knotted rope and was nearing the cedars below. On the very next three-foot descent, I felt the jerk of my stop and, then, additional movement as if slack in the rope above was taken up. By this time my hands were weary and the next descent slipped by the knot and I went down six feet grabbing for all I was worth at the next knot. Above something came loose and soil and pebbles rained down on me.

Then I was falling. Then I was upside down, snagged and twisted in the harness and falling along a totally slack rope. The fir tree was coming down. I crashed into the first cedar below, grasping at everything, ripping fronds and bark as I bumped down toward my death.

If I was saying good-bye to the twins, I stopped in mid-sentence. I stopped. Stopped falling, stopped tumbling. I just stopped and the fir tree whizzed by me carrying the top end of the rope with it toward the gorge. I found myself in the grip of a great, hairy arm round my waist. Another arm holding a long knife blade flew at the rope, slicing it off, letting the line pass through the harness and to go down to the stream with the falling fir. I was tossed like a sack of potatoes onto a damp stony floor of a cave, shaken but alive.

As true as ever, Roscoe met me at the nexus of living or dying, in concentrated intensity, and, somehow for me, with inexplicable force. He stopped my fall.

Stunned and bruised, I collapsed on the granite floor, staring up at the man who saved me. I hadn't found Roscoe, he had found me.

"Ya never took the easy way," he said.

I stared at him. "Are you real? Am I alive?"

"Next time, come in the back door," he said, sweeping an arm toward the back of the cave where he had a small fire burning. The coals radiated an amber light on the walls, but sunlight played around the floor over the fire. By that light I saw and followed a rope ladder better than the one I'd just fashioned leading to an opening above. Roscoe's chimney was his second entry.

It is hard to accuse someone of murder who has just saved your life, but I grew more confident as I realized I was bumped about but whole. I'd come to avenge Morgan's killing. No, that was not it. I'd come to expose Roscoe's solitary damnation. Not that either. Truthfully, I'd come to finish something already in motion before I'd met Morgan, a fear dressed in native garb, instilled in me through my father's mother, Banook, who'd brought me to a Mik'kmaq storyteller during my father's funeral. The same day I saw Roscoe go under the ice, I'd banished fear of my father and his ghost and years later with Shookii learned to listen to him to protect my children. I still feared. I feared the irrational, the spirits of nights and the unreasoning. That was what Roscoe embraced, what made him live against all odds. I'd come to face that.

"I saw you drown," I said.

"Because you banished spirits, mine and your father's," he said. "I've lived long and suffered 'from three t' one.'"

"What does that mean?" I said.

"Alone."

"I don't get it, Roscoe."

"Morgan was never guilty. She was against the windigo chase all along."

"She left the lake," I reminded him, "because she was guilty."

Roscoe shook his great bear head. "No. She felt guilty. Hiding does that."

"I understand that, but still don't get it."

"It was always three to one: Mary, Morgan, and Jay against me. They followed me on my chase, to protect me. In the end, Mary saved *me*, not Morgan, by diving into that horrible light."

"So, you believe you killed Mary?" He nodded.

"I saw you stab Jay. And now you've burned Morgan to death," I finally said. "Is that why you've stayed alive all these years? To wipe them all out?"

"No. It was for you. For you and the twins."

Now I was totally confused and angry. "For me?"

"You are from outside the lake and so a steady protector of Windsong's children. For twenty-years, remember, I thought Windsong was my child, not Jay's. Learning about a lie is different than living a lie. You don't give way so easily. When you stayed at the lake to help Morgan raise her daughter's daughters, I watched. Just as I had seen their mother grow to womanhood. They are my children as much as yours and more than they are Morgan's."

This was too much for me. "Bullshit, Roscoe. You are crazy. You killed their mother."

"Yes, but not Morgan."

"What? She was as much their mother as I was their father."

"I'm sorry Tatty, but that's not right either."

"Why?"

"I knew for years before that Windsong was not my child. But her children are. I killed her with childbirth. I couldn't prevent Morgan from raising them and couldn't have them myself, but I kept you here to shepherd them to adulthood. You did well."

I couldn't stand it. His lies were a blasphemy on my family, on my whole life. I rose slowly to my feet and, when I felt steady, I took a great breath in and charged. I hit Roscoe square in the stomach which was like a rock but knocked him down. He rolled and came back to standing right at the cave mouth. Still furious I screamed, "Liar! Dirty liar!" And reckless of danger, I charged again.

Roscoe could have feinted and dived aside, but the man stood loose and unbraced for my butting. Perhaps, I thought later, he understood my rage was the kind that had guided his hand to stab his partner and friend Jay. He took my flying block full force, and we both tumbled out of the cave's mouth.

It was as if he had known, had planned it. He rolled up into a ball, not flailing or reaching for a branch . He crashed through the cedars and fell to the canyon floor.

Clinging to a large cedar limb I'd reached out for, I looked down and saw him land on the granite slabs below. The current swept him off those rocks, and Roscoe disappeared for good.

I felt weak and would have wept had I not been in such a horrible place. I carefully climbed up again to the cave mouth and wormed my way in, kicking against branches and clutching the nearly smooth crannies of the cave entry. I collapsed again, rested, and regained sanity if that could ever be.

Roscoe had saved me at least twice, and his last grace had been the rope ladder up his improvised chimney. It was hard work going up but much easier than it had been coming in. An S-shaped exit was closely guarded by low growing fir branches which I crawled under to find myself not twenty feet from my toboggan.

Almost totally drained, it took me hours to recross the river and drag myself home. There, both Shookii and Popcorn were waiting.

Popcorn's Last
(Biini)

The year that Mama died in Tillie's fire was a hard one for me. I learned to pray in a new way, to pray for the souls of the dead as well as the reform of the living. Death camped on my doorstep and surprised me by refusing to move off, proving, I supposed, that those gone will not be forgotten.

That year—one that taught me every day to cherish the fathers and mothers of our world—is also one of the most beautiful in my memories of the lake. Along the way through troubles and loss as well as wonders and new life, I gained a refreshed bond with my dear sister, Dindii, and a new understanding of what it means to be a parent.

I had not known my own mother, Windsong, who died giving us birth. Mama, Morgan, who was really my grandmother became more my mother than my birth mom ever had a chance to be. Perhaps Morgan made up for not being present to bring up Windsong who was raised by Mama's Granny, my own great-great-grandmother whom I remember visiting (and inspecting) in my early years. So, instead of a looming mother figure as some children enjoy, I learned to see motherhood as a series of women aiding and abetting the tragedy and joys of raising children. I don't judge Mama's behavior now that I have truly forgiven her. Her wanderlust led me to a truer path both as a believer and as a mother.

I had not either known my father. Papa was there every day and still is, but he is not related to me by blood, unless you count hundreds of generations back when Ojibwe and Mi'kmaq people intermarried. For most of my young life I never wondered who Windsong's man was. I was told he was a local medicine man nearly twice Windsong's age. That was speculation. Windsong never revealed the father's name. No one at the lake talked much about him.

Even after Dindii and I learned who the man was, I didn't know him any better. My sister had been in his presence off and on for a couple years before he, as he had before, disappeared. His is just a name to me. Better to know him as the bear man of Thief Lake. Better to revere his spirit form than his difficult life or sullied name. After all, when Windsong died, Roscoe Lucci was mostly a specter to all at the lake. He had nearly ceased to exist in the physical world at all. Some said drink conquered him, but my Papa says the spirit world broke through when he was a youth and nabbed his life, though he continued to dwell on our earth.

I did not worry, and I did not grieve when even before he was born my son Timothy lost his father just as I had. Maybe because Papa had decided to stay at the lake to raise me, I was looking for a father for my son when I wrote to my friend Yaa about my last days with Teddy Good and about the impending birth of my boy.

The response to that letter did not come from Yaa who had returned to Africa. I received reply from Teddy's father, the founder and head of Planet Earth's Church of God, who losing a son was eager to gain another, especially one to call him grandpa. That Grandpa Martin is a good man and a much better Christian than Teddy ever was, helped me accept his care and generosity. I finally made that trip to Pasadena Yaa had proposed, and when Martin offered me work overseeing the summer camp at Orr, I made California my home for the other nine months a year.

I had already built my first church at Tillie's and accepted the blessing of wealth from Planet Earth's Church of God that allowed me to continue building small congregations in the northland where they are needed more than in Southern California. To keep my feet on the ground and my head out of the clouds there are Papa and my spiritual advisor, Old Borg. For love and companionship, I have Timothy.

For the legal questions, I have a sister.

Shookii's Last
(Dindii)

We rebuilt Tillie's. The place had become a point of civic pride, an affirmation of people accepting each other and getting along despite their differences. The project took on a life of its own attracting all sorts of talent across the northland.

It seemed that once all the long-ago denizens of the place, including my blood-father and my blood-grandmother, were gone their fate had no influence. The bear man had been right: the reopening of Tillie's set Mama free from herself. He could have pronounced the same doom or blessing on himself for what happened on a night thirty-six years distant from the windigo chase, the fire, allowed Roscoe the bear man to rest.

Papa told Biini and me about him. We knew he had gone after Roscoe for his own reasons, but what he learned in that cave was important to us all. Such as he was, we now had a father.

Papa though told no one else, maybe because most, even the old timers at the lake, knew little of him and, too, thought he'd been dead nearly two decades by now. Was it because no one was looking for him that his body was once again unfound? The elders might tell us to look carefully when we encounter one of our many Thief Lake black bears. Roscoe could inhabit any of them.

Though both Biini and I somehow gained Papa's penchant for visions and other-world sight, I acknowledge it in its Native forms and leave it at that. Like Papa, I grew to not desire that my second sight rule my existence. Life is hard enough without visions popping up everywhere. Nor have I been chained as was Mama to the curses of desire. Neither troublesome spirit nor ruinous emotion filtered through my side of Windsong's placenta, but reason and logic somehow did.

Whether or not that's true, my encounters with Roscoe and Papa's father and any temptations such as Biini fell to were tempered on my side by knowledge and reason. I figured out Teddy G in a hurry. I was able to make something of the bear man's appearance in the garage. I stood unafraid witness to Papa's last glimpse of his father. I knew by figuring where Mama had been each time she was absent, including the time she went off with the shotgun. And without knowing too much about Roscoe, I suspected he did more good than any suspected, including rescuing Cooley Jokkinen when he found him just short of the Kettle Falls Hotel, unconscious in the new fallen snow. Call it spirit-intuition, but it all stood to reason.

More importantly, though, I learned early the power of words, both for good and evil, harnessed them in my writing, and studied their authority in deeds, insurance lingo, and contracts, all to do with the reopening of Tillie's.

What amazed me most was the freedom, on one hand, and the constrictions, on the other, that words, simple scrawling on paper or birch bark, exerted. I'd always seen what effect they had on my dear sister, and not always with an approving eye, but also sensed the sway that, say Federal regulation on the Boundary Waters, had over the people at Thief Lake. You don't likely have to explain the US government's control through language to any Native in the country. They know better than any.

I restored the words of Tillie's mural not because I liked the jingle or understood what Roscoe composed or later repeated, but because language matters if for no other reason than it forms the basis of human memory. Without it, like Roscoe, we become bear men moaning our visions over the corner of a back country bar, instead of building what keeps us warm in winter and carefree in summer.

I did not become a journalist. The stories I related in the *Trout* and even the features I wrote, that many newspapers carried for the grand opening of Tillie's, were not enough for me, even as flattering as the initial praise they garnered felt. No. It was story telling, and as much as I love a story, simply, they come and they go. The lasting impression may linger a week, a month, perhaps, years, or even a decade, but those words do not bind, do not hold, do little to guide. They are much like Tillie's jingle: memorable, fun to recite, musical.

Since I wanted to build on something steadier than wind, I studied the law.

For the spiritual questions, I have a sister.

Postmaster's Coda 22

"Who cut the cheese?" Danny demanded. "Fer Christ-sake, open the door!"

Even in the generous environs of Cooley's Yeti, a prefabricated ice house, we were crowded. Danny and Cooley were of girth enough to fill the space, but Tiny and I had been invited over, too, and no one could turn around quickly without rubbing someone the wrong way.

"Look to yourself, Danny," Cooley rejoined, "We all showered this morning. Did you?"

"Shower?" Tiny asked. "That would mean stripping off his long johns well before winter ended."

Danny was laughing. "Okay, friends, I'll just hold my nose if you shush up about my underwear."

"This," I cashed in, "is why I won't retire. I'd have to fish with you guys every day, not just Sundays!"

Danny was good for the change of target. "Tatty, you just want to break Oliver McKinnon's sixty-year record. How many more you need?"

I did quick arithmetic. "I've served twenty-three years. I'd have to work til I am ninety-five."

"Nobody's in line for the job, Brother," Tiny said, "You might as well stay."

I moved toward the coffee pot across the room shouldering my way through and sat at the "kitchen" table which was just a corner between the propane stove and the window. All well designed . . . for smaller people. I let them jaw and jabber all they wanted as they checked their bait and tended their fishing lines. Too much company and too much jocularity put me in a funk.

I lost Morgan whose presence while not always welcomed filled my life with interest at the very least. I sent Shookii off to the university in Minneapolis for law school after four years at U of M, Duluth. Popcorn alternated homesteads and chapels in Pasadena and at the summer camp in nearby Orr. Over the last seven years, I had grown ever more solitary.

Even Timothy's vibrant and loving play on his stays with me during camptime were awfully long on my nerves. I was at my best when early winter closed in and most everyone but my "fishing buddies" filtered out of town to anywhere but here.

If August was good, it brought red and golden leaves at its end and opened the door to the first snows in September. Those were the times to light a fire in the porch-pit and snug up in a furlined deer hide waiting for the moon to rise to sparkle over the freshly fallen snow.

Sitting alone before a blaze, my thoughts often settled on Roscoe. Sometimes I found myself reciting his merry jingle from Shookii's mural. I banished Jay's death scene from my thoughts, and tried not to remember the sight of the bear man of Thief Lake lying below me on the floor of the gorge, washing into the rush of the river. At one time, just before I had consented to travel north for what I thought was a five-day trip, I called the lake "backwoods" and the people "yokels," expecting only chill and boredom of a long week. What I found, what I lived, were experiences that could fill a book or two, and far from dull and transitory, I find life at the lake sweet and contented.

I looked out the window of Cooley's Yeti, settling my gaze on the shoreline two miles over the ice, back toward town, now punctuated by pointed firs, then heaved by piled boulders glaciers had played with. I blew over the lip of my coffee cup and sipped the bitterness and maple sweetness of the brew.

"Hey, Tatty," Danny broke into my reverie, "Cooley's going to tell his wolf tale. Shake your blues."

My three musketeers had settled into their chairs aligned with their fishing poles staked to the ice each over a hole. Cooley spread his knees wide and brought his forearms to them supporting his prodigious belly.

"I'd got lucky with the first two wolves," he was saying, "but the other three kept circling making a tighter loop each time. If I was lucky, my last three shots would at least wound the trio. I missed the next shot, but then hit the two juveniles square on the nose. Then I realized I'd have to draw my knife on the biggest one when he attacked."

Danny was smiling a wolfish grin, "How many you say there were?"

"Five," reverberated through the Yeti, each of us telling the latest number.

"Salt 'n pepper," said Danny.

Author's Note

At the suggestion of my classmate Chuck Jurvelin, I revisited the setting and characters of *Listener in the Snow*, living with Tatty and Morgan for a chilly and wet California winter working on *The Nothing That Is Not There*. I sheperded them through the inevitable difficulties such characters in such a place will face. Not all of us made it out of Thief Lake this time, but we became, with the addition of the twins, a family of sorts for a while.

So have my critical readers and commentators become my family for a time. Many of them visited Thief Lake, reading *Listener* eight years back. I owe them a debt of gratidue and many, many thanks, especially, my historian friend, Jim Richter, my proofer and professor, Bruce Coyle, my designer and sweetheart, Carol Squicci who read draft upon draft, readers and commentators Kitty Fassett and Gary Durbin, and Marylene Cloitre and Bob Haus who joined at the end to make this book a grand experience in reading.

CPSIA information can be obtained
at www.ICGtesting.com
Printed in the USA
JSHW020631170723
44858JS00001B/2